---- ★ ----

THE MAN HAD TO
BE HERE SOMEWHERE

She approached the archway and shone the light into the room beyond.

Couches, chairs, coffee tables. The bar and stools at the end. A coatrack to the left of it. And over there, on a couch under one of the bay-side windows, lay a man....

Joanna froze. The man lay facedown in an awkward position, arms flung out above his gray head. He was very still, paying her no attention.

She stepped closer and saw the stains. They were brown, splattered all over the yellow flowered cushions above him. There were more on what she could see of the cushion beneath his torso. But the largest was on the back of his white shirt....

---- ★ ----

"Joanna Stark is a new heroine whose story shows the author at her best."
—*Washington D.C. Times*

The CAVALIER in WHITE

MARCIA MULLER

WORLDWIDE.

TORONTO • NEW YORK • LONDON
AMSTERDAM • PARIS • SYDNEY • HAMBURG
STOCKHOLM • ATHENS • TOKYO • MILAN
MADRID • WARSAW • BUDAPEST • AUCKLAND

Second edition August 1993

THE CAVALIER IN WHITE

A Worldwide Mystery/October 1988

First published by St. Martin's Press Incorporated.

ISBN 0-373-83304-0

For Lois Muller

ONE

NOVEMBER MORNINGS in northern California's Valley of the Moon are generally clear and sunwashed. The light has a peculiar watery quality and is further filtered through a gentle woodsmoke haze. They are days to delight the soul, even one as battered and ragged at the edges as Joanna Stark's, and normally one such as this would have filled her with enthusiasm and high hopes.

But on this Tuesday she walked across the Sonoma Plaza head down, feet scuffing the grass, leaning into the north-westerly wind. When she did raise her eyes she saw that the flag on top of the square basalt city hall had become entangled in its own ropes and drooped dejectedly, wrapped around its pole.

Trapped, she thought. Just like I feel. The trouble with Sonoma is that there's no place to hide.

She stopped, thrusting her hands into her pockets, and scanned the plaza. Its eight acres—containing the city hall, the chamber of commerce, playgrounds, and a duck pond—seemed wide open and threatening. The business establishments that surrounded it on four sides—ranging from Mexican-era adobes to false-fronted Western structures to the Depression-era Sebastiani Theatre—afforded plenty of old-fashioned charm, but little comfort. And the streets: In summer they were thronged with tourists who had been lured by Sonoma's ties to California history and tastings at the nearby wineries, but now the crowds had thinned; the very emptiness made Joanna feel vulnerable.

And that feeling in itself was ridiculous, she told herself. Just because a man had been asking for her at the post office, had known her box number but wanted her home address. A tall man, with graying hair. A man whose description matched that of any number of people she knew. A man who might be—

"Stop it," she said aloud. "Stop it right now."

A woman who was also cutting across the plaza gave her a peculiar look, then smiled and went on. It was one of the clerks from the Sonoma Cheese Company, where Joanna frequently had lunch. She decided to go over there and sit in the courtyard and think this through. The man didn't *have* to present any sort of threat; he could be a salesman or the census taker or even an old friend.

She crossed Spain Street and pushed through the doors of the Cheese Company. It was also less crowded than usual—only one pair of visitors stood at the back, looking through the plate glass windows at the stainless-steel tanks of whey—and she took a few minutes to snoop through the case offering Brie and Cheddar, Jarlsberg and Edam, Sonoma cheeses and those from all over the world, before choosing some Jack and a little salami. Then she got a glass of Chablis and went out into the patio to her favorite corner table. As she nibbled on her lunch, she leafed listlessly through a true-crime magazine which, along with a bulletin from the International Council of Museums and a bill from PG&E, had been the only mail in her box at the post office.

SHE ONLY KILLED THE ONES SHE LOVED.... SOUTH DAKOTA'S STRANGE DISMEMBERMENT DEATHS.... DISHWASHER VICTIM A SUICIDE—OR WAS IT MURDER?

Joanna closed the magazine, wondering why she still bothered to take it, or any of the other, similar ones that were delivered each month. For altogether too many

years now, they had contained nothing of serious interest to her, and it had been at least five years since she'd
enjoyed reading any of the articles for their sensational
value. She opened the ICOM bulletin, turned to its listing of recent art thefts, and quickly skimmed it. After
making a couple of half-hearted mental notes, she tossed
it on top of the magazine and her utility bill. It was time
she stopped this nonsense, and also stopped being
afraid—

"Hi, Joanna. May I join you?"

It was her friend, Mary Bennett, who ran the quilt
shop across the street from the Sonoma Mission.
"Sure."

Mary sat down, squinting in the sunlight that filtered
through the overhead latticework. She was a big woman
with unruly red hair, a former ad copywriter from "The
City," as San Francisco was called in these parts.

Funny, Joanna thought as she watched Mary unwrap
her sandwich, a lot of us who live here are former
somethings from someplace else. And we're divided into
two groups, those who are settled and belong and those
who don't. I don't; Mary does. Why? Probably because
she has a business to go about.

After a few minutes Mary—whose well-meaning nosiness was a source of both amusement and irritation to
her friends—pushed aside the ICOM bulletin and looked
at the lurid cover of the true-crime magazine. "So you're
still reading that crap."

"It's a hobby, like gardening."

"I suppose you've got an excuse, having been a detective."

"Not really. A security consultant to art galleries and
museums isn't a detective by any stretch of the imagi-

nation. Most of what I did was pretty mundane compared to investigating dismemberment deaths."

"Well, I bet it beat writing ads for underwear." Mary's biggest account had been a lingerie company.

"Maybe. Anyway, I'm thinking of letting my subscriptions run out." Joanna motioned at the magazine.

"Why?"

"I don't know. I guess I've outgrown them."

Mary regarded Joanna thoughtfully. "You seem down in the mouth today."

"A little."

"Is something wrong?"

Joanna thought of the man at the post office. He—whoever he might be—had merely served to raise an existing mild depression to anxiety level. She'd been meaning to discuss her low mood with Mary for some time now. "Yes and no," she finally said. "Mainly I'm worried about me."

"How so?"

She hesitated a moment before she said, "I'm not doing anything. After David died, I moved up here to establish an art gallery. I'd always wanted to, and I had plenty of money, and after years of working with gallery owners, I'd learned the ins and outs of the business—"

"I know all that," Mary said, "but that was three years ago. You never did anything about it, but you've seemed happy enough."

"Well, for a while I had lots of other things to do. First I had to fix up the house. And then there was the garden. And by that time I'd gotten used to my life here—get up late, grind the coffee beans, read the paper. Bicycle into town for the mail, have lunch, visit with friends, run errands. And then work in the garden, maybe take a nap, start dinner, read or watch TV or listen to music. Nice and slow and easy.''

"So why all this discontent now?''

She shrugged. "I guess I'm not cut out for a life of leisure. I've always worked, and worked hard. The idea of settling back into rich widowhood at forty-two horrifies me. I feel slothful—and bored.''

"I'd hardly call you slothful,'' Mary said. "Renovating that old farmhouse was a lot of work. You had to consult with the contractors and order the materials and, as I recall, supervise their goon squads when the boss was off at other job sites. It may not have been work for pay, but it was damned hard labor.''

"I suppose so.'' The trouble with friends, Joanna reflected, was that they felt obliged to defend you, even when you yourself were the one doing the criticizing. "But the house has been done for a year and a half now.''

"Then get on with the gallery.''

"That's part of my problem; the gallery idea has lost its appeal. I need work, but not that kind. And I don't know what—''

She broke off as she noticed a familiar figure standing in the door to the patio. Nick Alexander, her former business partner from San Francisco. So he was the man who had been asking for her at the post office, she thought, relieved.

Nick's thick black hair had more gray in it and his craggy face was more lined than when she'd last seen him at David's funeral three years ago, but otherwise he looked much the same, right down to the jeans and button-down shirt that were his habitual attire. When he saw her, he smiled and started toward the table. Immediately Joanna's relief evaporated. It was his sharklike smile, the one that made her nervous—and with good cause.

The smile always appeared when Nick was about to demand something of her. And Joanna was sure he would never have driven to Sonoma—which he considered a sort of uncivilized outpost—had he not wanted something badly. It would matter not at all to him when she explained that he could no longer make demands, that they were no longer business partners, save for the one-third financial interest that she had never gotten around to withdrawing from the firm. When Nick saw that an outright demand wouldn't work, he would then fall back on appealing to her sense of loyalty to him and their joint enterprise. And when she told him that she considered leaving her money invested to be loyalty enough, he would finally sink to cajoling, pleading, outright begging. These latter tactics were what Joanna feared most, because with them Nick stood a very good chance of succeeding.

He stopped next to the table. "Well, Joanna, fancy meeting you here."

"You were at the post office asking about me."

"If you'd list your street address and phone number in the city directory, or give them to old friends, I wouldn't have had to lurk around a government building." He pulled out a chair and sat down, stretching his long legs into the aisle.

Joanna sighed. "Mary, this is my former business partner, Nick Alexander. Nick, Mary Bennett." Pointedly she added, "Mary's a friend from the new life I've established here and like very much."

Nick grinned at Mary, who regarded him suspiciously. To Joanna, he said, "Why do I suddenly feel so welcome?"

Mary stood up quickly and said, "I'd better be getting back to the shop."

"No." Joanna put a hand on her arm. "Don't rush off."

Mary hesitated, looking dubiously at Nick. He spread his hands out and said, "I'm harmless."

She glanced back at Joanna.

Joanna sighed again, "It's okay, he's telling the truth. I guess you can leave me with him." She watched her friend carry the remains of her lunch to the trash basket, then turned to Nick. "So how are things at Security Systems International?"

"I sent you the financial report."

"I didn't look at it."

"Casual about your investments, aren't you?"

"I trust you." It was true; she and Nick had been through a lot together in the thirteen years she'd been with S.S.I., first as an employee and later as a partner.

Nick's face grew somber and more deeply lined. Joanna realized her initial impression had been false; he had aged swiftly in the past three years, looked older than forty-nine. "Perhaps you shouldn't have been so trusting," he said.

"Why? Is S.S.I. in trouble?"

"If you'd read the financial report, you'd know."

"Do you need to borrow money?" That was the one thing she was willing to do for him.

"No, I think I can pull it out without borrowing. But I do need your help."

"How?"

"With a theft that's just happened. It's a tough one, and you're the only person—"

"No." The word came out swiftly. "I told you I like my life here. And I'm not going back to San Francisco; there are too many memories—"

"I'm not asking you to move back, or to be there very long. You can handle this quickly, and then come back up here and sit on your fanny again."

The reference to what Joanna regarded as her worst and most ample feature irritated her, but she was also curious as to what kind of theft would make him come up here and hunt for her. But if she asked, he would only try to override her refusal....

Nick must have seen the indecision on her face and taken it as a hopeful sign, because he said, "Jo, you have to help me."

"No."

"This is vitally important to the future of S.S.I. The theft occurred last night at the de Young, and they've come to me and asked that we cooperate with the investigator from their insurance carrier."

The de Young was the art museum in Golden Gate Park where Joanna had worked on revamping part of the security system after a Rembrandt had been stolen years before. "What was taken this time?"

"A Hals painting—*The Cavalier in White*. It was removed from its frame before it was taken out of there. You remember it? It hung in the same room that the *Portrait of a Rabbi* was stolen from."

"Yes, I remember it." Frans Hals was one of Joanna's favorite Dutch painters, and the *Cavalier*—a foppish, smirking young nobleman dressed all in white—had held her attention even in the middle of the frantic process of shoring up the museum's violated security. "They didn't take it through the skylight, like the *Rabbi*, did they? No, they couldn't have; I made sure that—"

Then she caught Nick's expectant look. "I'm sorry about the theft, Nick, but I can't help you."

"Jo, don't you see, I need you. S.S.I. needs you."

Nick had quickly passed from the demanding stage to that of appealing to her loyalty. "It's just not possible," she said. "Besides, the police won't want S.S.I. interfering in their investigation."

"The police don't know about the theft yet."

"What? Why not?"

"It's too sensitive a situation."

"*Why?*"

Nick smiled at her. With a flash of annoyance, Joanna realized he had added extortion to his persuasive repertoire. "Dammit, Nick, that's not fair!"

He continued to smile, lounging indolently in his chair. "The museum people wouldn't want me discussing this any further with someone who's determined not to be come involved," he said.

She hesitated, then decided two could play his sly, manipulative game. With an elaborate sigh, she stood up. "I can understand why. But look, as long as you're in town, why don't you come by the house for a little while?"

His smile faded. Joanna went on, "I'd love for you to see it. It's a far cry now from the dilapidated old farmhouse David and I inherited."

He watched her, his eyes calculating. "I could come over for a few minutes."

Joanna restrained an impulse to laugh. They were indeed playing the same game—each of them buying time. Nick probably thought that if he came to the house, he might yet convince her to help him. And she hoped that if she plied him with some of the good red wine she had on hand, he would tell her more about the situation at the de Young.

As they left the Cheese Factory, Nick pointed to the left down Spain Street, toward a group of buildings erected in the 1830s by General Mariano Vallejo's forces. "My car's parked in front of the barracks."

"My bicycle's at the post office. Why don't I meet you at the house in about twenty minutes?"

His eyes widened. "Your *what*?"

"Bicycle. I ride it into town every day."

"My God, don't tell me *you've* turned into a physical fitness freak!"

"Not really. Anyway, I'm terrible at riding the thing. I fall off a lot. That's why I leave it at the post office— so I won't embarrass myself in front of the whole town."

"So why ride it at all?"

"I'm determined to conquer it."

He shook his head.

"The house," Joanna said, "is a big white one on Old Winery Road, about half a mile after you turn off Napa Street. You'll recognize it by the persimmon tree in the front yard. Do you think you can find it?"

"Sure. I'll just look for someone lying near a bicycle in the driveway."

TWO

As JOANNA ROUNDED the bend on Old Winery Road, her two-story white farmhouse came into view. It was a dignified relic of the Victorian era, replete with elaborate gingerbreading and a wide porch wrapped all the way around. The gnarled persimmon tree in the front yard added a burst of color to an otherwise sedate scene. Nick's blue Mustang was parked next to the tree, and he was leaning on the car, his arms folded across his chest.

Joanna got off her bicycle and began walking it toward the graveled driveway; the turn from the road was difficult to negotiate and she didn't want to demonstrate her lack of skill. As she walked she surveyed the house with pride. She, by her own efforts, had made it the showplace it was today. This was home, and she didn't want to leave it—even temporarily.

When she and David had first seen the house, it had been a decaying wreck, with peeling paint, tumbledown front steps, a crumbling chimney, and a weed-choked garden. It had come into their hands as an inheritance from an uncle of his, unexpected and, quite frankly, unwanted. They'd made minimal repairs and hired a neighbor to watch over it, then departed for the city, intending to put the place on the market the next spring.

The matter of the house, however, had become unimportant because before spring could come, David had learned he had bone cancer. He was a number of years older than Joanna—fifty-nine to her (then) thirty-eight—but still the possibility and then the probability and finally the certainty of his death had stunned her. David, thoughtful and practical to the last, had gone about his affairs methodically—winding down his law practice, which dealt mainly with clients in the art world, selling off portions of the extensive and valuable collection that he had acquired as an outgrowth of that practice, arranging trusts for Joanna and his son E.J. It was David, in fact, who had suggested that once she was alone she might be better off leaving the city and S.S.I. and living in the Sonoma house for a time. There would, he had said, be few memories attached to the place and a great deal of work to keep her mind occupied.

And now, three years later, the house sparkled with new paint, the yard was tidy, the branches of the persimmon tree—which had been half dead—leaned low to the ground with their burden of orange fruit. There was smoke rising from the chimney....

Smoke? She certainly hadn't left a fire burning. Joanna dropped the bicycle on the lawn and hurried up the brick path to the front steps. Nick pushed away from his car and followed her.

"What's the matter?" he asked.

Without answering Joanna ran up the steps, crossed the porch, and went inside to the living room. A fire blazed cheerfully on the grate. She turned, brushed past Nick, and went to the little bedroom off the kitchen. There, in the former maid's quarters that was now one of the guest rooms, an orange backpack leaned against the antique oak dresser.

"I knew it," she said, running her fingers through her short dark curls in frustration. "E.J.'s arrived. How like him to light a fire and then run right out again!"

When she turned, Nick was standing in the doorway. "Your stepson is here?"

"None other than the mercurial Elliot J. Stark."

"What's he doing these days?"

"The same thing he's been doing ever since David died—wandering around the country with that backpack, picking up odd jobs here and there."

"He must be . . . twenty-two now. No plans to go to college?"

"None that he's bothered to inform me of."

"Does he do this often—show up without giving you any warning?"

"Oh, I usually know more or less when he'll appear. E.J. travels fairly predictably. For instance, you can count on him to turn up whenever he senses a big feed is about to be put on the table. He's early, though; I didn't expect him until next week, for Thanksgiving. Well, at least you and I are here to enjoy the fire he's made."

They went back to the living room, and Nick took one of the overstuffed chairs. Joanna curled up on the couch, tucking a rough-woven blanket around her feet.

"How are you and E.J. getting along now that David's gone?" Nick asked.

"Fine as ever, when we see one another. That is, as long as we stay off the subject of what he's going to do with his life."

"Well, I suppose all this wandering has something to do with losing his father so suddenly, and at a critical time in his life. Young men need guidance—"

"He also has a mother."

The words had come out sharply, and Nick seemed surprised. "Well, yes, a stepmother. But you've got to remember, he lost his real mother when he was only ten. The combination of the two deaths has to have had an adverse effect—"

"He wasn't motherless long; David and I were married the same year that Eleanor died. And I was always there for E.J."

"I didn't mean to imply that you weren't."

Ashamed of her snappish reaction, Joanna quickly said, "Oh, Nick, I know you didn't. Don't mind me; I'm just touchy about E.J. because I worry about him. But in spite of his wandering ways, I'm pretty proud of him too. Even though David left him a substantial trust, he earns most of his own money and asks for very little. And he's charming and caring. It's just hard to picture him growing up or living in one place or leading a normal existence. I suppose that's what worries me. When he's forty-five, will he be able to get by on charm alone?"

"Maybe he'll snap out of it. Most kids do."

"Yes, except E.J.'s not a kid anymore. When I was twenty-two...but enough of this." Joanna paused, staring into the fire and hoping Nick would take the opportunity to reopen their discussion of the theft at the de Young. Perversely, he didn't, and she wasn't surprised. The reason Nick was such a good game player was that he varied his basic strategy from time to time; in the thirteen years they'd worked together she'd never quite figured out all the ground rules because they changed so frequently.

She was about to lead him into the subject by asking more about the financial problems at S.S.I. when Nick motioned at the oil painting over the fireplace and said, "A Rodriguez, isn't it?" Rodriguez was a well-known Filipino artist who was currently enjoying a vogue in the United States.

"Yes. And appreciating in value every day."

"Ever think of selling it?"

"Never."

He smiled. "No wonder you haven't started the gallery you were talking about—you'd never be able to part with any of your precious stock. Too much love of art. On the other hand, your knowledge and enthusiasm made you an excellent security consultant."

Ah, Joanna thought, now he's using a subtle approach that incorporates flattery. "Oh, did it now?"

"You were terrific—in spite of the fact I didn't want to hire you at first."

"I remember that well. You thought anyone who had studied art history couldn't possibly install burglar alarms in galleries."

"What did I know? Besides, you've got to admit you didn't look very promising. You came in late for your appointment, all bedraggled, with a chip on your shoulder—"

"I think it was more like with a hole in my shoe."

"Oh yeah?"

"Uh-huh. It was pouring rain and I had a hole in the sole of my only pair of good shoes, and the water kept seeping in. The buses were running off schedule, and I'd stood waiting for one for half an hour. You could hardly blame me for being late and bedraggled in that kind of storm."

"Late, bedraggled, and *mean*."

"I just seemed mean—actually I was desperate." She had been down to her last five dollars and had no place to turn. Her father had disowned her when she'd run off to Europe at nineteen—actually she had disowned *him* by doing so—and she had no friends in the city, and the rent on her apartment was two months overdue. It was either get the job or jump off the Golden Gate Bridge. And she was afraid of heights.

"So you bullied me into hiring you," Nick said. "I figured you were so persuasive that you'd probably talk the customers into buying bigger and better alarms once you got tidied up and over your bad temper. After all, you could speak the gallery owners' language, knew a Matisse from a Soutine." He paused, looking faintly surprised, as if he'd never thought of it until then. "Damned if you didn't make a good installer, too."

"Well, it's not that difficult once you study the instructions and try it a few times."

"I know, but that was in the days when I thought women couldn't learn things like that. But you were a good employee and an even better partner. If you hadn't bought into the firm when I needed capital and then convinced me that we should expand into comprehensive security planning, we'd still be nothing more than a burglar-alarm outfit."

"It was David who gave me the money to invest."

"David's money, your business sense. If it wasn't for you, we'd never have been approached by the de Young after the Rembrandt was stolen."

She's been wondering how long it would take him to get around to the museum. "That's true."

"Or this time, about the Hals."

"Right."

"Jo, won't you consider—"

"Tell me more about the Hals."

"It's confidential information."

"How can a person consider taking on a job when she knows nothing about it?"

She almost felt guilty when she saw the flicker of satisfaction in Nick's eyes. Almost. He leaned forward in the chair, his elbows on his knees, big hands dangling, and said, "I told you it was a sensitive situation. That's because it has the earmarks of an inside job. There's a security guard missing.''

"Who is he?''

"Name's Wilson Reed. He disappeared during his shift—the twelve-to-eight—last night. No one knows exactly when, but it was around five A.M. that the *Cavalier* was missed. Do you remember Reed? He's been with the museum for years.''

"Only vaguely.'' She pictured a stocky, gray-haired man. "He was on vacation when the Rembrandt was stolen, so I only had brief dealings with him. Do the museum officials think he stole the Hals?''

"They're not sure what to think. Like I said, he's worked there a long time and has a good record. And frankly, his supervisor doubts he's smart enough to have pulled such a thing off. Still, he could have been coached by someone who did the actual planning.''

"Or seen the thief and met with foul play because of it.''

Nick nodded. "But there's something else about Reed. He's connected with the inner circle of the San Francisco art world.''

"A security guard? Wait a minute—that's not the man whose wife was housekeeper for the Wheatleys?''

"Yes, it is. And Marshall Wheatley is the one who got him his job at the museum.''

"I see.'' Joanna closed her eyes, feeling a sudden nostalgia. Since she'd moved to Sonoma, she'd only given brief thought to the Wheatley family—usually when their annual Christmas card arrived—but once they had been very much a part of her life. Marshall Wheatley, the sixty-five-year-old patriarch of the clan, was one of the city's most prominent and reputable art dealers, and had been David's first client and closest friend. Wheatley's wife, Phyllis, had for many years been on the board of the museum; even now that she had retired from such time-consuming work, she was active in setting up special loans and exhibits of objects from the family's personal collections. They had two sons, Douglas and Michael, both of whom must be in their twenties by now. Douglas had broken with family tradition and gone into the business world—banking, was it? Mike, however, was an artist—and, she had heard, something of a black sheep.

Nick said, "You see how that complicates things?"

"Not really. I'm sure the museum officials don't believe the Wheatleys were involved in the theft."

"Well, there's something else—"

The back door of the house opened and closed. E.J.'s voice called out, "Jo, are you home?"

Joanna rolled her eyes and stood up. "E.J. always did have a fine sense of timing. Let's go back to the kitchen and say hello, get a glass of wine. We can continue this discussion later."

Nick nodded and followed her to the big country kitchen at the rear of the house. E.J. stood at the central chopping block—a slender young man with rumpled blond hair and a bushy beard. His turquoise blue eyes sparkled when he saw Joanna, and he left the two sacks of groceries he'd been unpacking and crossed to give her a bear hug that nearly suffocated her.

"Hey, Jo," he said, "you're looking great."

"You too." Indulgently she surveyed his worn plaid hunting shirt and faded jeans, more pleased to see him than she was willing to let on. "You remember Nick Alexander?"

E.J. looked surprised to see Nick there, but held out his hand. "Sure. How you doing, Nick?"

"Pretty good. Yourself?"

"Just great."

"When did you get into town?"

"Couple of hours ago. Hitched in from Eureka a little early for Thanksgiving."

Joanna went to the wine rack and inspected the bottles that were stored there. "What were you doing in Eureka?"

"Waiting tables at the Samoa Cookhouse. Good chow and plenty of it."

What Joanna really wanted to know was *why* he'd been in Eureka, but E.J. had never been good at answering such mundane questions. She let it go and said, "Well, this calls for a celebration," and pulled a bottle of Buena Vista Zinfandel from the rack. "From the vineyards just up the road. It's a red wine day, right?"

"Right," both E.J. and Nick said.

As she worked the corkscrew, she motioned at the sacks on the chopping block. "What's in those?"

"Dinner."

"Ah, you're cooking. What are we having?"

"A new recipe I thought up while I was waiting to hitch a ride outside Willits. You take some boned chicken breasts, sauté them in the marinade from those Italian artichoke hearts, then add mushrooms, black olives, Parmesan, lots of garlic—you'll love it."

"How do you know what it'll taste like if you've never made it before?"

"I've been imagining it for eight hours. It took a long time to get a ride."

Joanna passed around glasses of wine, and they toasted one another. Then Nick asked to use the phone. She motioned at the one on the kitchen wall, and while he placed a collect call to S.S.I.'s number in San Francisco, she and E.J. sat down at the round oak table in the breakfast nook.

"Well," she said, "it sounds like a wonderful dinner. Nice of you to buy."

E.J. looked embarrassed and gulped his wine.

"What's the matter?"

"The groceries—I, uh, asked them to put them on your tab at the store."

There were certain advantages to living in a small town where the shopkeepers let you run tabs—and certain disadvantages. Joanna tried to look stern, but her happiness at seeing E.J. made it impossible.

He spread his hands out and grinned helplessly. "I lost my last week's wages in a poker game in Arcata the night before I left."

"So that's why you're here early."

"'Home is the place where when you go there, they have to take you in.' Or something like that."

"I'm glad to see you haven't forgotten all your schooling."

Nick hung up the phone, came to the table, and drank up the rest of his wine. "Joanna, I'm sorry, but I've got to go."

"But you haven't finished telling me about the—"

He shook his head, glancing pointedly at E.J. "Why don't you walk me out to my car? Nice to see you again, E.J."

Joanna got up and followed him out. When they reached the Mustang, he turned. "There isn't much more to tell, but the rest is the important part. Late this morning, the insurance company that carries the policy on the Hals got a phone tip. A certain party claims he has information about the *Cavalier*'s whereabouts and is willing to part with it for a price."

"Who?"

"Mike Wheatley, Marshall and Phyllis's renegade son."

She bit her lip. "That's bad."

"It sure is."

"Have you contacted Marshall or Phyllis to see what they might know about this?"

"No. Mike specifically said that if we did, it would blow any negotiations. With the safety of the painting at stake, we have to honor that. Anyway, Mike said he would call back this afternoon and arrange a meeting with the insurance carrier's investigator, a fellow named Steve Rafferty, but so far he hasn't recontacted them. That's why I have to get back to town—to confer with Rafferty."

"What insurance company is it?"

"Great American."

"They're good at this sort of thing; they've negotiated several returns on valuable stolen items. But I don't know this Steve Rafferty."

"New man in the region, came out from New York last year. That's why they—and the de Young—want you on the case. You could help Rafferty a lot because you know the museum, the local art scene. More important, you know the Wheatleys."

Joanna thought of her old friends once again. She was awfully fond of Marshall and Phyllis. They had been nice to her when a lot of David's friends hadn't, when she married him so soon after his first wife, Eleanor's, death. Actually, they were more like parents to her than her own people ever had been. She hadn't seen much of the boys in recent years, but had heard there had been a lot of trouble with Mike. Whatever it was, she didn't know the particulars. Marshall and Phyllis weren't ones to air their family problems to their friends.

"You don't suppose this means Mike was in on the theft, do you?" she asked.

Nick shrugged, in a hurry to leave now.

Joanna looked back at her house and the smoke curling up from the chimney. She thought of E.J. and the special chicken dinner he had planned. Then she thought of Mike Wheatley and the lives that might be shattered if somehow he really were involved in the theft of the Hals—valuable lives, ones that mattered a great deal to her personally. Perhaps if a friend of the family were involved in the investigation...

"What time are you meeting with Rafferty?" she asked.

Nick hesitated, halfway into his car. "Five o'clock, at my office."

"I'll be there." The words were out before she had made a conscious decision.

THREE

IT WAS BEGINNING to get dark when Joanna arrived at the Fifth and Mission parking garage in downtown San Francisco. She left her white Fiat convertible in one of the basement stalls—as she had the succession of cars she'd owned in the years she'd worked at S.S.I.—and climbed the urine-stinking stairway to the street. The temperature here was noticeably colder than the crisp fall chill of Sonoma evenings; wind gusted up the side street, blowing discarded newspapers and other city debris against her legs. She pushed up the fur collar of her coat until it brushed her curls, jammed her hands deep in her pockets, and started across the intersection.

For more than a decade Joanna had crossed Mission toward Market on her way from the parking garage to her office; usually she had been caught up in thought—making mental lists of phone calls and appointments, planning the flow of her day, oblivious to the street scene around her. But now she looked about eagerly, with the curiosity of the long absent.

At close to five o'clock the streets were crowded: tired-looking workers stood in lines at the curbs, waiting for Muni and shuttle buses; shoppers streamed toward the parking lots and garages, sheltering from the wind behind their parcels; convivial groups pushed in and out of the bar at the Pickwick Hotel; diagonally across the street in front of the *Chronicle-Examiner* building, a newsie hawked the evening paper; and of course there were the derelicts and bag ladies. As she approached the corner of Market Street, Joanna spied an old wino known as Max who for years had spent his days and nights patrolling this single block on the north side of Fifth Street. When she came abreast of him, he made his standard pitch: "Loan me a dollar, lady, and I'll buy you a beer."

"No thanks, Max," she said, as she had many a time in the old days.

And as he always had, Max nodded philosophically and went to corral someone else.

S.S.I.'s offices were a block away on Market Street, in a narrow stone building that had been built in 1907, rising up from the rubble left by the great earthquake. In spite of its age and the declining fortunes of most of its tenants, much of its turn-of-the-century charm remained: The facade was ornamented with a frieze of angels and cherubs, all of them with windblown hair and beatific expressions that could still be seen through their surface grime; the lobby floor was white Vermont marble, worn dull in the center, still lustrous toward the walls where no feet passed; the gold filigree work around the elevator cages and the clock above them remained, even though the clock no longer worked and the hand-operated cars had been replaced with self-service ones. Even the old codger named Bill who manned the security desk was still there; he glanced at Joanna and grunted for her to pass as if she'd been in to work only yesterday.

She got into the first elevator and pressed the button for the seventh floor, fighting off a hollowness in her stomach and an almost dizzying sense of disorientation. Everything was the same; things had gone on in their normal course without her. But she had changed; where she had once belonged she now felt out of place.

And where she should belong by now—Sonoma—she didn't fit either.

Maybe now that David was gone she was never going to feel at home anywhere. Maybe she was destined to live in the world as a stranger, the way she'd felt during those lonely, sad, wandering years in Europe and Asia. Wandering, like E.J. Only E.J. was fortunate: He had inherited a sense of self, of roots within his own person, and thus he could be at home anywhere. She needed something external and concrete to cling to.

When the elevator came to rest at the seventh floor, Joanna shook her head hard—an old trick that usually banished bad feelings. The disorientation and threatening pressure of tears behind her eyelids vanished; the hollowness remained. She got out of the cage, turned right, and crossed to the door of S.S.I.'s suite.

The door was open and the little reception room was deserted. Everything looked the same here too. The decor of the reception room had been one of Joanna's contributions, creating a genteelly quiet area carpeted in soft beige with warm brown chairs, all designed to inspire confidence and soothe troubled or anxious clients. Framed posters from local museum and gallery openings subtly stated S.S.I.'s solid connections with the art world. But as Joanna stood in the door taking it all in, she began to notice slight differences: Two of the posters hung at odd angles; the leaves of the large philodendron plant were dusty; the secretary/receptionist's desk looked as if a pack rat had taken up residence.

Small signs, she thought, but unmistakable evidence that S.S.I. is indeed in trouble.

She skirted the untidy desk and went into the narrow hall beyond it. To one side was the darkened conference room that served as communal working space and gathering ground for the staff of security consultants. Next to it was the closed door of her former office. Who was using it now? she wondered, and was surprised to feel a faint twinge of possessiveness. Pushing that thought aside, she went to the end of the hall, knocked on the frame of Nick's open door, and went in.

Nick sat behind his big metal desk, his right foot propped on its corner. In one of the chairs across from him sat a man with a thick silvery gray mane and a tanned, youthful face that belied his hair color. He stood up, smiling coolly and professionally when Joanna came in, and she saw he was over six feet tall, trim and muscular under his well-tailored blue suit. Nick, never one to stand on ceremony, merely motioned at her and said, "Joanna Stark, Steve Rafferty."

They shook hands—his handclasp was brief but firm—and Joanna sat in the other chair, shrugging out of her coat and hanging her shoulderbag over the armrest. "Am I late?" she asked.

"Not really. Steve came over early because he wanted to report some news."

Joanna looked at Rafferty. "Mike Wheatley made contact?"

Rafferty looked back at her with level hazel eyes; his gaze was appraising, neutral. "Not Wheatley. A woman."

"Who?"

"She wouldn't identify herself, but she claimed to be calling for him."

"What did she say?"

Rafferty began ticking points off on his fingers. "First, that the Hals is safe and that the party who has it has no intention of taking it out of the country."

That was reassuring, Joanna thought. Generally most major stolen artworks could be presumed to have left the country of origin within twenty-four hours of their theft.

"Second, that Mike Wheatley is not in possession of the Hals, and will deny any knowledge of it if questioned by the police or his family. That was merely a reiteration of what he already said in his phone call this morning."

"Some chutzpah," Joanna said, "to give his name in the first place."

Nick said, "I think he did that for a reason. Wheatley is a big name in art circles; he knew if he gave it that we'd take him seriously. And with his connections at the museum, he probably knows how they—and their insurance carriers—operate in the case of a major theft, that they wouldn't go to the police if they thought there was a chance he might lead them to the Hals."

"Still, it shows a lot of confidence."

"Or stupidity," Rafferty suggested. "Anyway, the third point was that we continue to keep the police out of it and, since the painting is not destined to be taken abroad, that we not have the theft circularized by Interpol."

"Which could be a ploy to get us to hold off until it *is* out of the country and gone forever," Joanna said. "We may be cutting our own throats by not bringing in the law enforcement agencies."

Something that might have been approval flickered in Rafferty's eyes. "That's true. Unfortunately, the decision is out of our hands. The museum officials are adamant about how they want this handled."

It was not an unusual way of handling a theft where there were indications of an inside job, Joanna knew. Especially one like this, where there was a strong possibility that the painting would be recovered. And because of the connection with the Wheatley family, museum officials would exercise extra caution; they wouldn't want to risk besmirching the name of two of their most beloved—and generous—patrons.

"Anything else about the woman's phone call?" she asked.

"Yes. Wheatley will contact us with his demands tomorrow morning. Once we comply, he'll arrange a meeting."

"Did she give any indication of what those demands might be?"

Rafferty shook his head in the negative. "Her final point was that Wheatley is willing to negotiate only with Great American's representative."

"Did she seem certain that Great American was the carrier?"

"Yes."

"Then she and Wheatley have inside information. The artworks at the de Young aren't all insured by the same carrier; it would be difficult for someone who wasn't an insider to know who wrote the policy on the Hals."

Nick asked, "Could Mike have learned that from his mother?"

"I don't think so," Joanna said. "When she was a board member, Phyllis would have had access to the information, but it isn't likely to be something she would have concerned herself with. And it's been several years since she quit the board. Also, she wouldn't reveal such facts to Mike without knowing exactly why he wanted to know. Phyllis is a sharp lady; few people—and certainly not her own son—can fool her."

Nick grunted.

To Rafferty, Joanna said, "Tell me, did this woman speak knowledgeably? Did she sound like she was using her own words, or as if she'd been coached?"

He considered. "I'd say she was speaking more or less extemporaneously. I had no impression that she was following a script or notes, for instance. I'll be glad to let you hear our tape of the conversation."

"Thanks, it might help." Joanna was silent, thinking over what Rafferty had related of the conversation. The woman who had called could very possibly be an insider at the museum. Perhaps she, Mike Wheatley, and the missing security guard had engineered the theft. Certainly her insistence on not calling in the police and negotiating only with the insurance carrier indicated she was well versed in how such delicate situations were typically handled.

While some major U.S. cities had art squads whose primary function was to recover stolen works unharmed, San Francisco did not. Any investigation of the theft would be handled by the police department's burglary detail. And because they were not schooled to protect the artwork at all costs, the squad's first objective would be apprehension of the thief, or thieves. On the other hand, Great American had significant financial interest in seeing the painting restored safely to the de Young, and would be prepared to ransom the work at a high percentage of the face value of the policy. Until that was accomplished, they would not jeopardize the *Cavalier* by going after the thieves.

Rafferty said, "What about this Mike Wheatley, Mrs. Stark? You know him. Does he really have the knowledge and ability to have stolen that painting and negotiate its ransom?"

"I never thought I'd say this, but I really do wish I'd known Mike better. As I remember him, he was a horrid boy, always disrupting his parents' dinner parties. I recall one time when there was a frog in the soup tureen...." She closed her eyes, trying to dredge up any details she might have heard about the trouble Marshall and Phyllis had had with their younger son. "I think," she finally said, "Mike's been involved in the usual rich-kid scrapes. Getting kicked out of schools, drunk driving. There may even have been a paternity suit."

"He drinks heavily, then?" Nick said.

"Yes, and when he does he loses all his judgment and takes chances, mainly with expensive automobiles."

"What about drugs?"

"I don't know."

"And he's some sort of artist?"

"Some sort, but I doubt he's very successful. I would have heard if he were."

Rafferty said, "Frankly, he doesn't sound like the sort who could pull off a sophisticated art theft, even with an inside accomplice. What he does sound like is someone who might run a bluff."

Joanna turned to him. "You think he heard about the theft—perhaps from his mother—and is trying to extort money by pretending to know who stole it?"

"Yes."

"On the other hand," Nick said, "maybe the woman who called is the one with the know-how and coached Mike."

Joanna shrugged. "We could sit here all night speculating. None of us really knows Mike or how his mind works. Until we find out more about him—and I intend to look into that—we have no idea where the Hals may be. If Wheatley *is* running a bluff, the painting could be anywhere. For all we know, it could be in Argentina by now."

At the mention of South America, both Nick's and Rafferty's expressions became grim. It was a common destination for many stolen artworks—and one from which they were notoriously difficult to recover. That continent's reputation for harboring escaped Nazis, lunatic millionaires, high-level criminals, and every imaginable breed of power-crazed politico may have been greatly exaggerated, but the fact remained that the authorities there were maddeningly uncooperative in assisting investigations of art thefts.

Joanna continued, "This theft was a sophisticated one. It would have taken exhaustive planning to remove that painting from the gallery where it hung. I ought to know, because I helped revamp the security system in that room. So I think we can rule out theft on a whim."

Nick nodded. "For one thing, those kinds of capers happen during the hours when the museum is open to the public. A person's walking through a gallery and gets an urge for a Monet. He grabs it, stuffs it under his jacket, and gets caught right away. Or if, by some fluke, he gets away with it, he doesn't know what to do with his plunder and ends up taking it home and hiding it in the laundry hamper, or abandoning it where someone will find it and return it."

"Like that small Madonna and Child," Joanna said. "The marble sculpture that was stolen from the Oakland Museum last year and later abandoned in the courtyard of Mission Dolores. Remember?"

"Uh-huh. I think we have to agree that no amateur could have engineered this difficult heist. So we can also rule out a museum-goer who has been lusting after the *Cavalier* and just decided to break in and take it."

"Then what we have left," Rafferty said, "is high-level professional theft. The Hals was stolen either for some type of ransom, or on order from a broker."

Nick said, "Well, as far as ransom goes, we can be fairly certain it hasn't been taken for any sort of political statement. You know—'Send two million dollars to the starving Ethiopians and I'll return your painting.' Such a demand would have been made public by now."

The word "broker" had made Joanna sit up straighter. "I think we should canvass some of the less reputable local dealers to see if any of them have been approached about making arrangements with a Fagin." A "Fagin," named in honor of the Charles Dickens character, managed a string of thieves—usually young men—who worked on a commission basis. Contrary to romantic notions, the actual thief was the lowliest link in a chain that could start with a multimillionaire collector who placed orders with his art broker in the same manner he would buy stock. The broker—or "private dealer"—would contact a middleman, most likely an art dealer, in the city where the work was located; and in turn the middleman would contact the Fagin, who would contact the thief, who would then begin laying—casing—the place where the desired artwork was housed.

Joanna looked at Rafferty. "There are some dealers with whom I have a rapport and can talk personally, but I'll have to ask you to check out the ones who might become suspicious or panicked if I showed up asking questions."

"Fine with me. But let's reserve that until after Wheatley's call tomorrow morning."

They were silent for a moment while Rafferty scribbled some notes on a pad. Then Nick said, "What bothers me about this theft is the missing security guard—Wilson Reed.''

Joanna nodded. ''I take it efforts are still being made to locate him?''

''Yes,'' Rafferty said, ''both by museum people and my staff. His disappearance bothers me too. It doesn't fit. Most professional thieves prefer to work alone, without a contact inside the museum.''

Most professional thieves, Joanna thought, but not all. She had pushed the idea to the back of her mind as soon as Nick had mentioned the missing man that afternoon. Pushed it there and kept it there, not wanting to take it out and examine its implications. She cleared her throat and said, ''There *is* one thief I know of who used that modus operandi. But as far as I can tell, he's been inactive for almost a decade.''

Both men looked at her curiously, probably because of the way her voice had altered in pitch, becoming high and nervous. Then comprehension passed over Nick's craggy features. ''Oh Jesus, Joanna, not this again!''

Rafferty frowned as Nick said to him, ''Joanna has this...obsession about an Italian thief named Antony Parducci. She's been after him for as long as I've known her. Reads every bulletin issued on art thefts, even subscribes to true-crime magazines that have been known to favor write-ups of museum heists.''

''How do you know I still do that?'' she said defensively.

''I know, like I know my own name. You're the kind who will never let go of an obsession of that magnitude.''

''It's not an obsession, it's a hobby. Really more of a game that I play.'' She felt her cheeks turning red, wished she'd never brought it up.

Rafferty looked at her; surprisingly, his expression was sympathetic. "I've played games like that myself. In fact, I still do. There's a guy whose name I don't even know who vanished into—where else?—South America with two of MOMA's finest Picassos eleven years ago. I can't tell you how it hurt to deliver Great American's check for that one. I'm still living for the day I get my hands on him."

"But that's a professional grudge," Nick said. "Parducci never stole anything from any of our clients—or from Joanna."

"All right!" She held up her hand. "Let's drop it."

"Gladly," Nick said. "You want to go looking for Antony Parducci behind every pillar at the de Young, go ahead. But do it on your own time. Right now, I need you to stick to the task at hand."

Joanna breathed deeply to calm herself before she spoke. "Yes, the task at hand—tomorrow morning Mike Wheatley is due to call. If he hasn't by noon, Mr. Rafferty and I will canvass the art dealers. In the meantime, I'll try to get a better handle on Mike—which means paying Marshall and Phyllis a visit."

The men exchanged concerned looks. Nick said, "You're not going to tell them about Mike's call? Remember what he said about blowing any negotiations—"

"No, of course not. Since they're old friends, I should be able to extract any information I might need fairly subtly."

"Okay, then you might as well go directly to the de Young," Nick said. "There's an opening tonight—new acquisition for the American galleries—and Marshall and Phyllis are supposed to be there. You can talk with them and size up the situation at the museum at the same time.''

Joanna nodded. ''I'll do that, as soon as I make myself more presentable.''

''You have a place to stay?'' Nick asked.

''Yes.''

''Where?''

''The apartment.''

He raised his shaggy eyebrows. ''You still have that dump?''

''Yes. In a way it's similar to my one-third interest in S.S.I.—I simply forgot to give it up.'' She nodded to Rafferty and left the office.

In a sense, she was going home.

FOUR

THE APARTMENT was a tiny studio on Jackson Street, a few blocks up the hill from Chinatown. Dark, poorly ventilated, and unheated, it was on the third floor of an ugly stucco building that also housed what had to be San Francisco's only Samoan bar, the New Apia. The owner of both bar and building, Rex Malauulu, had rented the studio to Joanna in 1970, when she had arrived in the city after a year's stay in Manila. He had asked no questions when she had announced her decision to keep the apartment after her marriage four years later; every January he simply mailed her a bill for the annual rent, which she promptly paid. If Rex wondered about her comings and goings—or the lack of them in the past three years—he had never raised the issue. Recently Joanna herself had begun to wonder why she hung onto the place, but she told herself it would be handy if and when she began to come to the city on buying trips for her art gallery.

It was nearly seven o'clock when she wedged the Fiat into a parking spot on Powell Street and lugged her suitcase around the corner. The pink and green neon lights of the bar—its name, flanked by two scraggly-looking palm trees—gleamed through the mist that was typical of San Francisco evenings. Joanna went up to the door and looked in, standing in shadow so she wouldn't be seen.

Here, as in the South of Market area, nothing seemed changed. Rex—an enormous man with a Forty-niners cap on his head—stood behind the bar, clad in a huge expanse of white apron. The TV mounted on the far wall was blaring a sitcom, but the regulars—old men in baggy suits and old women in strange hats—hunched over the bar, ignoring it. Plastic bowls of popcorn were positioned at three-foot intervals all along there, but no one was having any of that either. The popcorn, Joanna thought, had probably been there since she left town.

She fumbled in her shoulder bag for her keys to the apartment, then went to the side door and unlocked it. It opened onto a steep flight of linoleum-covered stairs that led up to a landing outside the Malauulu apartment. From inside came the sound of the syrupy music from the forties and fifties that Rex's wife Loni was so fond of. Joanna tiptoed past the door and climbed a second, narrower flight to the third floor. Four studios opened off the hallway beyond the fire door, and as she passed the others, she wondered briefly who lived in the building now.

When she went to unlock her own door, the key stuck. For a moment she entertained the panicky thought that Rex had changed the lock and rerented her apartment, but then the key turned with a protesting squeak, and the door swung inward. A musty odor of old wood and dust and long dead cooking smells assailed her. She stepped into the tiny foyer and immediately felt transported into the past.

Without even having to think where it was, she reached for the light switch. The paper lantern that covered the bare bulb in the room directly ahead of her glowed brightly. Joanna stood still, her fingers tightly gripping the handle of her suitcase, her pulse slightly elevated. Feelings were washing over her—nostalgia, distaste, pleasure, sadness—all the feelings she could expect upon a return to a home where she had experienced intense pain and sorrow, intense joy and hope. After a moment, she set the suitcase down and closed the door behind her, then turned and surveyed the room.

The light blue draperies that she had made from embroidered fabric she had brought from the Philippines were tightly drawn. Not that it would have mattered had they been open; the one window afforded only a view of the brick wall of the next building. A darker blue blanket and a pillow in a flowered slip lay neatly at one end of the closed sofa bed. On the white enameled chest of drawers stood an antique crystal perfume atomizer and a photograph in a silver frame—her only relics of the parental home she'd abandoned so long ago.

Joanna dropped her coat and her bag on the sofa bed, then went to look at the picture, wondering what slight of sentimentality had prompted her to pack it and the atomizer—which had been her mother's—away in her duffel bag the night she had fled her father's house in New Jersey for good. It showed two people she now could scarcely remember—John and Ellen Scherer—standing proudly beside their 1953 Oldsmobile. Joanna Scherer, then aged nine, had taken the photo of her parents with her father's Kodak box camera. The day the new car had come home had been one of the last happy times for the Scherer family.

Joanna turned from the bureau and looked over at the tiny Pullman kitchen. Everything was as she'd left it. Coffee mugs hung from hooks under the cupboards; a copper tea kettle sat on the two-burner stove; old-fashioned metal canisters decorated in a red checked design lined up on the little counter next to the Mixmaster. With a shock, she saw the half-full bourbon bottle from which she'd drunk the night after David's funeral—the night she'd fled to the apartment from the big house in Pacific Heights for the last time.

The base of her spine began to tingle, and she went over and looked in the sink for the glass. She remembered she hadn't rinsed it the next morning when she'd awakened with an aching head and red, swollen eyes, had merely placed it in the sink, gathered her things, and gone back to face a houseful of David's disapproving relatives. The bottom of the glass was now coated with dust that had stuck to the residue of the bourbon. Joanna picked it up and looked at it thoughtfully for a moment, then returned it to the sink.

Did I ever intend to stay away from here so long? she wondered. No, of course not. How could I have known I'd go back to Vallejo Street house, have a frightful argument with David's Aunt Louise—who was so angry at being left out of his will—and decide then and there to have everything packed and moved to Sonoma? How could I have known that once there, I'd have no reason to run away anymore—no reason to flee to this shabby little haven?

She remembered the first time she'd broached the subject of keeping the apartment to David. While he'd been puzzled, she'd sensed no disapproval. "But why, love?" he'd asked.

"Because I need something of my own, a place where I can go when I want to be alone."

"A room of your own, you mean? Like Virginia Woolf wrote about?" He smiled when he said it, laugh lines crinkling, eyes kindly in the candlelight.

They were at their favorite dimly lit restaurant out in the Avenues, one of many they'd discovered after beginning their affair two years before. His wife Eleanor had recently died, their marriage plans had been publicly announced, and yet they'd kept going back there, as if they were unwilling to let go of the past. Joanna reached for his hand, missed it in the darkness, and ended up with her fingers in the butter dish. After wiping them off—while David attempted to control his amusement—she finally succeeded in making contact.

"That's exactly what I mean," she said. "I've been alone my whole life—almost—and being married is going to take some getting used to."

"I understand that. But you know, my house *does* have fifteen rooms. Surely in all those there's one that is isolated enough to suit."

"I'd really rather have the apartment."

He shook his head, blond hair gleaming in the light from the candle. "As long as we've been together, you've done nothing but bitch about the apartment. Cockroaches, you've said. The noise from the bar. The toilet that won't stop running. The refrigerator that freezes your lettuce. What is it, really?"

She took her hand back and toyed with her fork, pushing half-eaten veal parmigiana around on her plate. Finally she said, "The apartment's me."

"What? I refuse to believe I'm marrying a woman who identifies with that rat trap."

"Make light of it if you like, but it's true. It's *me*, and I don't want to lose it."

David apparently heard the seriousness of her words, because he stopped smiling, his hand arrested halfway to his wine glass. "Lose it—or lose yourself?" he asked.

She was silent.

"I'm beginning to understand now. You're afraid that you'll lost some part of your identity in this marriage, unless you have the apartment there to remind you who you are."

She nodded. "I know it sounds stupid—"

"It's not stupid at all. You're moving into another woman's house, to a certain extent assuming another woman's role in E.J.'s and my lives. But you also know I'm marrying you for who *you* are. I don't want you to change. So if it helps you to remain the woman I love, keep the apartment. Keep it for the rest of your life, if you want."

And so far she had. During nine years of marriage the apartment had been there for her. In both stormy years and calm years, on both good days and bad ones, she had fled there often—rushing through the Broadway Tunnel from the rarefied atmosphere of Pacific Heights to a more earthy world that she belonged in and understood. After the night when David had agreed she should keep the place, he had never set foot in it again—nor had anyone else, not even E.J. And for the past three years she herself had deserted it, left it devoid of life. But it had always been there for her, as it was tonight.

FIVE

JOANNE LEANED IN THE ARCHWAY at one end of Hearst Court, the great central hall of the de Young. The court—so named after a family whose tastes had definitely run to the grandiose and medieval—had always activated an embarrassingly gothic side of her imagination. The vaulted masonry ceiling rose upward into shadow where, she was sure, vampire bats hung. The oppressively dark tapestries probably concealed assassins with long, wicked daggers. At any minute, Lady Macbeth would enter, hands dripping with blood.

In reality, the hall was peopled with no one more sinister than about fifty Museum Society members, who were clustered to one side around a buffet table, their voices echoing in the vast space. They were an ill-assorted group—old and young, elegant and tattered, wearing anything from haute couture to Salvation Army chic. Listening to their unintelligible chatter, which at this distance gave the impression of a flock of hysterical chickens, Joanna decided she would have preferred the company of the clan Macbeth.

She had arrived at the museum an hour ago and spoken with various members of the security force, checking and rechecking the known details of the previous night's theft. Everything they could tell her—and that was precious little—pointed to what she had already surmised: professional theft, well planned and carefully executed. That task completed, she had joined the reception, gotten a plastic cup of wine, and taken up this vantage point to wait for the arrival of Marshall and Phyllis Wheatley. So far, neither had put in an appearance. Nor had anyone else she knew.

As receptions went, this one was poorly attended. Joanna wished the planning committee had chosen to hold it in the more cozy entrance or perhaps in one of the galleries. The cavernous hall was chilly and oppressive, the small group of attendees dwarfed by their surroundings. And the new acquisition—a small Copley portrait—sat on an easel in the place of honor opposite the buffet table, totally ignored.

Feeling sorry for it, Joanna left the archway, descended the stone steps, and went up to the portrait. It was of a woman dressed in red, with high-piled hair. Her pearl-like face glowed and her lips curved upward in a self-satisfied, almost smug manner. She looked ready to speak, to confide age-old secrets meant for Joanna's ears alone. She leaned closer, pretending to study the brushwork, but actually straining to hear the ghostly whispered words. Another flight of fancy, she thought, agreeable but hardly proper for one here on urgent business. She winked at her newfound friend and turned, scanning the hall for the Wheatleys.

Marshall must have come in while she'd been studying the portrait. A big man with faded blond hair and fluffy white sideburns, he wore a loud green plaid sport coat that stood out even in this crowd. When Joanna spotted him, he stood by the buffet table stuffing a cheese-heaped cracker into his mouth. Marshall was in no way a typical patron of the arts: He preferred bourbon on the rocks to fine wine; serious discussions to polite chitchat; golf clothes to formal attire. More important, he knew how to laugh—both at the pretensions of the art world and at his own reverse snobbism.

While Marshall delighted in bursting societal bubbles, Phyllis sallied forth to heal the puncture wounds, all the time laughing at her husband's harmless iconoclasm. Together the Wheatleys made an extremely effective and refreshing team.

Joanna made her way to the buffet table, where Marshall was washing down the cracker with a gulp of bourbon. His eyes brightened when he saw her, and he set down his glass and grabbed both of her hands, smearing them with a little Brie. "Joanna!" he said. "Welcome back!" Then he held her away from him, surveying her gray suede suit and nodding approval. "You're looking damned good, girl."

"So are you, Marshall." It was a gentle lie. He looked tired, his eyes shadowed and sunken. His color was bad, and he seemed to have lost weight. Was he ill? she wondered.

"It's about time you came back to the city," he said. "Are you here for good?"

"No, only a few days."

"On a buying trip for the gallery?"

"The what? Oh my God, Marshall, I've really been out of touch! I haven't even opened the gallery yet, and now I doubt I ever will."

"Well, Phyl and I wondered why we didn't get an invitation to the opening. What *are* you doing these days?"

She had thought over how to explain her reason for being in town and had decided the best approach was to be straightforward—up to a point. "At the moment, I'm working on a special assignment for S.S.I."

His eyes lost some of their shine. "Ah, they've called you in about the *Cavalier*."

"You've heard about it, then."

"Phyl found out. She's working over here this week—preparations for removing some of the furniture we've had on loan from our collection. Naturally there was talk. Can't keep a thing like that secret."

"Of course not," Joanna said, trying to keep the irony out of her voice.

Marshall picked up his glass and motioned at the buffet table. "Try some of the Brie. It's not bad, as Brie goes. But beware of the crackers in that little basket—tbey're as stale as old toenail clippings."

Mentally Joanna gagged on the analogy. "No, thanks. I think I'll just have some more wine." She went and got a fresh glass, then turned her attention back to Marshall, asking about the other members of the family. His eyes flickered when she inquired after Mike, but he merely said, "He's fine. Still painting."

There was an awkward silence, the kind that often happens between old friends, who have grown apart, but Marshall—always the easy conversationalist—said, "You still own part of that security firm?"

"Yes, more by default than for any real reason."

"Thinking of going back to work?"

"Not really. My partner—Nick Alexander—needs extra help on this *Cavalier* thing, so I came down."

"What have you been doing in Sonoma?"

"Not much. Fixing the house up, gardening, things like that."

"Got a steady fellow?"

She smiled at the outdated terminology. "No fellow at all."

Marshall frowned.

"I've been busy," she said defensively. "And besides, I'm not ready for any kind of emotional involvement yet."

"Huh." He turned and went to help himself to more bourbon. The volunteer who was tending bar merely smiled and let him alone. Marshall was a well-known figure around the de Young, beloved by even the most stuffy Museum Society members, and the consensus on how to handle him was simply to let him have his way.

When he returned to her, his eyes were troubled. "Joanna, I don't want to butt in.... Well, yes I do. What are you trying to do—make yourself into some kind of living monument of David?"

Coming from anyone else, the question would have enraged her. But because Marshall had asked it, she had to consider it seriously. Slowly she said, "I don't think it's anything that...maladjusted. I guess it's just difficult for me to think of being with another man. David was the only one—"

Marshall raised his shaggy white eyebrows.

"All right, obviously he wasn't. But he was the only man in my life who counted, who was a lover and also a friend."

"And you think you can't find another like that?"

"I think someone like that would be hard to find. Maybe I'm not willing to expend the energy for the hunt."

Marshall looked as if he were about to say something, but then seemed to think better of it. Joanna seized the opportunity to bring the subject back to the business at hand. "Listen," she said, "how about giving me a tour of the galleries? I haven't been here in years, and I'd like to see the room where the Hals hung, as well as how the collections have been rotated."

He looked surprised, but nodded. "Sure. Fill up that glass, and we'll go."

She did as he told her and followed him up the steps from the court and across the entry to the west corridor. Marshall stalked ahead of her, past the galleries labeled The Ancient World.

"The hell with the antiquities," he said. "They're not art, just artifacts. Besides, there's never anything new in there."

Joanna hung back a little. "Do they still have the mummy?"

He stopped. "Sure. You want to go in there and visit the mummy, little girl?" The words were teasing, his smile fond.

"No, I think I've kind of outgrown it."

They continued down the deserted corridor, Marshall's leather soles making squeaking sounds on the tiled floor. At its end a guard in a navy blue blazer and gray pants was patrolling with his walkie-talkie. His posture became more alert when he saw them, then relaxed; when Joanna had interviewed the security personnel earlier, she had warned them that she would be touring other areas of the museum than those open for the reception.

Joanna lengthened her stride to keep up with Marshall. "You don't care for artifacts, then?" she asked.

"They're all right, but they're just household objects. Bore me. Of course, you could say the same about our furniture collection. Maybe that's why I've always let Phyl deal with it."

"I don't know, I like the room interiors." The museum had a number of authentically decorated period room displays.

"Oh well, those are just plain fun. You can try to imagine living in them. Most of them, the chairs are too spindly for my taste and there isn't any place I could put my pipe or slippers, but I can see myself inside nevertheless. Here's one, though, that totally eludes me.'' He stopped at the door to a display on the left-hand side of the corridor. ''Could you live in *that*?''

It was at once the world's busiest and dingiest room. All the wooden surfaces were gray, and over that pastel garlands and flowers had been painted. A saccharine-faced winged angel smiled down from the central ceiling panel, and his lesser cousins graced the wall where it canted up toward a small leaded-glass window. What light it admitted was feeble, and the lack of furniture gave the room the appearance of a not very well appointed funeral chapel.

Joanna shuddered. ''What *is* it?''

''Northern Italian. Alpine. Explains the small window—protection against the harsh weather.''

''Its size also leaves more surface to paint doodads on.''

''True. Frankly, that room would send me running stark naked into the snow.'' Marshall started walking again, more slowly now. His shoulders slumped and despite his animated conversation, he seemed weary. Joanna wondered if everything was all right at his gallery, or at home. Perhaps Mike was giving them trouble again; Marshall might even suspect his involvement in the theft of the Hals—whatever that might be.

She wished she could be honest with Marshall, simply come out and say, ''Look, what do you know about your son's connection with this business?'' But she knew how he would react: He'd go to Mike and demand an explanation. And then, as Mike had threatened, he would feign innocence, and there would be no negotiations for the Hals. In no way could she jeopardize the careful balance Steve Rafferty and Great American wanted maintained until the *Cavalier* was safely home.

Marshall turned down a side hall and stopped abruptly in front of an imposing veneered bureau. "Speaking of our collection, this is one of the pieces Phyl and I have had on loan for the past six months. It's about due to come back to us."

"It's lovely." Joanna ran a hand over the dark satiny finish.

"German. Late seventeen hundreds." He reached into his pocket, took out a key, and unlocked the bureau's doors. Pulling them open, he revealed a small altar, complete with a cross. After a moment he said, "One of my favorite pieces. Says a lot about the practicality of the Germans: You can get your daily prayer over with while tying your tie."

"It's too bad it has to be kept locked so the average visitor can't see the altar. But I suppose it's a precaution you have to take."

"Unfortunately, yes. All the furniture that can be opened is locked. Prying fingers are hard on delicate hinges." He shut the doors, then motioned to a nearby room interior, which was dominated by an ormolu and rock-crystal chandelier. "Most of the stuff in this room is ours too, on permanent loan. French Regency. The harp's my favorite."

"Your collection must be larger than I'd realized."

"It's pretty extensive. Some of the pieces have been donated outright to the museum, others are here temporarily, like the bureau. I'm not sure which are which: like I said, the collection is really Phyl's baby. In fact, that's why she's not here tonight: too tired after making arrangements for the semiannual rotation." Earlier he had mentioned that Phyllis had begged off attending the reception; now Joanna could understand why. Phyllis was a seemingly tireless worker, scheduling her days with a minute-by-minute precision, while still managing to seem gracious and unhurried. She was in her early sixties, however, and owed it to herself to slow down a little.

They continued through the galleries, with Marshall pointing out both his favorite artworks and pieces of furniture from the family collection. His gallery on Sutter Street dealt primarily in modern American art, but his personal tastes were as classical as David's had been. Joanna was pleasantly surprised when he stopped in front of an Abraham van Beyeren still life and waxed eloquent about its fine detail. The painting—a hodgepodge of fruit, peeled and moldy-looking cheese, a half-sliced roast, and a large red lobster with an evil eye—had always been a favorite of hers. Often she'd spend time staring at it and wishing she could reach in and rescue the obviously displeased crustacean.

Finally they turned and went to a corner archway that led to a gallery that was temporarily closed to the public. Marshall unhooked the red velvet rope that barred the entrance and motioned for Joanna to enter. "The scene of the crime," he said.

It was a small gallery—no more than twenty feet square—with a parquet floor and earth-toned walls. During the day, the central skylight—reinforced and wired with a high-quality alarm at Joanna's recommendation several years before—admitted soft light that complemented the subdued and often moody paintings that hung there. A massive grandfather clock, flanked by four Dutch landscapes, stood at the far end; a ponderous dark walnut wardrobe and four side chairs occupied the left wall; to the right were four portraits of ladies and gentlemen in dark clothing and ruffs, and a big empty space where the *Cavalier* had hung. Joanna stared at it for a moment, saying nothing.

"They knew what they wanted," she finally said. "While they were at it, they could have grabbed those Hobbemas or the Ruysdael. But they didn't. All they wanted was the Hals. And they were clever; they took the time to remove it from its frame so it would be smaller and easier to handle." She pivoted, reinventorying the gallery's contents. "I've always liked this room. Sometimes I'd come in here and sit for a while. Didn't there used to be a bench?"

Marshall was staring at the empty space. Joanna repeated the question and he turned slowly. "Yes. I don't know why they took it out."

"The furniture's different from how I remember it too. Are any of the pieces yours?"

He shrugged. "You'd have to ask Phyl."

"Actually, I'd like to see her. Will she be working here tomorrow?"

"I think so."

"Maybe I'll stop by."

"She'd like that."

The empty space seemed to hold a fascination for Marshall, and Joanna had to admit she also felt a magnetic pull from that part of the room. "God, I hate to see this happen," she said. "I remember when the *Portrait of a Rabbi* was stolen; it was like losing an old friend. And now the *Cavalier's* gone too."

"Rembrandt and Hals are particular favorites of yours, aren't they?" Marshall said.

"Yes, especially Hals. Oh, you can't help but admire Rembrandt's works—he *was* the master. But Hals's technique is so wonderful. He painted very quickly, you know, and what he produced is a total entity, rather than the sum of composition and color and form and so on. It's all one, as if the people are really living beings.''

''It's the genre paintings I like,'' Marshall said.

''Me too. *Malle Babba*, the witch of Haarlem—the drunken old woman with the owl perched on her shoulder and the huge stein in her fist. And *The Drinker*.''

''Alias *Monsieur Peecklheering*.'' Marshall smiled fondly, as if they were speaking of an errant but well loved mutual friend.

'' 'Pickled herring.' It's wonderful how playful Hals could be—and how the Dutch responded to it. I think he actually may have taught a few of those stuffy Haarlem burghers to laugh at their own pompousness.''

''He did have a wonderful sense of humor, considering the fact that he lived under severe financial duress all his life.''

''Poor Hals,'' Joanna said. ''You know, I remember reading once that he—and, mind you, this was one of Holland's most celebrated artists—got sixty florins for a really good portrait. At the same time, farm animals like oxen were going for half again that much.''

''The eternal plight of artists.''

''Yes, and Hals's was worse than most.'' He had been in debt all his life—constantly being sued for overdue bills for bread, shoes, rent, even canvases. While he had been a master painter, he was also a financial dunce. It must have been a great relief to the beleaguered artist when in 1662 the City of Haarlem recognized this fact and provided him a subsidy of 200 florins a year until his death in 1666. On the personal side, his life had also been a series of misfortunes. He had had at least twelve children by two different marriages, two of whom ended up in the Haarlem workhouse: a son, Pieter, had been an

imbecile and eventually a danger even to his fellow in-
mates; a daughter, Sara, had borne an illegitimate child
and the family had petitioned she be incarcerated "in the
hope of improvement." Hals's second wife, Lysbeth,
had been brought up on charges a couple of times for
tavern brawling; the artist himself had spent a fair
amount of time in drinking establishments. It was no
wonder, Joanna thought, that the lowly subjects of his
genre paintings came fully alive, with all their foibles.

Marshall's comments had given her the opening she
needed to ask more about Mike. "Speaking of the eternal plight of artists," she said, "how is Mike's painting
coming?"

Marshall's shoulders seemed to sag even more. He
went to the entry, unhooked the red velvet rope and
motioned Joanna out of the gallery. "Oh, he's plugging
away at it, for what it's worth."

"Who's handling him?"

"Galerie des Beaux Arts, two blocks down Sutter
from me."

"I don't know them. I take it you couldn't handle him
yourself—nepotism, or whatever you call it?"

Marshall seemed at a loss for words. They had crossed
the larger Dutch gallery and were halfway down the
corridor before he spoke. "I didn't want to take him on,
Joanna. Mike's just not very good. There's a lot of
emotion in his paintings, but he never could be bothered to learn his technique. As a result, the feeling there
is raw and undisciplined—and very strange."

"Strange?"

"Yes. Mike's paintings are disturbing and unpleasant. If you see one, you'll know what I mean."

"I'd like to. And I'd like to see him. Where does he
have his studio?"

"In a warehouse near those old piers in China Basin. Now that shipping in San Francisco is pretty much kaput, a lot of those buildings have been taken over by artists and craftsmen."

"Do you know the exact location of the warehouse?"

If Marshall saw anything odd in her eagerness to look Mike up, he didn't show it. "No, I don't. Phyl might—ask her. Frankly, we don't see much of Mike these days, except when he turns up drunk and passes out in his old room or on the living room couch."

"I'm sorry about that."

"Don't waste your sympathy; it's our own fault."

Marshall bypassed Hearst Court, where the reception had dwindled to a couple of dozen people, and Joanna followed him out to the reflecting pool in front of the museum. The night was chill and misty; she could hear moisture dripping from the leaves of the nearby palm trees. They stopped at the edge of the pool and looked silently into its depths for a moment. Then Marshall put a hand on her shoulder.

"It's good to see you again, girl," he said. "Next time, don't stay away so long."

"I won't."

He squeezed her shoulder and started around the pool toward the sidewalk, raising a hand in farewell.

Joanna remained where she was for a few minutes, staring at the hazy reflection of the museum's lights in the water and listening to people saying their goodbyes in the foyer.

Marshall might be glad to see her now, she thought, but how on earth would he and Phyllis feel toward her if she were forced to expose their son as a thief?

SIX

WHEN JOANNA GOT into her car, she checked her watch in the light from the dashboard. Nine-thirty, too early to go back to the apartment and sleep. Besides, sleep was an impossibility now that she'd talked with Marshall; their conversation had left her strangely unsettled, her emotions fragmented. Part of her wanted to reach out for the genteel, well-regulated world she'd shared with friends such as the Wheatleys; another part wanted to flee to the snug nest she'd built for herself in Sonoma. But there was a third Joanna, one whom she'd thought long dead, who insisted on rushing forward into an uncharted and risky future, regardless of the price she might have to pay for that foray. It was in response to the demands of that reemerging self that she checked the address she'd noted down for the missing security guard and then drove through the quiet, misty streets to the Miraloma Park district of the city.

It was an area at the very top of Market Street, near the turnoff for Twin Peaks. The houses were good-sized stucco structures, and their neatly trimmed lawns and well-tended gardens spoke of quiet middle-class pride. Wilson Reed's address was on Juanita Way—a yellow house with brown trim around the bay window that bowed out over the garage. The porch lamp was on and light showed around the drawn draperies, but when Joanna rang the bell, she got no response.

She hadn't expected to find that the guard had returned home, but Reed's supervisor at the museum had told her the missing man lived with a seventy-year-old cousin, Frances Cathcart. Thinking that the woman might be hard of hearing, Joanna rang the bell again. Still no answer. Finally she went back down the steps and checked the garage through the mail slot in its door; there was a car inside, a humpbacked shape that suggested a VW. Not Reed's; according to the supervisor, he drove an old Chevy. Probably it belonged to Mrs. Cathcart; an old woman alone might not answer her bell after dark.

As Joanna started down the driveway to her car, she noticed a shaft of light coming from a window on the ground floor toward the rear of the house. A path led back there, past a row of rosebushes, and stopped at a gate in the fence. Beside the pull chain for the latch was a hand-lettered card that read N. Stevens. An in-law apartment, Joanna thought. Perhaps the tenant could tell her where Mrs. Cathcart was.

She pushed through the gate and followed the continuation of the path to a door that faced the back yard; a floodlight illuminated a barbecue and a set of lawn furniture, and the windows, while curtained with what looked like flowered sheets, leaked light. Joanna knocked on the door, and it quickly opened.

The woman who stood there appeared to be in her early twenties—thin, clad in jeans and a sweater, and clutching a textbook into which a pencil had been thrust as a marker. A second pencil was stuck through the unruly bun on top of her head. "Yes?" she said impatiently.

"I'm looking for Mrs. Cathcart—"

"She's not home." The young woman made a move to close the door.

"Please, it's important—about her cousin, Wilson Reed."

The woman paused, her eyes narrowing. "Are you from the museum?"

"From their security firm. My name's Joanna Stark." Briefly she wished she had not thrown out all her S.S.I. business cards while on a housecleaning binge two years ago.

The woman seemed to take her at face value, however, opening the door wider and leaning on its jamb, book propped on her hip. "It's really something, isn't it—him disappearing like that? Fran—Mrs. Cathcart—is really upset."

"I imagine so. Can you tell me when she'll be back—"

"Who would have thought that old Will had it in him, to make off with a valuable painting? And to act so cool about it yet."

"You know about the theft, then?"

"Sure. It's not the sort of thing Fran could keep to herself. But she told me it's confidential information, and I'm not about to gossip. Don't have time to, what with a poli sci midterm tomorrow." She nodded at the book.

Joanna was about to ask Mrs. Cathcart's whereabouts again when what the woman had said earlier registered. "You say Mr. Reed acted cool about the theft?"

"Yeah. That's why I could hardly believe it when Fran told me."

"When was this?"

"Right after the insurance company guy was here. Fran came down and knocked, all upset—"

"No, I mean Wilson Reed. When was he acting so cool?"

"Oh, that. This morning early, maybe about five. I'd been up cramming all night—another midterm—and remembered I'd forgotten to put the garbage can out. That's one of my jobs, in exchange for the low rent. Anyway, I dragged it out to the curb, and he was just leaving."

"Did he say anything to you?"

"Sure. Good morning, how are you, that sort of thing. I asked him where he was going so early, and he said fishing. And then he laughed, as if he'd made some big joke."

"*Was* it a joke?"

The woman shrugged. "It must have been. Will likes to fish, but he didn't have any of his equipment with him. And it wasn't in the car either, because I would have seen it when he got in and drove away."

Not a very funny joke, Joanna thought, but then maybe the guard didn't have much of a sense of humor. "Was Mr. Reed carrying anything?" she asked.

"Just a canvas flight bag."

"And was there anything else in the car?"

"Not that I could see."

That didn't mean anything, of course. The painting could have been concealed in the trunk. "Did you tell the man from the insurance company about this?"

"I never talked to him. I've been at school pretty much all day."

Joanna made a mental note to inform Steve Rafferty of the conversation, then said, "What about Mrs. Cathcart—where is she now?"

"At the church—one of her ladies' committee meetings. I had to talk her into going, she was so upset." The woman glanced at her watch. "Come to think of it, I'd better get over there and pick her up. She doesn't drive, so I play chauffeur when Will can't.''

Quickly Joanna said, ''Look, I've interrupted your studying, so why don't you let me pick her up? It's the least I can do.''

The woman looked uncertain, eyeing Joanna hesitantly and then glancing down at her textbook. ''All right,'' she finally said, ''the church is St. Brendan's, over on Laguna Honda, right off Portola. Do you know it?''

''Spanish style with a school attached, right?''

''Right. Fran will be waiting out front. She's wearing her bright pink coat, so you can't miss her. There aren't two coats that bright in the entire city.''

Joanna took out her car keys. ''Good. I'll tell her you sent me. Your name is . . . ?''

''Oh, sorry. Nancy Stevens. Thanks for fetching her. You know how it is with midterms.''

As she went down the path and through the gate, Joanna smiled wryly. Once she had indeed known how it was with midterms, during the two brief years she'd spent at Wellesley. But the memory had long ago receded, until it now was as dim as the fog-hazed light from the corner lamppost.

UNLIKE THE LAMPPOST, the tip of St. Brendan's spire defied nature, gleaming a clear iridescent blue in spite of the mist. Several groups of women stood in the floodlit plaza in front of the church, but none of them wore a bright pink coat. Joanna pulled the Fiat to the curb and sat studying them.

Mostly old and stout, the women were bundled in cloth coats, gloves, and kerchiefs, and carried large purses that matched their sensible dark shoes. While tonight their attire was necessary protection against the fog, Joanna knew they would dress the same in any weather, keeping their coats neatly buttoned even on those rare days when other San Franciscans went sleeveless and barefoot. There was a constancy about these women that was reflective of the older, bedrock neighborhoods of the city: Some spoke in accented English even though they had left their European homelands decades ago; many had attended the church school, as had their children and now their grandchildren; year after year they inhabited the same neat homes, went to the same Sunday service, shopped in the same produce store, banked at the same savings and loan. And while they viewed newcomers—young professionals, minorities fleeing their respective ghettos, college students like Nancy Stevens—warily, they also treated them with tolerance and respect. Theirs was a forbearing tradition—and that too did not change.

Joanna waited in her car for five minutes, but there was still no sign of a bright pink coat. The groups of women began to break up, walking off in twos and threes toward the parked cars. Just as she was about to conclude that Mrs. Cathcart had gotten another ride home, the door to the church opened and a heavy woman in shocking pink came out, supported on the arm of a priest. The woman's kerchiefed head drooped and she walked wearily; the priest, a tall man, inclined his face toward hers, talking as he patted her gloved hand. They stopped a few feet from the door, spoke a little while more, and then the woman turned and made her way slowly across the little plaza. The priest stood watching her, then went back inside.

Joanna got out of her car and crossed toward Mrs. Cathcart, calling out her name. The older woman looked up, her plump, curiously unwrinkled features registering confusion. Quickly, Joanna said, "Nancy Stevens sent me to pick you up, Mrs. Cathcart. My name is Joanna Stark."

The confusion turned to alarm. "Is Nancy all right?"

"Yes, she's fine—"

"It's Will, isn't it? They've found Will."

"No, no one has seen him."

Frances Cathcart pursed her lips—a baby's mouth in a round baby's face—and hugged her black handbag protectively against her chest. "Are you from the museum? I already told the man from the insurance company all I know."

"I work with Mr. Rafferty, the man who spoke with you earlier. Please, won't you let me drive you home?"

Mrs. Cathcart hesitated, her lips still pursed, but then weariness seemed to take over. "All right," she said, and let Joanna lead her to the Fiat. She eased her bulk into the passenger seat, arranging her legs carefully under the dashboard. When Joanna got in, she was staring straight ahead, her purse clutched in her lap. Joanna started the car and drove toward Portola.

Frances Cathcart didn't speak until after they had made the turn onto the larger street. Then she said, "It's a nice little car."

"Ma'am?"

"This car. It's a pretty little thing. My son had a sports car once. It caused a terrible row with his father."

Joanna downshifted and turned into the Miraloma Park district. "Why was that?"

"George—my husband—hated that car. He called it a 'selfish automobile.' And he told George Junior he was selfish too, for buying a car that would only hold one other person. That was the start of the rift between them." She paused, then looked at Joanna, an odd mixture of amusement and pain in her eyes. "*I* always thought that my husband secretly coveted that car. For years he'd driven a big Ford that would hold the entire family. A man couldn't help but envy someone who could get into a little car and just drive away all alone, now could he?"

"I guess not."

"Lord knows there's been many a time when *I* would have liked to do that—drive away and never come back. When George Junior had his final quarrel with his father and left for good. When my oldest daughter had that terrible drinking problem and her husband threw her out. When George Senior had his final illness and none of our children came to visit him in the hospital. But it wasn't in me to run, it just wasn't in me." She was silent until Joanna brought the car to a stop in front of the yellow house, then added, "Do you think that's what Will has done?"

"I'm sorry?"

"Do you think maybe things got to be too much for him, and he just climbed into his car and drove off?"

"I don't know. Was he under some sort of pressure?"

"That's what my priest—Father Tierney—asked me. He could have been; he'd been spending more time alone in his room than usual. But whatever it was, he didn't discuss it with me."

"Could it have been financial pressure, perhaps?"

"I don't think so. He was as prompt as ever with his room-and-board payments, and just last week he bought me a beautiful flower arrangement for my birthday. But still, there had to be something. I can't believe he's disappeared because he stole that painting. It has to be something else that made him go."

Joanna had no answer for that. She got out of the car and went around to assist Frances Cathcart. When the old woman was standing on the sidewalk fishing in her handbag for her housekeys, Joanna asked, "May I come in for a few minutes and talk about your cousin?"

Mrs. Cathcart shrugged. "You may as well. After all, you were nice enough to give me a ride home."

Feeling slightly ashamed, as if she'd just bribed a child with some candy, Joanna followed her up the steps and into the house. The front door opened directly into a living room. Its furnishings were several decades out of style—blond wood and yellow and green floral-patterned slipcovers on the furniture. A grandfather clock stood against the wall opposite the door; another old-fashioned clock in a walnut case sat on the mantelpiece. There was a nautical clock with brass fittings on top of the console TV, and a small timepiece encased in black lacquer and mother-of-pearl on the coffee table. As Joanna took all of this in, the clocks began to register quarter to the hour: a cacophony that included West-minster chimes, a stolid bonging, a lilting tinkle, and—from another room—the squawking of a cuckoo.

Amazed, she turned to Frances Cathcart. The stout old woman was hanging her coat in a closet next to the front door, oblivious to the racket. When she saw Joanna's expression, she smiled. "One thing I'm always sure of is the time," she said.

Gradually the noise stopped, the melody of the West-minster chimes reverberating in the quiet. Joanna said, "I've never seen so many clocks in one place, outside of a store. And they all keep the exact same time."

Frances Cathcart sat down on an overstuffed chair opposite the TV set and motioned for Joanna to take the sofa. "It's Will's hobby, rebuilding old clocks. He keeps them synchronized and in perfect running order."

"He actually refurbishes them, works and all?"

"Yes. He's been doing it for years. He could probably get a job as a clocksmith, but he prefers to keep it a hobby. Says that tinkering relaxes him. Most of these clocks cost hardly anything at all, they were in such bad condition when he came upon them. That one he found in the city dump." She motioned at the mantelpiece.

Joanna got up and went to look at the clock, then turned her attention to a framed photograph beside it. It was of two couples in their late middle age. Dressed in casual clothes, they stood on a dock next to a somewhat ramshackle building, fishing gear in hand. Immediately Joanna recognized a younger version of Frances Cathcart, and the other woman—Margaret Reed, the Wheatleys' former housekeeper. Both of the men were stocky, gray-haired, and in every respect ordinary looking. One was vaguely familiar—Wilson Reed, the security guard she'd briefly interviewed at the de Young after the theft of the Rembrandt.

She said, "This picture—it's you and your husband and the Reeds?"

"Yes, that was taken at the Bayshore Rod and Gun Club a few years before Mr. Cathcart and Mrs. Reed died."

"Is fishing another of your cousin's hobbies?"

"Oh, yes. For years we all belonged to the club. It wasn't just for sports—there were social events too. Those were happy years, we had a lot of fun. Of course, now those days are gone...."

"Does Mr. Reed still fish?"

"A few times a year, no more. Will doesn't enjoy fishing alone, and my arthritis prevents me from going with him."

Joanna returned to the sofa and sat down. "Does he still belong to the Bayshore Rod and Gun Club?"

"Oh, no. That closed three years ago. The property was run down, and they couldn't afford to keep it up."

"I see." And that, Joanna thought, made it highly unlikely that Reed had been going fishing at five o'clock on a cold November morning. Why the comment to Nancy Stevens, then? A joke, as the young woman had thought? Not a very funny one.

"Mrs. Cathcart," she said, "did Nancy Stevens tell you about meeting Mr. Reed this morning?"

She frowned, pursing her lips in concentration again. "She *did* say something, but frankly, I was so upset I didn't listen. I remember being surprised that he had been home at all; I hadn't heard him come in. But then, I *am* a heavy sleeper."

"You mentioned before that Mr. Reed might have been under some kind of pressure, that he was spending more time in his room than usual. Was there anything else that was different about his habits?"

"Well...no. He goes to work and comes home and sleeps. Then he gets up and eats and tinkers until it's time to go to work again. Sometimes he works in the yard. You have to go through it to get to Nancy's apartment, and we like it to look nice for her. She's such a good girl and looks after so many things around here. I don't know what we'd do without her—or without the rent money she pays us."

"What about phone calls? Has your cousin had any unusual calls? From people you don't know, for instance?"

"That's the same thing the man from the insurance company—what's his name?"

"Steve Rafferty."

"Oh, yes. It's what Mr. Rafferty asked me. No, I don't recall any." She hesitated, her little mouth trembling. "You think he stole that painting, don't you, Miss Stark?"

Joanna shook her head. "Actually I don't. But I think he may have known who did, and that's why he went away. I want to find him to make sure he's not in any danger."

The words seemed to relieve Mrs. Cathcart, because her lips stopped trembling.

Joanna said, "Let me ask you this: Does Mr. Reed know a man named Antony Parducci?"

The old woman looked surprised at the question, but her face didn't register any recognition. "Parducci? I don't recall Will ever mentioning the name. He has a few Italian friends . . . this man *is* Italian?"

"Yes. Tall and thin, with straight black hair. Bright blue eyes. Mid-forties." She tried to think of anything more distinctive about Parducci and felt a mild surprise when she couldn't.

"Is he from San Francisco?"

"No, Italy. But he speaks English well, so you'd hardly notice any accent."

"Oh. Well, he doesn't sound like anyone Will has ever mentioned. He doesn't have many friends, and certainly none of them are foreigners. Most of the people he and Margaret knew well were from the rod and gun club, but since it closed, they're no longer in touch." She looked away at the photograph on the mantel and sighed. "It's strange, you know. You can be friendly with people year after year, fish with them on the week-ends, attend parties and cookouts, and then one day the reason you're drawn together is gone—and they're gone too. It's strange—and sad.''

Silently Joanna agreed, thinking of all the genteel, affluent friends she and David had shared gallery openings and dinner parties and occasional weekend trips with. Now, only three years after the reason she and people like the Wheatleys had been drawn together—David—was gone, the only ones she would have felt remotely comfortable with were Marshall and Phyllis. It *was* strange and sad—yet somehow a relief. She had kept two good friends from those easy, secure days, but now—at last—was moving on into the future.

She said, "I know how you feel. And I should go and let you get some rest, but I have one more favor to ask—may I take a look at your cousin's room?"

Mrs. Cathcart looked alarmed. "Why?"

"It may contain a clue to his whereabouts."

"Oh." Her eyes shifted away from Joanna's, and she looked down, picking at a bit of lint on her dark skirt.

"May I?" Joanna asked again.

Frances Cathcart raised her eyes; they were a little afraid. "I'm sorry, but I can't let you do that."

"Why not?"

"I would if I could. But I went to look at his room this morning, after your Mr. Rafferty left. And..."

"And?"

"Will has locked his door. Locked it and taken the key. Miss Stark, he's never done that before, and it has me ever so worried."

SEVEN

UNFAMILIAR SOUNDS AWOKE HER: footsteps and slamming doors, the hum of a garbage truck, the clang of a cable car's bell, the keening of a foghorn. The bed was strange too, lumpy, with a rough woolen blanket instead of soft quilts. And when she opened her eyes she saw a low ceiling webbed with cracks, and a tattered paper lantern. Where . . . ?

Oh, yes, the apartment. She was in San Francisco. A painting had been stolen from the museum, and she had come here to help Nick out.

It was cold in the dingy little room. Joanna pulled the covers up around her neck as the events of the day before came back to her. She'd gone to the de Young and talked with Marshall Wheatley, and then she'd paid a visit to the cousin with whom the missing security guard lived. When Mrs. Cathcart had told her Wilson Reed had locked the door of his room before he'd disappeared, she'd persuaded the woman to let her break a pane on a window, slip the catch, and climb inside. She'd found very little, except for a large stack of department-store and mail-order catalogs with numerous expensive items circled in red felt-tip pen. Cameras and videocassette recorders, televisions and stereos, oriental rugs and cut-crystal glasses, monogrammed silk bathrobes and cashmere sweaters—it seemed Wilson Reed had coveted all this merchandise. Whether the well-worn catalogs represented a fantasy shopping trip or whether Reed actually expected to have the money to acquire the objects was open for speculation. But the catalogs did reveal a side of his character that had previously been unknown even to his cousin.

Interesting as that was, the visit to Reed's home had met with a dead end. Today Joanna had decided to pursue the investigation from another angle, by attempting to track down Mike Wheatley. First she would talk with Phyllis and find out where Mike's studio was, and then—

Joanna moved her foot to one side and came up against something solid. She kicked out, and whatever it was fell to the floor. Struggling into a sitting position, she peered over the edge of the sofa bed. The box containing her files on Antony Parducci lay on its side, a few newspaper clippings spilling out onto the rug. She'd lugged it to San Francisco with her, intending to refresh her memory about the thief, should it appear he had something to do with the job at the de Young. And she'd left it on the bed when she'd tired of combing through the papers at about two that morning.

Of course, the files had told her nothing new, merely re-confirmed her suspicions. Parducci had been active as an art thief from the late fifties to 1976, eventually specializing in works by Dutch or Flemish artists because he had developed connections with a number of collectors who were interested in that particular type of painting. All of the jobs that could reasonably be attributed to him followed a pattern: He enlisted the aid of a museum or gallery employee. And all of these employees fit a certain profile: They were well beyond their middle years, reliable but not very bright, and of an extremely acquisitive nature, which they had not previously been able to indulge because of low income. It was a profile that

Wilson Reed fit very well, now that Joanna had seen the stack of catalogs in his room.

In total, Joanna had thirteen files on thefts that the authorities had laid at Parducci's door. But in 1976, following the disappearance of a Bruegel religious painting from a small museum in Brussels, Parducci had simply vanished from the underworld of art. Some investigators thought he was dead; others assumed he'd gone into a legitimate business with the proceeds of his crimes. Joanna doubted either theory; she believed that Parducci had become a broker, thus removing himself several steps from the actual thefts. And she had an equal number of files on thefts after 1976 that might have been ordered by him. They all fit his modus operandi, indicating he might have specified how they were to be carried out. And the theft of the Hals fell right into line except for one factor.

Mike Wheatley. He was the piece that didn't fit the puzzle no matter how hard Joanna tried to jam it into place. If it weren't for his telephone call to Great American, the theft would appear straightforward, almost classic. But Mike's involvement had muddied the picture, and it would stay muddied until she found out more about his connection. With that in mind, she got up, showered and dressed, and left the apartment.

On the second-floor landing, she came face to face with Rex Malauulu. Her landlord was wearing a garish red and yellow Hawaiian shirt that billowed out like a maternity smock over his giant belly. His khaki pants were rumpled, his tennis shoes torn, and on his head he wore a Forty-niners cap that almost covered a spreading bald spot. When he saw Joanna, he grinned easily at her, as if their last encounter had been only yesterday.

"I'm glad I ran into you," he said. "We need to talk about the rent."

"It's paid up through December, isn't it?"

"Yeah, but I'm going to have to raise it come January—higher maintenance costs, you know."

Uh-oh, Joanna thought, I should have known a good deal like this apartment wouldn't last indefinitely. "How much?"

"Well." Rex paused, taking off the cap and scratching his bald spot. "You pay two hundred now. What would you say to two-fifty?"

Joanna blinked in surprise. Apartments like hers went for upward of five hundred these days. "Two-fifty?"

"It's not too much, is it?" Rex peered at her anxiously. "I wouldn't want to lose you. You're my quietest, best behaved tenant." Then he laughed uproariously and punched her on the arm, a tap that nearly sent her reeling down the stairs.

"No, it's not too much," she said when she had recovered her balance. "Just send me the bill like you always do."

"Good. We going to be seeing more of you?"

"Maybe. For a few days, at any rate."

"Well, when you get a chance, stop by the bar. Drinks on the house."

"Thanks, I'll do that." She started down the stairs, but paused when Rex called after her.

"Hey," he said, "did that guy who was asking for you find you?"

"What guy?"

"Tall fella, graying hair. He came around yesterday, and I told him that as far as I knew you were living someplace in Sonoma. I hope it was all right to give him your box number."

Joanna smiled. "It's okay; that was my business partner. And yes, he found me." She continued down the stairs, still smiling. Nick was as insular a San Franciscan as existed in this strangely provincial city, disliking even to cross the bridge to Oakland unless it was absolutely necessary. Trust him to start looking for her close to home, on the off chance she might be in town and thus save him a trip to Sonoma.

She stepped outside into a brilliantly clear day. Unlike fall weather in Sonoma, where the sunlight had a filtered, moody quality, November days in San Francisco were often crisp and bright, the sun making colors more true and defining everything with a hard edge. But come evening the fog would inevitably creep in, and even now the wailing of the horns outside the Golden Gate was a reminder that a gray bank of mist hovered there, waiting. Still, the fog was infinitely preferable to rain. It had been an unseasonably wet fall, and already several landslides—those yearly disasters that swept away homes that Californians nevertheless insisted on building on hazardous hillsides—had been reported, especially along the coast.

A minor annoyance waited on the windshield of Joanna's car—a parking ticket. She snatched it off and scanned it, then glanced up at a sign a few yards away. A no-parking zone this morning, due to the weekly street cleaning.

"Damn," she muttered, tossing the ticket into the space behind her seat. Inconveniences such as a multitude of parking regulations and overzealous meter maids were only some of the reasons she'd been glad to leave the city, and as she drove across town to the de Young, dodging reckless motorists and foolishly confident pedestrians, she began to compile a list of others. By the time she had parked in the lot next to the Music Concourse, she was regretting telling Rex Malauulu she'd keep the apartment. Why pour money into the economy of a place that annoyed you so much?

But then she got out of the car and surveyed the impeccable lawn that sloped down to the grove of gnarled plane trees in the concourse. And glanced at the majestic shape of the band shell. Across the avenue that skirted the concourse was the museum, surrounded by tall palms, its graceful tile-crowned tower rising against the hard blue sky. Because she'd been away so long, Joanna took the scene in as if she'd never viewed it before—and immediately reversed her position on the city. There was no place quite like San Francisco, annoyances and all; perhaps taken only in occasional small doses, it was at its charming best.

She crossed to the museum, spoke with one of the security guards, and found that Phyllis Wheatley was in the eighteenth-century British gallery near the rear of the building. The room was closed to visitors, but Joanna entered anyway. Phyllis stood at the far end, supervising two women as they removed a set of china from a massive mahogany breakfront bookcase. She was a tall woman—almost as tall as her husband—wearing slimly tapered slacks and a long sweater coat that emphasized her angular frame. When Joanna spoke her name, she turned, reaching for a pair of horn-rimmed glasses that perched on top of her stylishly upswept white blond hair and setting them on the bridge of her nose.

"Oh, Joanna!" she said. "Marshall told me you might stop by." She hurried over, enveloped Joanna in a hug, then removed the glasses—which were for farsightedness—and plunked them back on top of her head. Her brown eyes, curiously girlish in an older woman's face, sparkled as she surveyed Joanna from head to toe. "You look lovely."

"So do you." Having seen how bad Marshall looked, Joanna had been afraid Phyllis would have suffered a similar change, but she was relieved to find her much as she'd always been. The brown eyes were clear, her color was good, and her face—its cheek and jaw bones too pronounced for it to be truly handsome—showed no signs of tension. Whatever had wrought the change in her husband had left Phyllis untouched.

Phyllis smiled at the compliment. "Why, thank you. Tell me, will we have a chance to visit with you while you're in the city?"

"I hope so. I guess Marshall told you I'm here on a job for S.S.I."

Phyllis glanced back at the two women, who were lowering a flower-patterned soup tureen into a packing case. "Yes, he did. Look, why don't we go to the cafe for a cup of coffee? I don't have much time, but I think I can trust these ladies not to smash the crockery." She signaled that she was leaving, then led Joanna into the hallway, linking arms with her as they walked along. "I didn't want to discuss your... business in front of my helpers," she said in a low voice. "They're volunteers and don't know about the theft."

"Frankly, I'm surprised it hasn't made the headlines yet. This museum has always been a nest of gossips."

"Frankly, I wish it had. I've never been one for keeping these matters from the police, regardless of who is involved." Phyllis sounded uncharacteristically grim.

"I tend to agree with you," Joanna said.

They entered the museum's cafe, got coffee, and went out into the little courtyard, taking a table next to the reflecting pool. Phyllis adjusted the red and blue striped umbrella so it did not block the sun, and they both leaned back in the wrought iron chairs, savoring the warmth for a moment.

Joanna said, "When you speak of who's involved in this... business, do you think Wilson Reed did it?"

"I do not. His wife was a fine woman, and we've known him for years. He would never do such a thing."

"He was married to your housekeeper, right?"

Phyllis nodded. "In fact, he lived in the apartment over our garage up until Margaret died. In those years he worked for the Muni, driving a streetcar. But when they put the Metro in, he couldn't adjust to the new type of cars, so Marshall spoke to the head of security here and got him his job. There has never been the slightest complaint about Wilson's work."

"So I've heard. What do you think happened to him, then?"

Phyllis's eyes clouded. "I think he saw the thief and was forced to accompany him when he left with the painting. To tell you the truth, I'm afraid he may have been harmed, possibly killed."

"That's what I'm afraid of, too." Joanna paused. "But let's talk about more pleasant subjects. How is your family?"

Phyllis reached down and fumbled in her handbag, a leather one which—like her working costume—had seen better days, and pulled out a pack of cigarettes. She didn't speak until she had finished lighting one. "The family is fine. Douglas is doing well at the brokerage firm; in fact, he's in New York at the home office right now. I believe they may be discussing a promotion, but I don't dare ask until he announces it. Douglas so likes to spring a surprise on us."

"And Mike?"

"Mike is the same as always." But the fine lines around her mouth had tightened.

"I understand from Marshall that he's still painting and has a gallery to handle his work."

Phyllis drew deeply on her cigarette. "Oh, Joanna," she said, "I can pretend to most of our friends, but not to you. Yes, Mike is still painting, and yes, the Galerie des Beaux Arts is handling him, but it's on a very small scale, and that's only because the owner is also his girlfriend. I believe what he really does is spend most of his time at Islais Creek Resort, drinking up what's left of his trust from his grandmother."

Joanna sat up straighter. "Islais Creek Resort?"

"Yes. It's a bar and restaurant on the water near his studio—"

"I know the place. Where is his studio, anyway?"

Phyllis frowned at her abrupt response. "He rents space in one of the old warehouses in China Basin. He's never bothered to inform us which one. But what's the matter? You've gone positively... I don't know, rigid."

Joanna was silent. The Islais Creek Resort, on the shores of one of the inlets that extended off the bay near the old Hunter's Point Shipyards, was better termed a waterfront dive. Its owner, Tony Capello, was known as an amiable drunk who supported starving artists and other hangers-on by giving them odd jobs, credit, and an occasional free meal. Joanna knew Capello from her days at S.S.I., however, and she was aware of a darker side of his patronage: Those who accepted these favors from him owed him a debt, and said debt was usually worked off by performing sub-rosa errands. The most innocuous of these, delegated to the least skilled, were drug deliveries; the adept, she knew, were enlisted in thefts of various kinds—including art thefts.

"Joanna?" Phyllis said.

"Oh, I'm sorry." She put a hand to her forehead. "I'm not feeling well. It must be from sitting in direct sun."

"Here, I'll move the umbrella." Phyllis started to get up.

"No, that's all right." Joanna made a show of looking at her watch and then shrugged into her jacket. "I have to be going now anyway. I . . . have a meeting at the office."

Phyllis nodded and told Joanna to come by the house when she could spare the time. Her words were unconcerned enough, but when Joanna glanced back at her old friend from the door, she saw that she had her glasses perched on her nose and was staring after her with worried eyes.

ISLAIS CREEK RESORT WAS a two-story weathered frame building on the edge of an oil-slicked inlet on the industrial east side of the city. Downstairs was a pool room generally inhabited by shabby, sullen men who took their beer and their bank shots seriously; upstairs was a bar and an outdoor deck with rickety, mismatched tables and chairs. When Joanna entered the bar at a little after eleven, it was already crowded with an odd mixture of working-class types from the nearby warehouses and shipyards and members of the business establishment who had apparently gotten lost on their way to the more chic eating places such as Mission Rock Resort. Most of the tables on the deck were occupied, and waitresses—one of them in the dirtiest T-shirt Joanna had ever seen—hurried up to the window behind the bar shouting orders for beer and burgers, then rushed off again.

A friend of Joanna's had nicknamed the place the Last Resort; looking at it now, she had to agree that the label was apt.

There was one stool still vacant at the bar. She climbed onto it and looked around for Tony Capello. He was at the far end, pouring white wine into a smudged glass—a short, bald man with a fringe of curly, grizzled hair. She hadn't seen Capello in more than five years, but he didn't appear to have changed much; perhaps the beer belly that protruded under his dirty white apron was larger, but otherwise he looked much the same.

A second bartender came up and took Joanna's order. She asked for a Budweiser, thinking it safest to drink out of a bottle rather than a glass. When the beer came, she sipped it slowly, keeping an eye on Capello. He was making his way down the bar toward her, exchanging jokes and wisecracks with the patrons as he went. About two feet away he stopped and began telling a long joke about a Jewish widow haggling over funeral prices; at its conclusion, which was reasonably dirty and involved a lot of dramatic hand gestures, he glanced expectantly to both sides—and saw Joanna.

Capello's eager expression faded. The nearby patrons, who had been laughing at the joke, quieted and looked at Joanna too. The other bartender noticed the sudden silence and tensed. Capello stepped in front of her, bracing himself on the bar, palms down, arms stiff.

"Well, well. Mrs. Stark," he said. "What brings you here?"

Joanna raised the bottle and sipped her beer, then placed it carefully on the coaster in front of her. "I'm slumming, Mr. Capello."

His expression didn't change. "Still the smart ass, aren't you?"

"Sure am."

He leaned closer, lowering his voice. "What do you want?"

"Information."

"Nothing changes." Then he motioned at the bartender. "Give this lady another beer, Jim, and cover for me, will you?" He ducked under the plank and came around behind Joanna. When she had her beer, he took her arm in a forceful grip and steered her toward an isolated corner table that was always kept reserved for him. Joanna's stool was instantly taken, and the conversation at the end of the bar resumed.

Capello seated Joanna and took the chair opposite her, leaning forward on the table, thick fingers laced together. "Information, you said."

"Yes. I want to know if anyone's tried to place any orders lately."

"Orders? My customers place lots of orders—for beer, for booze, for hamburgers. You name it—"

"You know what I mean, Tony."

"Mmm." It was Capello's characteristic way of giving himself time to think. "I thought you quit that business."

"I like to keep my hand in."

"Mmm."

"Tony, we both know what I'm talking about."

"A gentleman in white?"

"Right. What do you know about him?"

Capello spread his hands out and smiled innocently. Joanna sipped beer.

Finally Capello said, "All right, you've always been straight with me. In fact, I owe you one from that time you kept my name out of that mess at the Ross Galleries. But one is all I owe you."

"So pay up, and you'll be debt-free."

Capello laced his fingers together again and leaned closer. "All right. No one's tried to place an order here. In fact, the whole thing came as a surprise, and that's strange because I usually get wind of it beforehand when something like that's about to go down."

"When did you hear about it, then?"

"Yesterday. There was a young fellow in here who talks too much when he gets a few bourbons in him."

"Mike Wheatley."

Capello raised his eyebrows. "Good, Mrs. Stark. Very good."

"What did he say?"

"Mmm. Nothing that made much sense. Just that he was going to get rich and get even because of the fellow in white."

"Get even?"

"Yeah. The young man had revenge on his mind, and from the look on his face, I think the revenge will be damned sweet. To him, that is; I pity the poor bastard—"

"Tony, did he give any indication *who* the person might be?"

"No, only that he'd been waiting years for the opportunity."

Joanna frowned, sipping beer. "What did he say about the actual theft?"

"Just that it had happened."

"Did you have the impression he himself had done it?"

"Mmm."

Joanna waited.

After a moment Capello said, "I'm thinking back to the conversation, and you know, it's funny. The way he talked about it, it was as if he was reporting something he'd seen in the newspaper. If I had to make a judgment, I'd say no, he didn't do it."

"You're sure?"

"Well, that judgment would be colored by what I know about the guy. He's a drunk. Now I've got nothing against drunks, being one myself at times, but for something in that class, he's unreliable as hell. Takes an organized type to pull something like that off. That's why I've never used him for anything."

Joanna nodded; it matched her own impression of Mike Wheatley. "I hear he has a studio in a warehouse around here."

"Yeah, over at China Basin. An old warehouse with a wharf attached. Has an orange-striped door, so you can't miss it. Usually you can either find him there, or here propping up the bar."

Joanna finished her beer and stood up. "Thanks, Tony. Now I owe *you* one."

"Mmm. I appreciate it, but I'd just as soon call us even."

"Why?"

"Because every time you do me a favor, I owe you an even bigger one in return. You want to repay me, do it by staying out of my bar."

"But Tony!" Joanna gestured around at the shabby, smoke-filled room. "I find your place irresistible."

"Yeah," he said gloomily, "that's what I'm afraid of. But seriously, kid, if you go over there to see our friend, be careful. The guy used to be a harmless drunk, but lately he's become a mean one."

"I'll remember that."

"Good. And now get the hell out of here, and don't come back!"

EIGHT

BEFORE LEAVING THE BAR, Joanna stopped at the downstairs pay phone and called S.S.I. Nick, the secretary told her, was at Great American's offices awaiting Mike Wheatley's promised call. Joanna dialed again and spoke with Steve Rafferty, who said Wheatley had so far failed to phone. She told the insurance investigator—who sounded tired and on edge—that she was following up some leads, and hung up before he could ask what they were. Then she drove north on Third Street to China Basin.

Named in honor of the Pacific Mail Steamship Line's China Clippers, which were berthed there in the 1860s, the basin is surrounded by freight yards and a wide assortment of industrial concerns. A long channel, spanned by two bridges and a freeway, extends inland from it, making the area seem cut off from the mainstream of life in the city. Hard hit by the decamping of the bulk of the shipping industry from San Francisco to the Port of Oakland, the present-day China Basin also seems far removed from its exotic past, when large fishing boats from such faraway home ports as Nome, Sitka, and Gig Harbor would winter there to escape the storms to the north.

The old warehouse that Tony Capello had described was on the water's edge near Pier 48. A loading dock extended the length of it, and while the large overhead doors were closed and secured, a smaller orange-striped door stood propped open with a brick. Joanna went up and studied the sign posted next to it.

It was list of the various craftsmen who had studios there: C. Condor, Sculptor; M. Zimmerman, Weaver; A. Eddy, Goldsmith. Close to the bottom was Mike Wheatley's name, followed by the equally simple notation Painter. The sign gave no hint of how to locate any of these people, so Joanna stepped into the cool, dark hallway and followed it as it led haphazardly among plywood partitions that had been erected to subdivide the space. Here and there doors were cut into the walls; some bare plain signs, others were brightly painted, one had even been decoupaged with illustrations from slick magazines that she assumed to be the work of the graphic designer within. In adherence to what she'd observed as a strict law of nature, Wheatley's studio was the farthest from the entryway. Its door was rough planking, and an index card hand-lettered with his name was tacked to it an an odd angle, imparting an impression of neglect and haste.

Joanna knocked and waited. After a moment, she heard shuffling sounds within, and then the door opened. The barefoot man who looked out at her was in his mid-twenties, with a stubbled chin, bloodshot eyes, and sandy hair that stuck out in thick tufts. He wore jeans and a wrinkled shirt, the tail of which hung out. When he saw Joanna, he made a feeble attempt to smooth his hair. This was an older Mike Wheatley than she remembered, and from all appearances, he was suffering a massive hangover.

"Hi, Mike," she said. "Remember me—Joanna Stark?"

"Uh." Once again he ran his fingers through his hair. "Uh, sure. Your husband was my father's lawyer."

"Right. How are you?"

"Uh, actually I'm not sure. I was just waking up. Come on in."

She stepped past him into a cramped space whose walls seemed to lean at strange angles. It took her a moment to realize that the effect was created by stacks of large canvases that were propped against them. To one side was a cot whose sheets hung to the paint-splattered concrete floor, an old cracked leather armchair, and a card table that held a hotplate, dishes, and utensils. But the rest of the room was jammed with canvases, most of them over four feet high. One stack was turned toward the wall, another was covered with a stained tarp, but directly ahead a painting faced into the room. Joanna drew in her breath when she saw it.

It measured some six feet square, and its background color was an iridescent reddish-orange. Superimposed on that were three black silhouettes of people who appeared to be engaged in a struggle. And across this scene at six-inch intervals were vertical black lines, like the bars of a cell.

Joanna stepped forward, studying the figures. The one at the left was holding the central one by its shoulders. And the one at the right stood poised on the balls of its feet, arm raised, ready to plunge a knife into the helpless person. A shiver ran through her and she turned away. Mike Wheatley had closed the door and was watching her, strangely alert in spite of his wasted state.

He said, "You like it?"

"It's . . . powerful." The truth, but not all of it. The painting was bizarre, disturbing—and quite sick. As for the technique, Marshall had been correct in his assessment of that: Mike had not bothered to learn his craft; this looked as if it had been sketched in outline and then painted with an airbrush. The precise form negated the turbulent emotion embodied in those figures, and that made the leashed violence seem all the more disturbing. Joanna wondered if Mike was aware of its effect.

He stood there, arms folded across his chest, nodding in satisfaction at her reaction. Then curiosity flooded his haggard features and he said, "Joanna Stark. I remember you from years ago. You and your husband were a couple of Mom and Dad's favorite people. I remember him especially."

"Oh?"

"Yeah. My parents were giving this big dinner party four or five years ago. Dad and I had just had a fight because I'd been kicked out of school again, and I was feeling shitty. David saw what was going on, and he grabbed a bottle of wine and took me out into the garden and talked to me. We sat there on those stone steps overlooking the lawn and the sea and drank the whole bottle and afterward I felt better."

Joanna remembered the occasion now; the recollection brought a warmth and, at the same time, a hollow pang of loneliness. In the past three years she had found the two emotions strangely compatible. She said, "What did you talk about?"

Mike's face had softened when he spoke of David, but now he drew it into cynical lines and shrugged. "Hell, I don't know. He probably gave me some advice that I never followed."

Joanna sighed. Apparently Mike had never been known for his ability to take advice.

Mike said, "He died soon after that, didn't he?"

"Three years ago last summer."

"I'm sorry. Didn't you move out of the city, or something?"

"Yes, I've been living in Sonoma. I went there to establish an art gallery."

"Oh." Mike's glance strayed to his painting, then returned to her. "Are you here on business? I mean...it's been so long and I don't really understand why you looked me up."

"I heard about your paintings, and I thought I'd take a look at them."

"Oh. Well, the best ones aren't here; they're at the gallery that handles them—" Suddenly he broke off, looking at his wrist. There was a band of light, untanned skin bisecting it, but no watch. "Damn! You have the time?"

"Twelve-oh-five."

"Damn!" Frantically he began tucking his shirt in, while slipping into a pair of loafers that lay pigeon-toed next to the cot. He then went to the table and rummaged around on it. "Where are those goddamn keys?"

"What's wrong?"

"Appointment at eleven. Overslept."

The appointment, Joanna thought, was probably to make his call to Great American. And thinking of the gallery that handled his paintings had triggered his recollection of it. She looked around the room, but saw no phone; Mike would have to go out and make his demands.

He stopped pushing things around on the table and stood still, his eyes closed. "Keys," he said. "Keys."

"Look, if you can't find them, I'll drive you wherever you're going."

He snapped his fingers and started for the door. "I know—must have left them in the van last night. Listen"—he stopped, looking back at her—"I can't talk anymore now. Come back or—no, call Suzanne Mackenzie at the Galerie des Beaux Arts. She'll show you my stuff.'' And then he was gone, leaving the door ajar.

Joanna went after him, but by the time she got to the loading dock, Mike had climbed into a beat-up red VW van that was parked there and was pulling away. She noted the license plate number as she ran for her car.

The red van traveled along Third Street, crossed the Lefty O'Doul Memorial Drawbridge at the channel, and proceeded through the South of Market district. It moved slowly—more because of a sluggish engine, probably, than a lack of haste on the driver's part—and none of Wheatley's maneuverings through traffic gave any indication he knew Joanna was behind him. He crossed Market and turned off Kearny onto Sutter, into the heart of the city's gallery district. Here in roughly, a five-block stretch were located some three dozen of San Francisco's art retailers; the surrounding streets all well lined with shops offering anything from traditional European paintings to contemporary works by local artists to tribal artifacts from farflung corners of the world. With the same hollow pang she'd experienced earlier, Joanna noted the neat brick building where David had had his law office.

David, she thought as she waited at a stoplight two cars behind the van. It was interesting that Mike had remembered him so well, spoken of him with apparent fondness. That conversation in the garden during the dinner party must have meant a great deal to Mike, regardless of the fact he professed not to remember what had been said. Whatever the actual words, she could imagine the tenor of them: reassuring, never condescending, indicating liking and respect on David's part. She'd seen him take that approach with E.J., particularly during the bad time when the boy had seethed with resentment over his father's marriage to Joanna so soon after Eleanor's death. Or later, when E.J. was in high school and had realized that Joanna and David had been lovers long before Eleanor had fallen ill.

The light changed. Mike's van moved on for half a block, then stopped, signaling a left turn. When traffic cleared, he drove into a side street. Joanna went past slowly and saw the street was actually an alley that dead-ended some twenty yards from the sidewalk. Mike had pulled his van off to one side and was climbing out.

Joanna put on her brakes and stopped, scanning the adjacent building. It was similar to the one where David had had his offices, four stories with a wide storefront on the ground floor; the storefront's windows were draped in a plain white fabric, and each displayed a brilliantly hued contemporary painting of the school that Joanna privately referred to as "splash and splatter." Gold lettering on the right-hand window said this was the Galerie des Beaux Arts; a sign on the door read Closed.

So Mike's appointment had been with someone at the gallery that handled his paintings. What was the name he had mentioned? Suzanne Mackenzie. Probably she was his girlfriend, the owner—and possibly the woman who had made the call to Great American for Mike the day before. Or was that too great a leap in logic? Maybe, maybe not.

A horn honked behind her. Joanna looked up and down the street and saw all the parking spaces were taken. The horn honked again, more insistently. She took her foot off the brake, drove to the corner, and made a right turn, uphill. Circling the block quickly, she returned to Sutter. The van was still parked in the alley, and a truck was pulling out of a loading zone a few car-lengths ahead. Joanna took the space it had vacated and debated what to do.

The gallery was closed—odd for a Wednesday afternoon—but she could always ring the bell and ask to view Mike's paintings. But wouldn't he think it too great a coincidence for her to arrive without calling, and while he was there? And what if he were on the phone, in the process of making his demands on Great American? Her arrival might panic him, upset any arrangements being made—and ultimately jeopardize the Hals. It would be better, she decided, to wait it out and continue to monitor Mike's movements.

Her wait was not a long one. Within five minutes Mike had emerged from the gallery's side door and climbed into the van. He backed down the alley and eased into traffic, narrowly missing an *Examiner* delivery truck, then continued along Sutter—past his father's gallery—to Van Ness. After following that main artery north toward the bay, he made a series of jogs around Fort Mason—once a military installation and now a cultural center—toward the Marina Green. By the time he was passing the yacht harbor and about to enter the Presidio, Joanna guessed his destination was the Wheatley home in Sea Cliff.

What had Marshall said about Mike last night? That they seldom saw him unless he turned up drunk and spent the night on the couch. At the moment he was neither intoxicated nor in need of a place to sleep. Why pay this uncharacteristic visit, then?

The road ascended a hill and wound through the Presidio, high above the Golden Gate and the sea. The land was thickly forested with eucalyptus, and wind-bent cypress clung to the rocky outcroppings. Beyond their twisted, tortured shapes the water on the Pacific sparkled with deceptive calm in the early afternoon sunlight; further out, looming on the horizon, was the patient, waiting fog. The van labored up the steep incline, forcing Joanna to fall farther back. It only gained in speed when it emerged from the military reservation and turned on Twenty-fifth Avenue into the affluent residential area.

The homes solidly perched on the cliffs overhanging the Pacific were large, but set uncomfortably close together; as in the rest of the city, land in Sea Cliff was at a premium and not to be used wastefully. The Wheatley home, set on a promontory above the protected expanse of China Beach, was no exception. A square Italian-style stucco, its grayish beige color, sculpted medallion between the second-story windows, and massive urns guarding the entry had always reminded Joanna of houses she'd found quietly mouldering on once elegant side streets in Florence or Rome. The shade of the two large cypress trees in the front yard imparted a broody but not unpleasant atmosphere that further put her in mind of those European cities. Today the house seemed even gloomier, its walls moss-grown, its yard littered with dead leaves from the neighbors' mulberry trees, but she chalked that up to both her long absence and her less than cheerful mood.

Mike pulled his van into the driveway and stopped under the larger of the trees. Joanna waited three houses down the street, watching as he loped across the small lawn to the front entry, rang the bell, and was admitted by an older woman in a gray and white uniform. Margaret Reed's replacement, undoubtedly.

Joanna smiled, thinking of all the things that had not changed in her three years' absence from the city; the Wheatleys still followed their practice of not carrying keys to their own house. She had found that extremely odd the first time Marshall had brought David and her here and had rung his own doorbell.

"What is it with you?" she had said to the big, kind man who—in spite of their social set's outrage at the upstart who had married David only months after his wife's death—had made her feel welcome. "Are you afraid you can't keep track of your own house key?"

He grinned at her, eyes twinkling at her obvious bewilderment. "Phyl and I have both been known to lose key rings. I drop them down sewers or elevator shafts. She just plain misplaces them. Makes it mighty handy for a burglar."

"But goodness, what if there's no one home?"

At that point, the door had opened and Margaret Reed stood there, plump yet curiously trim looking in her uniform. "This lady," Marshall said, "is always here. I swear she never goes out, eats, or sleeps."

"Now, Mr. Wheatley," Mrs. Reed said, "you know that isn't so. Mr. Reed and I have our bowling night, our Bingo night, and the functions at the rod and gun club. What I am"—this to Joanna, with a brief smile at David—"is a good manager. I pull rank and delegate door duty to the maid."

Marshall and Phyllis had started to make Joanna feel accepted; now Mrs. Reed had finished the job. Joanna said, "I could install a burglar alarm for you, and then the maid could go bowling, too."

Marshall laughed. "You've already installed one in the gallery. But at home, I'm old-fashioned, even if it means a high turnover of maids."

The recollection of that conversation warmed Joanna now, and it was a good three minutes before she remembered to turn off the engine of the Fiat. Then she settled down to wait for Mike to come out of the house. Fifteen minutes passed, half an hour. How long should she wait? she wondered. Mike might be paying an extended visit; even though Marshall would still be at his gallery, Phyllis should have returned from the de Young by now. They would be sitting in the sunroom overlooking the sea, chatting and perhaps sipping some of that wonderful chamomile tea that Phyllis was so partial to. . . .

She checked her watch, waited five minutes more, then restarted the Fiat. Sitting here was a waste of precious time, and besides, she was anxious to talk with Nick and Steve Rafferty, to see if Mike had indeed made his call to Great American.

NINE

THE RESTAURANT WAS CHINESE—and old-fashioned. Jade green and gilt painted wood. Lanterns with stylized scenes and red tassels. Black lacquered tables. Lotus blossom crockery. And high-backed booths with bead curtains for privacy. In any other city it would have been a cliché; in San Francisco it was a classic. For years it had been one of Joanna's favorite eating places, and she had been pleased and surprised when Steve Rafferty had suggested they have an early dinner there.

Now Rafferty took a sip of red wine, set his glass down, then picked it up again. "Have another slug of wine, Steve," he said. "Don't mind if I do," he answered himself.

Joanna smiled. Rafferty was tired and frustrated and more than a little angry, but he still managed to handle those emotions with humor, and that—like his choice of restaurant—pleased her. And he had a right to those feelings, given the events of the afternoon.

When she'd reached Rafferty's office at Great American a little before two, she found that Mike Wheatley had called—at approximately the same time she'd been waiting for him outside the Galerie des Beaux Arts. The conversation had been another stall: Wait until five, and then he would have ascertained the exact whereabouts of the Hals. When Rafferty had attempted to elicit any further information, Mike had hung up.

Joanna had then gone over the tapes of the three phone conversations with Nick and Rafferty, verifying that it was indeed Mike's voice on the first and the third. The woman's voice—assured and cool—was totally unfamiliar. Mike's first call had been similarly confident, but during this afternoon's conversation he had sounded less in control. Joanna was inclined to chalk that up to his being hungover and late in making the phone call, but—as Rafferty pointed out—it could also indicate some hitch in his plans.

So, with a couple of hours on their hands, she and Nick had proceeded to dig: While he attempted to find out all he could about Suzanne Mackenzie and the Galerie des Beaux Arts, she canvassed a number of the less reputable dealers in the Sutter Street vicinity. And she returned to Rafferty's office empty-handed; if anyone had tried to place an order for the Hals, he hadn't contacted any of the dealers whom she could count on to be reasonably open with her. While she didn't believe that the city's art underworld had been as quiet recently as they all claimed, she was fairly certain that no one had so much as mentioned Dutch art, much less the *Cavalier*.

In the meantime, Nick hadn't returned from his researches and Rafferty had met with further frustration. It was six o'clock; again there had been no call from Mike. At five-thirty Rafferty had scheduled a meeting for eight o'clock with both Great American and de Young officials. Its purpose was to convince them to go the police; Rafferty was certain that any further details would only result in the loss or destruction of the Hals.

Now he poured more wine for both of them and said, "The son of a bitch is playing games with us. I know you're close to the family, Mrs. Stark, but we can't continue to protect them."

"You're right; we can't." She studied Rafferty across the table. His hazel eyes were red-rimmed; his face, which she had thought so youthful the evening before, was crimped with weariness; even his silver gray hair looked as if he'd been clawing at it. She knew the negotiations for the return of the Hals—if and when they occurred—would probably mark a crucial point in his career. Successful arrangements could solidify his position at Great American, but a failure could destroy it.

"It doesn't matter who the family are," he said, as if trying to convince Joanna of the validity of his position.

"I'm not disagreeing with you." She reached for the menu and scanned it. It was another thing that had not changed in her absence from the city. When she glanced questioningly at Rafferty, he shrugged, looking disinterested, so she said, "Potstickers, kung pao chicken, eggplant, sizzling calamari. Okay?"

He brightened a little. "Shrimp, rather than potstickers."

"Mr. Rafferty, you're a connoisseur."

"Call me Steve."

"No, you're just plain Rafferty; I can't think of you any other way. I'll drop the 'Mr.' though. And you call me Joanna."

He quirked his lips up in one of his infrequent, slightly lopsided grins. "Some people are just last-name guys, right?"

"Right."

"Well, here's to a good working relationship."

They clicked their glasses together. Joanna sipped, then leaned against the high back of the booth, feeling the warmth of the wine spread through her. Had she been imagining it, or had Rafferty stressed the word "working"? The man seemed to be all cool professionalism, avoiding any conversation that was remotely personal. An hour earlier in his office, she'd attempted to question him about a picture of a little girl that sat in a gold frame on a side table, and he'd abruptly steered the subject back to her visits to the art dealers.

The waiter came. Joanna had to order; Rafferty had forgotten what they'd chosen. She'd noticed there was a kind of person who got rattled in Chinese restaurants, always said something like, "Oh, God, now what *did* we decide on?" and then fumbled with the menu. David, for all his urbane ways, had been one of those. So was E.J. She was not, but she liked Rafferty for being one, and forgave him his earlier reticence.

She said, "Number two, fifteen, twenty-seven, thirty-one, and more wine, please."

The waiter—an old, stooped, balding man who had worked there since Joanna had moved to San Francisco—said, "I remember you."

"Really?"

"Yes. It is always the eggplant and more wine." Then he repeated the order and shuffled toward the kitchen.

Rafferty said, "You really *have* come here a lot."

"Off and on for twelve years."

"You make me feel like a rank newcomer. I only found this place six months ago."

"That would be right after you came out from New York?"

"Yes."

"Why did you come to San Francisco?"

"A promotion. And to get away from things."

"Oh?"

At the inquiring syllable, he looked annoyed with himself, as if his brief comment had revealed more than he'd intended. "Uh-huh. Are you a native San Francis-can?"

"No, I've been here only a couple of years longer than I've been coming to this restaurant."

"And before that?"

She hesitated, realizing one of the reasons she felt so comfortable with Rafferty: Like him, she had things she preferred not to talk about. "I was traveling for a few years. Originally I'm from New Jersey—Tenafly."

"Interesting. My wife and I lived in Teaneck for a while."

"Oh?"

"We were divorced, two years ago."

"I see." Probably one of the "things" he'd wanted to get away from.

The shrimp came. Rafferty waited until the waiter had gone, then said, "Since you're also a transplant to the city, tell me what you think of it."

"How do you mean?"

"Well, this case has pointed up one of the things that disturbs me about San Francisco. It's an impression I've had ever since I arrived here. There seems to be a little upper crust in-group that takes care of its own. They think they *are* San Francisco, and the rest of us can go to hell for all they care. The Wheatleys are part of that group—hence all the protecting of them. I guess in a sense you're part of it too."

Joanna pinched a shrimp between her chopsticks and ate it slowly, thinking. "You could be right, but I think the group you're talking about is just more visible. The city is actually comprised of a number of in-groups, on different societal levels. And they *all* take care of their own. In a sense, it's a very caring town."

"What do you mean?"

"Well, look at the gay community. Or the Asian refugees. The Chinese Six Companies. The Irish Cultural Center. Hell, even the Yuppies got together for a big dance last year."

Rafferty looked skeptical.

"Take my own experience, if you want something that illustrates it better," Joanna went on. "When I came here, I didn't have a dime or a job or any other claim to respectability. But I found a little apartment in a building owned by a kind man, who saw right away what my circumstances were and didn't demand a deposit or much rent. And then I applied for a job I wasn't qualified for and was hired by Nick, who also saw my circumstances and took a chance on me. When I married my husband—well, I didn't exactly have the social connections or spotless past of most members of his set, but they eventually accepted me, with very few questions asked. That's the kind of town it is—from people like my landlord to the opera-going set."

The rest of the food came. They waited, passed platters around, began to eat. After a while Rafferty said, "Well, your experience has been very different from how it would be, say, in New York."

"Of course. People don't realize when they first come here that this city isn't so very different from the rough-and-tumble Gold Rush outpost it started out as. We've got a lot of museums and the opera and the symphony hall, and we get all gussied up for opening nights. But basically—in comparison to people in a place like New York—we're really little kids dressing up and acting fancy in Mom and Dad's castoff clothes. And we admit it."

Rafferty smiled crookedly. "Maybe I'll like it better here, now that you're explained it."

"I hope so." And she meant it. She liked Rafferty, liked him a lot. As they ate, she became aware of a growing warmth that had nothing to do with the food or the wine. Rafferty was a comfortable man, equally easy to talk to or be silent with. And she sensed he was a private man, had the same reservations about his personal life that she had. He was a man who would never intrude where he was not wanted.

Once when she glanced up from her plate at him, he smiled, and she smiled back, feeling no need for idle, forced conversation. Another time she reached for the wine carafe, and their fingers met. He took the carafe from her and poured into her glass, his hazel eyes serious in the foolish red glow from the lanterns.

My God, Joanna thought, is the man attracted to me? And I to him? It was an intriguing idea. Since David had died, she'd been too busy trying to maintain life on an even keel to think of other men. She'd avoided any involvements that might throw her daily routine off its carefully charted course. But in the last two days, that life had begun to change. With it, she supposed, would come the possibility—

"Mrs. Stark?"

Joanna looked up. The man who peered through the red bead curtain was diminutive—less than five feet tall—with thinning dark hair and a mustache so fine that it looked as if it had been penciled on. His slight frame was clad in what had to be a custom-tailored black suit, and he carried a furled umbrella under one arm. The umbrella was a sensible precaution in this overly rainy fall season, but Joanna knew that Malcolm Halsey, art dealer, was never without it, even in the dry months.

She introduced Halsey to Rafferty, adding, "Mr. Halsey was busy with a customer when I stopped by his gallery this afternoon, but he offered to talk with me this evening. I called him from your office while you were winding things up with your secretary and suggested he meet us here.''

The two men exchanged pleasantries, and the art dealer sat down next to Joanna, placing the umbrella between them and folding his delicate hands on the table. Malcolm Halsey owned a gallery on lower Grant Avenue, between Chinatown and Union Square; he carried one of the better selections of Oriental art in the city—ivory and jade carvings, temple bronzes, Imari porcelains, Chinese scroll landscapes, Japanese silk screens. The gallery itself could be said to be a work of art: spacious, effectively lit, and well arranged. The high prices that Malcolm Halsey charged for his wares were always discreetly discussed; and just as discreet were his underworld contacts, which could be used to acquire that "something special" for an old and trusted client.

If Halsey now felt he had ventured into enemy territory, his demeanor didn't show it. The dealer was no stranger to those delicate and quasi-legal negotiations that went on between insurance companies and those who happened to possess stolen artworks. He accepted a glass of wine graciously—although his nose wrinkled at his first sip of the house red—and listened as Joanna explained what sort of information she was seeking. When she had finished, Halsey pursed his lips thoughtfully before he spoke.

"Of course," he said, "there are rumors about the theft at the de Young. Some say a member of a prominent family has involved himself, thus necessitating that the museum officials protect him." Halsey waited, but when Joanna didn't confirm or deny what he had said, went on. "That, however, does not concern us here.

What you are interested in is whether anyone was inquiring about the Hals before its disappearance.''

She nodded.

Again the dealer pursed his lips, his eyes closed contemplatively. ''To my knowledge,'' he finally said, ''no such inquiries were made. The primary sentiment in the art district is surprise that such a theft could occur with none of us having had prior knowledge.''

Joanna sighed and shot Rafferty a disappointed look. It was the same thing the other dealers had told her.

''It has been very quiet in the district for some months now,'' Halsey said. ''There was one inquiry, however.''

Simultaneously Joanna and Rafferty said, ''What?''

Halsey sipped wine, then took out a handkerchief and patted at his lips. ''It has nothing to do with the Hals. I only mention it because of its oddity. Possibly it wouldn't interest you.''

''No,'' Joanna said, ''please go on.''

''A gentleman was inquiring after an art dealer who has an adopted son. The boy, he said, would be in his twenties. He was most anxious to locate the dealer.''

Joanna felt a sudden tingling at the nape of her neck and looked at Rafferty. The insurance investigator seemed puzzled at this unexpected piece of information. It surprised her too—and interested her very much.

''I don't suppose the gentleman identified himself?'' she said.

''Most certainly not.''

''When was this?''

''Perhaps three weeks ago.''

''You talked with him personally?''

''Yes. I could not help him, and as far as I know, no one else was able.''

Joanna said, ''Will you describe him, please?''

Again Halsey closed his eyes in concentration. "Tall and slender. Balding. Regular features. It was almost as if he had been manufactured for complete anonymity. There was a scar on his neck, immediately below the jawline on the right side, which spoiled the effect."

"Eye color?"

"He wore sunglasses, even in the gallery."

"How did he speak?"

"He seemed educated."

"I meant, did he have any kind of accent?"

Halsey considered. "If he did have, it was very faint. It would be difficult to tell, at any rate, because his voice was extremely hoarse, as if he had a bad cold."

Joanna glanced at Rafferty. He was looking at her with a peculiar expression. He probably wondered why she was so interested in this bit of information. Or maybe he knew what she was thinking; after all, Nick had told him about her so-called obsession with Antony Parducci. She hoped he wouldn't mention it in front of Halsey.

When Rafferty spoke, he merely said, "Is the fellow we've been discussing so much lately adopted?"

In her quick anxiety she hadn't thought of that. "I...don't know. If so, no one's ever mentioned it to me."

"Can you find out?"

She hesitated. "I can try. It will take some delicate handling. I mean, you don't call up a person—even an old friend—and say, 'Oh, by the way, is your son adopted?' "

Rafferty smiled faintly. Joanna glanced at Halsey and saw he was taking in the exchange with bright, interested eyes. She said, "I think that's about all I have to ask you, Mr. Halsey. Rafferty, do you have anything further?"

"No." He looked at his watch. "And I'm due in a meeting at eight."

Halsey picked up his umbrella. "I also have an engagement."

Joanna said, "Thank you for agreeing to talk with us."

"You're perfectly welcome. I'm as curious about this theft as either of you—for purely professional reasons, of course."

Joanna smiled distractedly at him. "Why don't you go ahead, Rafferty? S.S.I. will take care of the check."

He started to protest, but she waved it away. They all exchanged the necessary polite phrases, and the two men went out together. Joanna remained in the booth, listening as the strands of the bead curtains swayed and clicked against one another.

An art dealer who had an adopted son in his twenties, she thought. An *art dealer*. It could have nothing to do with the Hals. Or everything to do with it.

TEN

JOANNA WALKED UPHILL on Clay Street, in the general direction of her apartment. The fog, which had arrived on schedule, blew wetly against her face. It was close to eight o'clock, already dark, and the produce stores that lined this block above Grant Avenue were closing, shopkeepers removing the crates of vegetables from the outside bins. A fish store was still doing a steady business; Chinese and Caucasians alike swarmed around the refrigerated compartments where salmon and crabs, snapper and oysters and scallops lay on beds of ice. She paused, looking in the window at a tank of lazily swimming carp.

Fish, she thought. There was something about fish....

Oh, yes. Wilson Reed had told the tenant at his cousin's house that he was going fishing. Somehow in the day's activities she'd lost sight of the problem of the missing security guard.

Gone fishing.

And then the remark—intended to be darkly humorous, but really not very funny—began to make sense. Well, *maybe* it did. It was a bit of a long shot, and following it up would be a gamble, but she had plenty of time on her hands. Joanna began to run up the hill and around the corner to Powell Street, toward Rex Malauulu's bar, where she knew there was a pay phone.

The bar was peopled with the same old, shabby customers who were always there; some of them looked as if they hadn't left their stools in years. Rex was behind the plank, polishing glasses, wearing the same apron with the same stains on it. The sitcom on the TV was interchangeable with the one that had been on the night before. Joanna glanced at the popcorn in bowls on the bar, to see if it was draped in cobwebs.

Rex saw her and called, "Joanna, come over here and collect your welcome-home drink!"

None of the customers looked around; it was as if they were all deaf.

"I can't, Rex. I have to make a phone call." She started for the booth, then saw there was no directory.

"Nonsense," Rex said. "Red wine, right?"

She sighed. When Rex was determined to be a gracious host, there was no stopping him. Besides, he probably had a directory behind the bar. But the house red at the restaurant had left a sour feeling in her stomach—a consequence of having lived down the road from a really good winery for three years. "Make it white, and you've got a deal," she said, sitting on a stool between an old man in a fedora and an old woman with what appeared to be a moldy basket of fruit on her head. Neither of them noticed her presence.

What *was* it, she wondered, with the New Apia's customers and strange hats? One of life's imponderables; perhaps she was better off not knowing.

When Rex brought her the wine, she asked to see his phone book. Frances Cathcart's number was listed. Joanna copied it down on a cocktail napkin that pictured a hula dancer clinging to a palm tree on a tropic isle. Little parentheses-like marks indicated that the girl's hips were swaying, and the general effect was that the earthquake was going on and she was hugging the tree as a desperate, lifesaving measure. Joanna drank her wine quickly, thanked Rex, and went to the phone booth.

Mrs. Cathcart's voice was anxious when she answered the phone. For a moment she didn't seem to remember who Joanna was. Then, "Oh, you're the young woman who was so kind to me last night. Have you heard anything about Will?"

"Not directly, no. But I may have an idea. You said one of Mr. Reed's hobbies used to be fishing?"

"Oh my, yes. He'd fish any chance he got."

"But he hasn't done much of it in the past few years?"

"Not since the rod and gun club closed."

"Where was the club?" Joanna asked.

"South of Candlestick Park, on that little spit of land they call Punto Solidad. Solitary Point in Spanish, you know."

"What happened to the clubhouse?"

"It's still there. The members own the land, and nothing's been decided about what to do with it, although there's been some discussion. One developer—"

Joanna cut her off. "Can you tell me how to get there?"

"Young woman," Frances Cathcart said tartly, "I may be old and ramble a good bit in my conversations, but I am not senile. I went to that club every weekend for thirty years, and I can certainly..." And then the import of Joanna's question sunk in. "What does this have to do with Will?"

"I think he may be hiding there. Will you give me directions?"

"But *why* would he hide?"

Exasperated, Joanna said, "There are many possible reasons. For one, he may be afraid for his life."

There was a sharp intake of breath on the line. Then Mrs. Cathcart said, "Do you have a pencil?"

"Yes."

"Go south on 101 to the Cow Palace exit . . ."

THE ROUTE from the freeway by which Mrs. Cathcart had directed her crested a hill and then descended past the South San Francisco city limits, through an area of shabby stucco houses and storefronts with bars and iron mesh over their windows. Ahead lay the vast, barren expanse of freight yards, where long lines of boxcars hulked in the mist. As she drove past them, Joanna noticed that the buildings to her left were now the sort of light industrial concerns—drayage companies, small manufacturers, storage facilities—upon which South City's economy was based. All of them were dark and looked deserted, even though security personnel probably patrolled within. She felt a sudden sense of isolation, and she shivered.

She found the turnoff toward Candlestick Park with no problem. The potholed pavement led under a narrow overpass, then emerged in a Y at the freeway's frontage road; the left arm led to the stadium and a half-completed industrial park complex, the other ran between the freeway and the bay. The land between the road and the shore—a narrow strip here, a wide plain further south—was mounded with dirt and rocks, as if it had been bulldozed for future development and then abandoned. Scrub oak and other scraggly vegetation clung to the sides of the heaps and grew more thickly in the gullies; the tree branches waved like bony arms in the blowing mist. Joanna turned right and drove slowly, looking for the entrance to the lane that led out onto Punto Solidad.

Solitary Point. An appropriate name, she thought, especially on a foggy night when even the headlights of the cars less than a mile distant on the freeway barely penetrated the darkness. The mist had caked her windshield with salt, and when she turned on the wipers they only smeared it. She opened the side window for better visibility, and was startled by the silence outside. Except for her car's engine, the only sound was a lonely wail from a boat horn somewhere out in the bay. This was too far south for commercial shipping, so it must be a pleasure boat. Joanna imagined it lost out there in the mist and blackness, the passengers frantic. She shivered again and turned up the collar of her jacket.

About a quarter of a mile down the road, she caught sight of a graveled lane that was rapidly being reclaimed by the vegetation on either side. She turned in slowly, the Fiat's headlights illuminating a badly rutted track that snaked east toward the water. After a hundred yards or so, it came to a board fence that had collapsed on one side of its open gate. On the other side, it was spray-painted with graffiti: Death to pigs, Forty-niners 4ever, Impeche Regan, Fuck the Giants.

Joanna stopped the car and idled just outside the gate. The graffiti had brought home the riskiness of her undertaking. This abandoned point of land was only miles from Hunter's Point, one of the city's black ghettos. Already there had been vandalism here, and she couldn't be sure there weren't juvenile—or adult—delinquents inside. Still, the spray paint looked old and faded, and vandalism usually dropped off sharply on cold, foggy nights.

Finally she pressed on the accelerator and moved slowly forward, through the ramshackle gate and into a graveled parking area. Directly ahead was a long, rectangular building with a smaller ell on the right-hand side. She switched her headlights onto high beam so they would illuminate it.

The main building was of weathered gray wood, with a long porch extending the length of it. Large windows had once overlooked the parking area, but they were now boarded up, and the walls—like the fence—were crudely spray-painted. She turned the car to the right so the headlights lit up the ell, and saw that it was merely charred walls with roofbeams reaching bleakly toward the sky. Arson, as well as graffiti, was apparently part of the vandals' repertoire.

Joanna waited, eyes searching the shadows. There was no noise or telltale motion from the deteriorating building. If Wilson Reed was inside, he would have hidden upon hearing her car. But *was* he here? There was no sign of his old Chevrolet.

She stopped her car a few feet from the burned-out ell and reached into the glove compartment, where she kept a flashlight and a canister of Mace. She'd started carrying the Mace years ago, when she'd had to go out on late-night calls because clients' burglar alarm systems had shorted out and gone berserk, and periodically she replaced it with a fresh can. She put it inside her shoulderbag, within easy reach, then switched the flashlight on and got out of the car. The mist was blowing harder now; it swirled around, chilling her and reflecting the beam of the flashlight back to her eyes, as if she were shining it upon an opaque curtain. She felt her way to the front of the Fiat, and trained the light on the ell. Trash had blown in drifts against the blackened walls, and several of the more badly charred boards had fallen to the ground. Through the opening one of them had left, she caught the glint of metal.

She hurried forward and shone the light closer. It was the bumper of a car. Extending the flashlight through the gap, she moved it up and down the length of a yellow Chevy Monza. It had not been difficult to drive the car into the building, since the wall on the opposite side was almost totally collapsed.

So Reed *was* here. But where?

She turned and surveyed the main section of the building. There was a wide central door, but it was padlocked and further reinforced by two-by-fours nailed across it at close intervals. When she went over there and climbed onto the porch, she saw that the padlock was a relatively new one—and sturdy. Avoiding the places where the flooring had fallen through, she moved down the length of the porch in both directions, testing the boards over the windows. They too were securely in place.

On the bay side of the building, Joanna found that the porch—really more of a wharf here—continued. Two docks extended from it, leaning at crazy angles above the water. Next to one a decaying sailboat was moored; it was half full of water, and its mast had fallen against the dock. The door to the building and all the windows were boarded up on this side too.

The boat horn sounded again, far out in the bay. The mist was thick and still here, rather than swirling, as it had in the parking area. Water lapped against the pilings; it smelled brackish and fishy; the building itself exuded a stench of rotting wood. A sudden creaking sound startled her, and she swung her light toward it. Merely the frayed rope of the sailboat rubbing against the dock.

Joanna's hand shook and the flashlight beam skittered over the water. Her legs felt weak, her hands cold and clammy. She wished she were home in Sonoma in front of her fire. Or in the cozy little apartment in San Francisco. Or even perched on a stool in Rex Malauulu's weird bar. Anywhere but on this rotting wharf on this desolate spit of land in the bay.

You're an idiot, she told herself. This is foolish and dangerous. Who do you think you are, anyway? Nancy Drew, blundering into trouble? Nancy Drew—hah! More like a gothic heroine, about to get devoured by a werewolf in the attic. Or whatever it is that lies in wait up there these days.

Go home, Joanna, she thought. Go home!

Ignoring her own command, she started down the wharf toward the other end of the building. Behind her, the half-sunken boat tugged at its moorings again. She rounded the building, moving toward the burned-out ell, but stopped and ran her flashlight over the end wall of the main wing. One of the boards hung awry on a window there, and on the sill were what looked to be fresh pry marks.

All right, she thought, you've found what you came for. Now get out of here and call Rafferty or Nick.

But surely Wilson Reed had heard her car. By the time she returned with either man, he would have run. Besides, she doubted Reed was dangerous; more likely he was a frightened pawn in a plan that had—somehow—gone wrong. And to insure he would know that she was a friend, she had gotten a sort of password from Mrs. Cathcart.

She stepped up to the window, transferred the flashlight to her left hand, and tugged at the loose board. It didn't yield when she pulled it toward her, but she found it would slide easily to one side. Blackness greeted her from within. And cold—it was colder in there than here on the porch. There was an odor—heavy, sweetish, like rotting garbage. God, how could Reed stay cooped up inside there? He must either be very frightened or playing for incredibly high stakes. She suspected the former.

The main thing now was to reassure Reed. Joanna kept the flash in her left hand, placed her right on the canister in her purse, leaned through the opening, and called out.

"Willie-bird!" The name echoed in the darkness within and, in spite of her nervousness, Joanna felt ridiculous. It was a childhood nickname, part of a litany Mrs. Cathcart had said she'd used to comfort a small cousin who was the object of his father's abuse. If Joanna used it, the old woman had said, it was sure to tell Reed she meant him no harm.

The silence inside the foul-smelling building was ponderous. Joanna called twice more, but heard only the echo of her own voice. Finally she let go of the canister of Mace, switched the flash to her right hand, and shone it around the room inside.

The window opened into what appeared to have been a dining room: There was a bandstand with a small floor for dancing to the left side; tables for four stood under the boarded-up windows that had overlooked the bay; others had been drawn together for seating for larger groups in the middle of the room. Most of the tables were bare and had chairs stacked upside down on them; the remaining ones were still set with heavy serviceable crockery and cutlery. A sign draped limply behind the bandstand, its faded letters reading "Hail and Farewell: Bayshore Rod and Gun Club, 1950-1983." From it hung the corpses of deflated balloons, like so many little dead birds.

Evidence of a gala farewell party, yes. But no evidence of Wilson Reed.

The man had to be here somewhere, Joanna thought. Where? What was beyond the archway at the far end? Her flashlight beam wasn't strong enough to show her. She debated for a moment, then hoisted up her straight skirt and raised one leg to the window sill. As she was climbing through the narrow opening, she felt the seam above the kick pleat tear, grimaced in irritation, then ignored it.

Dropping off the sill, she raised her flashlight and once again surveyed the room. Dust was thick on the linoleum floor, but it was broken by a wide track of footprints. Someone in ripple-soled shoes had made a number of trips back and forth from the window to the archway—and recently.

She began following the footprints, her heels tapping on the linoleum squares. As she went, she swung the flashlight to either side, over the nearby tables. With surprise she saw that the plates on those that were still set were dirty and streaked; there were splotches on the tablecloths, and the white linen napkins were crumpled and smeared.

What had happened here? she wondered. Had the busboys quit halfway through cleaning up after that final party? Didn't anyone care enough to claim the furniture, linens, and cutlery? Perhaps the former members of the Bayshore Rod and Gun Club were an impractical and unsentimental bunch; once they were through with a place, they were *through* with it. Still, she found it incredible that the vandals who were so much in evidence outside hadn't broken in here and stolen everything that wasn't nailed down.

She approached the archway and shone the light into the room beyond. It appeared to be a lounge, furnished with the kind of lumpy-cushioned bent-rattan furniture you often saw in cottages at the seashore. The floor was covered in woven straw mats; even from here she could smell their moldiness. She raised the flashlight higher, noting that the walls were knotty pine and a bar bowed out into the room at the far end—

Abruptly a beam of light glared at her. Joanna started, heart pounding, and drew back into the dining room. The light disappeared. She waited—resisting a strong urge to run—then stepped forward and raised her flash once more. The beam reappeared, wavering as if the person holding it were trembling.

She felt a flood of relief, followed by an impulse to break into hysterical giggles. The light was merely a reflection of her own flashlight in the mirror behind the bar. No wonder the beam shook so!

Momentarily reassured, she stepped into the room and moved the light around it. Couches, chairs, coffee tables. Conversational groupings. The bar and stools at the end. A coat rack to the left of it. And over there, on a couch under one of the bay-side windows, lay a man....

Joanna froze. The man lay face down in an awkward position, arms flung out above his gray head. His legs were bent at the knees and canted off the cushions; the tips of his toes touched the floor so she could see the bottoms of his ripple-soled shoes. He was very still, paying her no attention.

She stepped closer, and then she saw the stains. They were brown, splattered all over the yellow flowered cushions above him. There were more on what she could see of the cushion beneath his torso. But the largest was on the back of his white shirt....

She drew in her breath sharply and backed away. Something nudged at the rear of her calves, and her knees went weak. She reached behind her and then sat down hard on a coffee table. Her stomach knotted, and she dropped the flashlight. Crossing her arms over her abdomen, she leaned forward, wracked by sudden spasms.

"No," a voice said, "oh *no*." It was broken, rasping. "No!"

Her voice. She tried, but couldn't stop it. It went on and on, repeating the same two words in torn, ragged syllables. "No, no, no, oh no...." She leaned forward, hugging her stomach, trying desperately to regain control.

After what seemed like a long time, she straightened. Somehow she remembered to look for the gleam of the flashlight. It had rolled away under a nearby chair. She dropped to her knees, went after it, then stood like an old, old woman. She wanted to look at the body again, to make sure he was really dead, but knew she couldn't.

Instead she ran through the archway and into the dining room, toward the window through which she had entered.

ELEVEN

ALL THE WAY BACK to Sonoma the next morning, she couldn't stop crying. It was stupid, she realized. She'd hardly known Wilson Reed; it wasn't for him she was grieving.

No, she was weeping for poor Joanna Stark, who had had to go through the terrible ordeal of finding his broken, bloody body. Poor Joanna, who had been up all night giving statements to the police and then conferring with Rafferty and Nick. Joanna, who had finally told Nick she could go on with the investigation no longer and had then started back to safety in the country.

Knowing why she was crying made her feel faintly contemptuous of herself, but the tears kept leaking from her eyes anyway.

By the South San Francisco coroner's estimate, Wilson Reed had been dead a little over twenty-four hours when she'd found him. He'd been shot in the back with a twenty-two caliber revolver, apparently while trying to flee his killer. The police, both of South San Francisco and San Francisco itself, had been enraged at the coverup of the theft of the Hals—which had had to come out when murder entered the situation. They implied that if the museum, S.S.I., and Great American had not collaborated in their silence, Wilson Reed might not have died. But none of them actually believed that.

It was ironic that when Joanna finally reached Rafferty at his office an hour after she had found Reed's body, the insurance investigator had just returned from the meeting with the museum officials—a meeting that had resulted in a mutual decision to contact the police in the morning.

Now Joanna drove blindly, mechanically, turning onto the Sonoma Highway on the last leg of her journey. During the night she had wondered about Reed's killer, posited a great many things, both to herself and others. She hadn't mentioned Antony Parducci, but he had been very much on her mind; and also on her mind was the firm conviction that whatever he was, Parducci, who was known to personally detest guns, was not a killer.

Besides, what evidence did she have that Parducci was even alive, much less anywhere near San Francisco, or involved in this particular theft? None, except for a few lingering suspicions that she hadn't been successful in banishing. Maybe she *was* obsessed with the man, as Nick had often said.

But no matter. If the last fifteen hours had taught her anything, it was that she didn't want her life to change after all, didn't relish any more adventures. She had chosen to withdraw from active participation in the larger world three years ago when she had retreated to Sonoma, and that was as it should be. She would stay in her country refuge from now on, with her books and music and garden. She would bicycle to town once a day, visit with her friends, spend time with E.J., when he was at home. Perhaps tonight she'd convince him to cook the special chicken dinner he'd planned before her foolishness had prompted her to rush off to San Francisco. And tomorrow she would call Rex Malauulu and tell him she didn't want to keep the apartment after all. He could rent it furnished; she'd already removed the few possessions she cared about.

As she was coming into town on Broadway, she slowed, briefly contemplating a stop at the post office for her mail. No, she decided, it could wait. All that would be in the box was perhaps one of the true-crime magazines that regularly arrived around the end of the month. And that was another thing: those magazines. She would cancel her subscriptions, as well as quit taking the ICOM bulletin. She was through chasing a phantom, through with chasing anything at all—save peace and relative solitude.

Solitude. Punto Solidad.

In spite of the warm, muggy temperature—which promised more rain—she shivered. Then she turned right at the Plaza, going home for good.

The first drops of rain splashed against her windshield as she turned into her driveway. She left the car under the sheltering branches of the persimmon tree and ran up the steps to the porch. In the hallway, she nearly collided with E.J., who was emerging from the rear of the house, orange backpack strapped in place. When he saw her, his elfin features darkened and his expression became closed and guarded.

"Where are you going?" Joanna said. "I thought you were staying through Thanksgiving."

He stood still, not speaking, staring at her in a curiously analytical way, as if he'd never seen her before.

Joanna grabbed his arm. "E.J., what's wrong?"

He shook off her hand and went into the living room, his stride stiff and jerky. She followed, stopping behind the couch that faced the fireplace. "E.J.," she said again, "tell me what the trouble is. Where are you off to?"

In front of the hearth he turned and faced her, feet set wide apart, arms folded across his chest. When she saw his expression, she drew in her breath. She hadn't seen such a look of resentment and rage on his face since he'd been in high school and busy hating her and David for what he considered their betrayal of Eleanor.

He said, "I was on my way to the city, to find you and demand an explanation."

"An explanation of what?"

"A man came to see me earlier."

"What man?"

"He wouldn't give his name. He was tall. Going bald. With a scar on his neck. He wore sunglasses all the time he was in the house and spoke with a sort of raspy voice. Mean anything to you?"

She had heard the same description just the night before: It was the man who had been making inquiries about an art dealer who had an adopted son. Oh, God. Her knees went weak, as weak as they had been when she'd found Wilson Reed's body. She went around to sit on the couch, feeling her way along the back of it, as if she'd suddenly gone blind.

E.J. was watching her, his turquoise blue eyes narrowed. "I thought it might," he said.

"What did the man say to you?" she asked.

"What do *you* think?"

"E.J., I'm not in the mood to play games."

He stepped forward, his stance becoming more aggressive as he loomed over her. "No, neither am I. Although that seems to be what everyone's been doing all my life—playing games with me."

She felt a hollowness replacing the panic inside her. The moment had come, as she'd always feared it would. Quietly she repeated, "E.J., what did he say to you?"

"He told me about the incredible fraud that Mom and Dad . . . Mr. and Mrs. Stark perpetrated on me. He told me they weren't really my parents." He paused, and for a moment she thought his eyes might fill with tears. Then he squared his jaw and added, "You must have known that. You helped them cover it up, too."

Joanna sighed and looked down at her clasped hands. When you fear something for years and then it happens, she thought, it isn't ever as bad as you've imagined. She felt no panic now, only the hollowness and a faint stir of hope.

E.J. stepped back and shrugged his shoulders, shifting the weight of the pack. For a moment Joanna thought he was going to remove it, sit down, and talk this through. But he only adjusted it and folded his arms again. That was the way he had always handled disagreements: standing up, in nose-to-nose confrontation, usually shouting. No reason he should change now.

Joanna studied him, not knowing what to say. If only she wasn't so tired; if only she could think more clearly. She should have planned for this day, rather than shut the possibility off in the dim recesses of her mind.

Finally E.J. said, "It's true, isn't it?"

"Yes, it's true."

Some of the aggressiveness went out of his posture. His mouth, in its nest of beard, trembled the way it used to when he was a hurt little boy. He struggled to control it.

Joanna said, "Did the man explain why he was telling you this?"

"He said he was a friend of my natural father, and that they both thought I deserved to know the truth, so he was bringing me a message from him. He told me I was born in Paris. And that when I was a few months old, Dad...David went over there and brought me back to San Francisco, where he and my...Eleanor adopted me.''

"Did he tell you who your father was?"

"He wouldn't."

"Or your mother?"

"No. All he said was to ask you."

She looked back down at her hands. The rain was falling full force now; she could hear it splashing against the windows on either side of the fireplace.

E.J. said, "Who were they, Jo?"

She didn't want to perpetrate any more lies—but this one was necessary. "I don't know."

"You don't *know*? The man said—"

"Look, I don't even know who that man *is*."

"You recognized his description."

"That's because he's been asking around San Francisco about you. It came up in connection with the matter I went there to investigate. But I swear I don't know him, and he can't possibly know me. He's probably someone who's checked up on the family, knows about me, and assumes that David told me—that's all."

E.J. was silent, except for his breathing, which was heavy and erratic. Joanna couldn't bear to witness his suffering, so she kept her eyes on her hands.

Finally he said, "Why would he do that—check up on us?"

She thought for a moment. "He may have some sort of extortion plan in mind. He probably knows we have money. Perhaps he and his friend—"

"My father."

"Your father. Perhaps they want to get their hands on your trust fund."

E.J. didn't say anything for a moment. Joanna stared resolutely at her clasped hands. Then he asked, "You knew I was adopted all along, didn't you?"

"Yes."

"And you kept it from me, even after David died."

"I promised him I would."

"Why? Most adopted children are told as soon as they can understand. Or at least when they become adults. It's no big thing anymore."

She looked up and immediately wished she hadn't. His face was rigid with pain.

"To understand why you weren't told," she said, "you'd have to understand what went on between your parents...adoptive parents. There were serious problems in that marriage long before David brought you home. Eleanor was in poor health, both physically and emotionally. One result was that she couldn't have children. And David badly wanted a child."

E.J. laughed harshly. "So on one of his business trips to Europe, he picked me up, like he would a stray puppy or kitten."

"It wasn't like that."

"Oh no? Maybe it was more like filling a prescription to save his marriage."

Joanna felt anger rising to replace the hollowness. "I said, David wanted a child. He wanted *you*. And he loved you."

"But she didn't."

"She had problems that interfered with her loving anyone."

He nodded, suddenly thoughtful. "You know, one thing finally makes sense to me. When I was a little kid, I'd hear them arguing. I'd be upstairs in bed, and their voices would be going on and on downstairs—angry, bitter. And the quarrels would always end with her talking about *his* son by *that woman*. And then he would storm out and leave. I never understood, and for years I haven't even thought of it, but now I realized she believed David had fathered me, and she resented both of us because of that."

"Yes, that was one of Eleanor's delusions. But it was *not* true."

He looked away, over her head. "She was a very sick woman, wasn't she?"

"If she'd allowed herself to be treated, they probably would have diagnosed her as a paranoid schizophrenic. And might have been able to help her. But she wouldn't permit that. Eleanor was very single-minded, about her condition—and about you. The only way she would agree to the adoption was that you never be told you weren't their natural son, and David wanted you so badly he went along with it. They even moved away from town for a couple of years, so all their friends would think you had been born in their absence. By the time Eleanor had died, David felt it was too late to tell you. Was afraid you'd turn on him if he tried to explain."

"And you just went along with that?"

"It was his right to make the decision."

And that, she thought, was at best a half-truth. She'd participated actively in the decision, had known it was wrong but had been relieved at not having to face the potential crisis.

Perhaps the thought showed on her face. Perhaps E.J. knew her well enough to be able to tell—at least in this instance—that she was lying. "I don't believe that. You and David decided everything together. Hell, you probably helped him pick out Eleanor's casket."

The anger she had been holding in check flared. "I realize you want to hurt me because of this, but that was a cheap shot."

"Was it? You'd been standing there in the wings for years, waiting for her to die."

She gasped and involuntarily drew back one hand, as if to strike out at him. She didn't really intend to, and it would have been a useless gesture anyway, since he towered over her. But its violence impressed him, and he took a step backward before he added, "If you'd really cared about any of us, you'd have left a troubled situation alone."

Youth, she thought, was always so idealistic and self-sacrificing—at least when it came to what others should do. She sighed and said, "We won't discuss this any further, E.J. You can't possibly understand a situation until you've lived inside it."

"I did, dammit! I was part of it, too, you know."

"But not as an adult. You can't begin to understand the dynamics of that marriage, any more than you can understand what went on between David and me."

He was silent for a moment. Then, bitterly, "You're right. I only know what you two told me, and that was precious little."

"You mean about us meeting by accident at Marshall Wheatley's gallery?" She had been installing an alarm system; David had gone there to get Marshall's signature on some papers.

"Yes, and how he recognized you from before...." E.J.'s voice trailed off and a startled expression came into his eyes. "*When* did you know him before, Jo?"

With a shock, she realized what he was thinking. "It was nothing like that. David...David and my father were best friends and roommates in law school. They were so close, in fact, that my dad had always told me if I were in trouble or needed anything, I should get in touch with your father.''

"My *adoptive* father."

She shrugged. E.J. seemed determined to reject the memory of David and Eleanor—as well as reject her. She would answer his questions—as fully as she could—but she was also through humoring him. This was one problem he would have to work out on his own.

He said, "So that's what you did—looked him up because you needed something?"

"Hardly. But David was a lonely and unhappy man. I was an equally lonely woman. It was a dangerous combination—but one that ultimately worked."

There was a long silence. Rain splattered against the windows, harder now. What was E.J. thinking? she wondered.

When he spoke, what he said surprised her. "Is your father still alive?"

"As far as I know."

"And living in New Jersey—Tenafly?"

"You remember where I was from?"

"Sure. There was a song you made up—'The Barfly from Tenafly.'"

In spite of her tension, she smiled faintly. It was only one of many nonsensical songs she used to improvise to amuse him, usually when they were off on a long and tedious car trip.

E.J. said, "You ran away from your father, didn't you?"

"Yes."

"Just like you used to run away from me and Dad...David."

"What do you—"

"To that apartment. You ran there."

Anger had come back into his voice, but she sensed he was forcing it now. E.J. needed to rage at her, needed to hate her. "Sometimes it was important that I be by myself," she said.

"I guess so. You would never let either of us go to that apartment. David always claimed what you just said—that you needed a place of your own. But when you took off, *I* thought you hated us. And it hurt him, even though he would try not to show it. I knew, because when you went, he wasn't really there at home with me anymore. We didn't have a life together without you."

She couldn't speak. She had never realized.

Her silence gave E.J. the additional fuel he needed for his anger. "That's the way you've always dealt with the people you supposedly love, isn't it, Jo?" he said. "Your father, David and me, David's relatives after his funeral. You run from them, hurt them, let them down. And then you claim you did it because you *had* to."

Perhaps it was an irrational assessment, but that didn't stop it from hurting. The pain seared her, and for a moment she wanted to lash out at him in an equally cruel manner. Then she realized her main concern right now should be with helping E.J.: He was at the point of flying apart. The controlled stance was gone; his face twitched with conflicting emotions. Words would not reach him.

She got up and went toward him. If she could hold him, it might calm—

"No!" He whirled, throwing her hand off his arm like a small child on the verge of a tantrum. "Don't you try to mother me! Not now—not after all these years. It's too late!" He started toward the door, the backpack swaying with each jerky step.

She stopped, aware that if she went closer to him, it would bring on a full-scale adult tantrum. "Where are you going?" she asked.

He threw the door open so hard it hit the wall next to it. "I don't know. Anywhere, so long as it's away from here."

"E.J., don't do this. We can work it out—"

He turned in the middle of the porch, his face astonished. "Work it out? What *is* there to work out? Your lies have turned everything I ever cared about to shit."

And then he was gone, running down the steps, striding across the lawn through the rain, turning down the driveway toward the road.

Joanna stood in the doorway looking after him. No good to chase him, beg him to listen to reason. Not now—maybe not ever.

She watched until he was out of sight, then closed the door and went back into the living room. Rain splashed against the windows and dripped down the chimney onto the dead ashes on the hearth. It was cold and cheerless here—and so was her life.

Lies, she thought. For years, lies. What good is a life built on that basis, anyhow?

TWELVE

THE RAIN TAPPED in steady rhythm on the flat roof of Mary Bennett's quilt shop. The corner woodstove—which Mary had installed herself—smoked because, as she had once reluctantly admitted, she had not fully comprehended the instructions for venting it. Unconcerned, the big red-headed woman fanned the smoke away and handed Joanna a mug of coffee that was laced liberally with Irish whiskey. Then she eased herself into a wicker basket chair—the companion of the one in which Joanna now curled—and stretched her long legs out toward the stove.

"Well," she said, "if you have to have a crisis, this is the day for it. No one's going to come shopping for quilts in this weather." Then she picked up her own, similarly laced mug from the table between the chairs and raised it to Joanna. "Cheers."

Although the word seemed singularly inappropriate to the occasion, Joanna returned the gesture and sipped the coffee. The warmth of the whiskey spread through her and went straight to her head in record time. Belatedly she remembered that she'd had no breakfast or lunch today—nothing, in fact, since the Chinese dinner with Rafferty. But what did it matter if she sat here and got drunk, anyway? She had nothing to do the rest of the afternoon or evening—or perhaps for the rest of her life.

"So," Mary said, "you had a big blowup with E.J., and he walked out on you."

Joanna nodded. It was as much of an explanation as
Mary had allowed her to give when she'd arrived here,
disheveled and wet and close to tears, driven from her
own house by its sheer loneliness. Her friend had immediately bustled around, tucking her into the chair
under an eight-point star quilt, fixing her some coffee to
match the mug she herself had been enjoying. Now she
was all sympathetic ears, and Joanna had begun to regret coming.

"You want to tell me about it? Or did you just come
by because you know I keep a bottle of Irish on hand?"
Mary smiled, taking the edge off her words.

Still Joanna hesitated. She was not—never had been—
a woman given to feminine confidences. Mary was the
only person in Sonoma who knew more about her than
what anyone could glean from the morgue of one of the
San Francisco papers. And that was due to Mary's own
nature, rather than anything in Joanna; the big woman's well-intentioned nosiness made it impossible to keep
her at arm's length.

In spite of their friendship, Joanna didn't intend to
confide everything about the quarrel with E.J. She said,
"E.J. is angry with me because I kept a secret from him,
and now he's found it out. I don't know if we'll ever be
friends again." She saw a familiar, avid look come over
Mary's face, and hurried on before she could ask what
the secret was. "But that's not what seriously worries
me; what's happening to E.J. is one of those coming-of-
age experiences, and if I know him, he'll survive it and
probably emerge all that much better."

Mary looked disappointed, but she and Joanna had
been friends long enough that she knew what was off
limits and what was not. "So what *is* bothering you,
then?"

"He accused me of something. Unjustly, I thought at the time. But after thinking about it for a while longer, I'm not so sure there isn't some basis for what he said."

"And that was . . . ?"

"That all my life I've been running away from people I care about, letting them down when they needed me. And then I turn around and blame my actions on them, say they forced me to do it, rather than taking the responsibility upon myself." It was a fairly sophisticated version of E.J.'s hostile rantings, but she was sure it was what he had meant.

"Hmmm." Mary got up and fed a couple of pieces of wood to the stove. "What evidence does E.J. base this on?"

"When I was married to David, I kept an apartment near Chinatown, and occasionally I'd hole up there. E.J. claims it hurt both of them. I never knew that. Neither of them ever said."

"So whose fault was that?"

She shrugged. "Then there were David's relatives. After his funeral, I quarreled with one of them and came running up here and refused to ever deal with any of them again."

"From what you've told me, they were a pretty greedy, motley crew."

"Well, yes."

"So?"

"Then there was my father."

Mary raised her eyebrows. Joanna had never mentioned her family before, and it was clear she relished this new information.

"My father," Joanna said, "was a cold man. A lawyer—very precise, methodical, unemotional. He and David were good friends in law school, and I've always wondered how that happened. David's main interest in his work was always his clients' welfare; over the years many of them became practically family. But my father didn't care for people; he lived for logic, points of law.''

"I know the type."

"It *is* a type, isn't it? Anyway, in spite of it, I loved him. So did my mother. But a lack of affection like that wears on you when you live with it year after year. For me, it wasn't so much of a problem—I was busy trying to grow up—but for my mother... she became an alcoholic.''

"How did your father deal with that?"

"He had her institutionalized." At Mary's horrified look, Joanna added, "Oh, not a state hospital. It was a nice, expensive place, but it was still an institution. And my father worked so hard to pay for it that he seldom had time to go to see her." She paused, hearing the bitterness in her voice even after all these years, and feeling faintly surprised by it. "Then he met someone else."

"And he divorced your mother."

"He didn't have to. When he told my mother his intentions, she killed herself."

Mary sighed heavily. The rain pelted the roof, loud in the silence.

Joanna went on, "Right after the funeral I left home and ran off to Europe. I was nineteen years old, attending Wellesley and not really liking it. I went to Tenafly and saw Mom buried, then packed a little bag and left for good. I've never seen my father since." She smiled wryly. "You notice how I'm always making major decisions right after funerals?"

Rather than answer that, Mary held out her hand for Joanna's mug and went to fix them more Irish coffee.

When she returned, her face was elaborately noncommittal. "Is your father still alive?"

"Funny, E.J. asked me that too. Probably. David kept in touch with him, but at my request didn't keep me up to date. The only thing he told me was that Dad had married his lady love a few months after I left. Otherwise, I know nothing. Nor do I want to."

Mary was silent, fiddling with the woodstove. Joanna knew it was her habit to engage in unimportant activity while she thought something through. Finally she returned to her chair and said, "So because of these incidents, you believe E.J.'s assessment of you. In two of them—with David's relatives and with your father—you were pushed to what any normal person would agree were unbearable limits. In the other—the apartment—you were perhaps selfish, but again within normal range."

"But selfish nonetheless."

"Let me ask you this: If either E.J. or David had told you that you were hurting him by running off and holing up there, would you have continued to do so?"

Joanna's response was automatic. "Of course not."

"I rest my case."

She stirred uncomfortably in the chair, pulling the quilt more closely around her in spite of the heat from the stove and the additional warmth of the whiskey. "Well, there's something else."

"What?"

"Just this morning I ran out on an old friend—my former business partner, whom you met at the Cheese Factory the other day—and on someone else who might have become a new friend."

"Why?"

Joanna told her: about Punto Solidad and finding Wilson Reed's body; about her horror and panic and her fear that she had handled things very badly; about her decision to withdraw from the real world for good.

When she had finished, Mary got up and busied herself with another of those rushes of activity that indicated intense thought. Joanna knew she was formulating an opinion of all this, and that—like most of Mary's opinions—it would be freely given, and both valid and valuable. She waited, content to sip her drink and watch the smoke rise from the woodstove while Mary plumped up quilts, made more coffee, and brought wood in from the back porch.

Finally her friend returned to her chair. She said, "I have a few questions for you. First, do you think E.J. will be coming back here soon?"

"Not for a long time, if ever. He's angry and determined not to deal with me. And for once, he has ample funds."

"What do you mean?"

"Before I came over here, I realized there was no booze in the house—you were right about your bottle of Irish luring me—and I also realized I was low on cash. So I went to the place where I keep my emergency stash, and it was gone."

Mary's eyes widened. "E.J. wouldn't *steal* from you!"

"Oh God, no. The money is there for household use. He's always known he was welcome to help himself. And he left an I.O.U." It had been a slip of paper torn off the grocery list pad; all he had done was write the letters in his bold hand. "But he took all of it, five hundred dollars or so, and that's what worries me. It's a lot of money for E.J. Normally he wouldn't think he needed that much. And he took it before I arrived at the house this morning, when he was still planning to go into the city and confront me. I can't figure why he felt he needed that much cash; I don't understand what he intended to do with it."

"From what I know of E.J., I don't understand that either." Mary frowned, and Joanna was afraid she might fly off into another of her manic fits of activity. Instead she shrugged and returned to the course she had originally been pursuing. "Well, be that as it may, my next question is: What about this investigation you've been assisting with? Now that there's been a murder and the police have been informed, would you still be able to help out?"

"Oh, for sure. Once all the furor over our concealment of the theft died down, the police admitted they would like our cooperation. You see, since they don't have a trained art squad, they don't know the nuances of the artistic world as we do. The department has actually consulted both Nick and me before on other thefts. Besides, Rafferty is still hoping to get the Hals back unharmed."

"Rafferty?"

"Steve Rafferty. The insurance investigator."

There must have been something in the way she said his name, because Mary's face took on a sly, inquisitive look. "What's this Rafferty like?"

"Oh, he's about my age, maybe a little older. From back east, New York. Nice looking, comfortable to be with, has a good sense of humor—"

"Single?"

"Yes . . . oh, Mary!"

"Well, at least it's occurred to you. You're not as badly off as you paint yourself." Mary sat up straighter now and added briskly, "But romance aside for the present, you admit you actually are letting Nick and this Rafferty down by fleeing the scene of the crime, so to speak."

"Yes...."

"And letting people down is what, according to you and E.J., you've been doing all your life."

"More or less."

"Well then, just this once why don't you try to change that?"

Joanna was silent.

"Yes," her friend said impatiently, "I know what you told me. You want to stay here and insulate yourself and never have to find a dead man again. You want to run—because running's a more comfortable way of behaving to you than facing up to a difficult situation."

Joanna's anger flared. She hadn't come here to listen to the same nonsense that E.J. had handed her. She frowned, but before she could speak, Mary held up one large hand to silence her.

"Now, don't get mad," she said. "Hear me out. Has running away ever really worked for you?"

"No," Joanna said grudgingly.

"And has hiding here in the country been the idyll you thought it would be?"

"God, no!"

"Well then, why don't you try a different solution for what ails you? Go back down there and see this thing through."

Joanna stared at the wisps of smoke curling up from the poorly vented stove. She thought of her house—cold and cheerless, no longer a home since E.J. had stormed out. She thought of Rafferty's and Nick's disappointment when she'd announced her decision to quit the case. And then she took a long time going over the argument with E.J. There was something there, a link between what he had said and the theft of the Hals. Something she'd overlooked in the heat of the quarrel.

It was possible she could make a difference in the investigation after all. She might be able to help them get the *Cavalier* back.

She looked at Mary, feeling a new closeness to her. They'd been friends for a couple of years now; she'd often sought the big comfortable woman's advice, had enjoyed her warmth and humor and wry observations. But she'd been too caught up in her own insular life to fully appreciate the value of those insights. Now it was possible that Mary had given her a gift of great value.

"Thanks," she said.

"For what?" Mary replied gruffly. "It's nothing more than common sense, and you've generally got plenty of that. More coffee?"

"Please." Joanna held out her mug. "But no Irish this time. I have a long drive back into the city."

THIRTEEN

SHE STOOD AT THE WINDOW of the apartment, staring out into the blackness between it and the brick wall of the next building. Rain sheeted down and splashed on the pavement below. The alley was a narrow one, composed of steps that scaled one of the irregular inclines of the lower reaches of Nob Hill; water rushed down them as if it were a small cascade. Joanna listened to it, allowing her mind to wander while she waited. The territory through which it roamed was pretty commonplace; she'd had enough of soul-searching on the drive back from Sonoma.

Thanksgiving: She'd already invited Mary and a couple of other friends, so it would go on even without E.J. What to have? Turkey—and then a week of tiresome leftovers? Ham? No, that was better for Christmas. Why not shock them with lasagna? The chimney: It needed cleaning. Better contact the Grim Sweeper, a too cutely named but efficient service. Firewood: Order a cord. Christmas cards: What had she done with the Metropolitan Museum catalog? If she sent for the cards she'd picked out at this late date, would they arrive in time to address and send? Stamps: She was out of stamps—

The expected knock at the door came. Joanna turned, fluffing out her short dark curls, smoothing down the ribbing of her blue cable-knit sweater. The anxiety she'd held in check with trivial thoughts returned as she went to admit the first visitor she'd had at the apartment in the past twelve years.

Steve Rafferty stood in the hallway, raindrops beading on his brown trenchcoat, an open umbrella in his right hand. He looked at Joanna, then glanced down helplessly at it.

"Just leave it outside the door; no one will steal it," she said. It wasn't the greeting she'd expected to give him. Somehow the words should have been more important. But when he grinned and set the umbrella on the floor, she knew what she'd said had been just right. Anything more significant would have set them both on edge; as it was, the comfortable rapport they'd had before was reestablished.

Rafferty said, "I wish someone *would* steal it. I've got a hankering for one of the kind that pop up, sort of like a giant switchblade."

She stepped back and motioned for him to come in. "Why don't you buy yourself one?"

"Why? I've *got* a perfectly good umbrella. Besides, I don't like to buy myself things." He looked around the room, nodded slightly in a way that seemed to say he liked what he saw, then began unbuttoning his coat.

Joanna held out her hand for the wet garment and hung it on an old coatrack that was wedged into the corner next to the door. "Maybe Santa Claus will bring you one."

Rafferty stepped further into the room and looked around some more, thrusting his hands into the pockets of his trousers. "I stopped believing in Santa Claus a few years ago."

"Funny—so did I."

He turned to face her, hazel eyes serious. "Do you envy people who still do?"

"Yes and no. In the long run it's better to see things the way they really are."

"Better—but sadder."

"Well, yes." There was an awkward pause, as if both of them were conscious of having revealed too much of themselves. Then she said, "Can I offer you a drink? I'm afraid all I have is some bourbon that's been sitting open for a few years. I don't really live here—"

"That's okay. You don't have to play hostess. It's enough to have you back on the case." He sat on one end of the sofa bed, pushing the folded blanket aside. "I can't tell you how glad I was when you called and asked me to meet you here; we can really use your help."

She sat down too. "Fill me in on what's happened today."

"Not a great deal. There's no new evidence in Wilson Reed's murder. That deserted old clubhouse was the perfect place for a killer to strike and get away without leaving a trace. The police have been looking for Mike Wheatley. Again, no progress. He's disappeared from his usual haunts, and the woman at the gallery that handles his work—Suzanne Mackenzie—claims she hasn't seen him in over a week. That's a lie, of course, since you saw him go there the other day, but we have no way of proving she was there."

"I suppose by now his family knows about his phone calls to Great American."

"Yes."

"How are they taking it?"

"With the requisite shock and disbelief—which doesn't quite cover a resigned acceptance that it's true."

Joanna sighed. "Those poor people. I take it no one else has contacted your company about the Hals?"

"No. It leads me to believe that Wheatley did know something after all. Maybe Reed had the painting with him at the rod and gun club, and Mike killed him and took off with it.''

''I can't believed Mike would kill anybody.''

''I recall some of the Manson family saying that about Charlie.''

She was silent for a moment, trying to picture Mike shooting Wilson Reed in the back, but failing. ''And that's it?''

Rafferty spread his hands out. ''That's it.''

''What's Nick been doing?''

''Continuing the job you started of canvassing the art dealers. He's had no luck, and claims it's because he doesn't have the kind of rapport with them that you do.''

''That's probably true. I spent years developing those contacts.''

''Will you take over for him tomorrow, then?''

''No, I don't think so.'' She got up, went to the window, and looked out again at the pelting rain. ''I want to follow up something else, and that means starting once again with the Wheatleys.''

''Oh? Does it have anything to do with what that art dealer—Halsey—was talking about last night? The man who was looking for the dealer with an adopted son?''

''In a way.''

''Do you think Mike *is* adopted?''

''I don't know.''

''Joanna—''

''Please, Rafferty, let me look into it my own way. If it doesn't work out, I'll know pretty quick, and then I'll go back to talking to the dealers.''

''Fair enough.'' He stood up, and she turned, afraid he was going to leave. But he just remained there, looking around the room, his eyes finally coming to rest on the framed portrait of her parents on the bureau. It was one of the few objects she'd removed from the apartment before her flight to Sonoma that morning, but was now back in its accustomed place.

He said, "How long have you had this apartment?"

"Since nineteen seventy."

He looked faintly surprised. "But you don't really live here?"

"Not since I married in seventy-four."

"Why do you keep it?"

"That's a long story. And not terribly interesting." She pulled the blue curtains across the window, shutting out the rainy night, then crossed toward the sofa bed again.

Rafferty stopped her, blocking her path. He placed his hands on her shoulders, and she felt a brief, unreasoning flutter of panic. "I'm interested," he said, "and I've got plenty of time to listen."

She drew away, sat down on the couch.

Rafferty added, "Nick told me you never let anyone come here. Not even your husband, once you were married."

She looked up at him, feeling small and vulnerable. "That's true."

He knelt down in front of her, bringing his eyes on a level with hers, again placing his hands on her shoulders. "Why me, then? Why let me come here now, Jo?"

She tried to pull back, knowing at the same time that the action was irrational. After all, wasn't this what—in the back of her mind—she'd wanted when she'd decided to ask him here?

"Why, Jo?"

"Don't call me that. Don't call me Jo."

"Why not?"

"It's what everyone calls me."

"What *should* I call you, then?"

She stared into his eyes; they had a soft, misty quality. "I don't know.... If you like, you can call me Janna. It's what I called myself when I was little and couldn't pronounce my name. It's what my mother called me before she..."

He waited. When she didn't speak, he took his right hand from her shoulder and stroked her cheek. "Before what, Janna?"

She felt a tightening sensation deep beneath her breastbone; it made her eyes sting and her throat close up. Good God, she thought, am I going to cry in front of him?

She closed her eyes, felt the tears pressing under their lids, and turned her face away. Gently he cupped her cheek in his hand.

"Before what, Janna?" he repeated.

She waited until the tears were under control and the tightness had left her throat. Then she said huskily, "That's also a long story."

"As I said before, I have plenty of time."

"You don't want to hear—"

"I do."

And then he kissed her—gently but insistently, his hand at the nape of her neck so she could not pull back. At first she felt frozen with shock, and before she could warm to the kiss, he had broken away from her and was pressing his face into her hair.

"We have all the time in the world," he said in a voice that was curiously edged with pain.

She twisted her neck so she could look up at him and saw a reflection of the pain on his face. This closeness was no more easy for him than it was for her.

He said, "You tell me all about the apartment and your mother and anything else you'd care to. And then maybe I can tell you about why I stopped believing in Santa Claus."

Again she felt the tightening sensation beneath her breastbone. Then it let go, and a flooding warmth washed away the last barriers between her and the future.

FOURTEEN

FRIDAY MORNING: subdued light filtering through the thin blue curtains; the sound of rain still pelting down in the alley; rumpled sheets and bunched-up pillows; a warm spot where Rafferty had lain.

Joanna kept her eyes closed, recalling the heat and the closeness. An emotional closeness; which only enhanced that of the body. A unity that made the touchings and explorations and joinings and completions all the more pleasurable. She lay there, savoring the sensation of a body well used and well shared, feeling fully alive again after all the years—

The door to the apartment opened and shut. Struggling to a sitting position, she saw Rafferty, barefoot and wearing trousers but no shirt. As she pulled the covers over her bare breasts, he grinned. She dropped the blanket, acknowledging that the gesture was uncalled for.

He said, "Guess what? I heard furtive footsteps and went out to find my umbrella's been stolen."

"Well, you got your wish. Now you'll *have* to buy a new one. But it's pouring outside. What are you going to do until you get to a store?"

"I thought I'd wait for you. You can deliver me to my car under your umbrella."

She reached for her robe where she'd always put it on the arm of the sofa bed, then realized she hadn't even unpacked it yet. With a shrug, she stepped out of the bed and moved toward the bathroom.

Rafferty's grin faded and another look came across his face—one she'd become more than familiar with the night before. As he intercepted her and put his arms around her, she said, ''That's a fine idea, but there's one drawback.''

''I hadn't noticed any.'' He began nuzzling her neck.

''No, I meant about the umbrella. You see, I don't have one.''

He pulled back and looked down at her. ''You're kidding.''

''No. I haven't owned one in years. When I carry one I'm a menace, always about to poke someone's eye out or get its spokes tangled in people's hair. So I finally gave up on umbrellas.''

''How do you get about in the rain?''

''Wear a waterproofed hat—and run a lot.''

''Then I guess that's what we'll both have to do. But not just yet. . . .''

THE SHOWROOM of the Wheatley Galleries was deserted when Joanna entered at a little past ten. She stood for a moment in the marble-floored foyer, shaking raindrops off her floppy hat, before stepping onto the thickly piled burgundy carpet of the main room. The space was rectangular, windowless, and white walled, with alcoves at either end for more secluded—and serious—viewing of paintings. She had not been inside Marshall's place of business in a number of years, and now it seemed larger than she remembered, the number of works on display fewer.

There was a good abstract by Stuart Davis positioned to the left of the entry, and an early Max Weber to the right. Joanna studied both of them, liking the Davis but deciding the colors of the Weber seemed curiously muddied compared to his later works. The subdued realism of a painting in the Andrew Wyeth tradition on the opposite wall was more to her liking, although a trifle sentimental. The other works offered here ranged from two poorly executed examples of the "soup can school" founded by Andy Warhol, to a bright, bold Pop Art painting, to a few as yet unclassifiable creations of contemporary—local?—artists. She made a full circuit of the gallery, and decided there wasn't one of them she would want on her walls at home. They must have their merits, however; Marshall's taste had always been unfailingly correct.

Hearing a rustling sound behind her, she turned to see a young woman emerge from the office at the rear of the gallery. It wasn't Jane Lake, Marshall's longtime assistant, but a newcomer, and someone who presented a marked contrast to Jane's understated elegance. This woman had a slicked-back, wet-looking hairstyle that suggested a punk influence, plum-colored fingernails, and two dangling silver earrings in each earlobe. She wore a satiny black dress that would have been more appropriate at a disco than an art gallery. And when she saw Joanna, her face remained deadpan, as if she were afraid she'd crack the bright, hard makeup that went with the hair.

She said, "Can I help you?"

"I'm here to see Mr. Wheatley."

"He's not in today."

That wasn't surprising, in view of the trouble Mike was in. "What about Jane Lake—is she in?"

"Who?"

"Jane Lake, Mr. Wheatley's assistant."

The woman drew herself up taller. "*I'm* his assistant."

"Oh, you must have replaced Jane."

"I didn't *replace* anybody." She examined her fingernails in—it seemed to Joanna—a deliberate gesture of rudeness. "Marshall didn't have any other employees when he hired me."

"When was that?"

"Six months ago."

And you lowered the tone of this establishment by several notches, Joanna thought. "Can you tell me—"

"Are you interested in a painting, or what?"

"I'm a personal friend of Mr. Wheatley."

"Oh." She shrugged indifferently. "In that case, you might want to check his home. His kid's in some sort of trouble."

"I know."

Joanna made a hasty exit and ran through the rain to her car. What on earth, she wondered, was Marshall doing with such an unattractive and disagreeable assistant? And what had happened to Jane Lake? Employees who possessed a knowledge of modern art and good selling skills were difficult to find, and maybe this woman—like Jane—had that rare combination, but Joanna doubted it. She certainly couldn't be doing the Wheatley Galleries any good; her contacts with potential clients were bound to leave a bad taste in their mouths—as the encounter had left in Joanna's.

The elegant houses of Sea Cliff looked gloomy and forbidding in the rain—empty piles of brick and mortar and stone, rather than homes where people lived comfortable and happy lives. As Joanna drove up to the Wheatleys' Italianate villa, a gray Buick Riviera passed her and turned into the driveway. A man in a brown overcoat got out, went around to the passenger's side, and removed a medium-sized suitcase.

Joanna got out of her car and went up the walk. At the sound of her footsteps, the man turned, and she recognized Douglas Wheatley, Marshall and Phyllis's elder son. He hadn't changed much since she'd last seen him at a museum function four years ago: brown hair that was best labeled nondescript; a gangly body that was odd in a man in his late twenties; thick glasses, a sharply pointed nose, and the kind of little pinched mouth that usually went with a humorless disposition. As he watched Joanna approach, his mouth became even more pinched with suspicion.

"Douglas," she said, "do you remember me—Joanna Stark?"

His lips relaxed somewhat. "Of course. It's been a long time. How are you?"

"Fine. You?"

"Fine also. Are you here to see Mother?"

"Either her or your father, if they're in."

He extended an arm toward the front door. "I don't know if they are or not. I just got back from New York—early flight out of Kennedy. But Enid will know."

"Enid?"

"The housekeeper." He pressed the doorbell and thirty seconds later they were admitted by the white-haired woman in a gray uniform whom Joanna had seen opening the door for Mike two days before. "Hi, Enid, I'm back," Douglas said unnecessarily. "This is Mrs. Stark. She's here to see Mother."

"Hello, Mrs. Stark," Enid said. "Mr. Douglas. I'm sorry but your mother isn't home."

"What about Father?"

"No, he's out too. I don't know when either of them will be back."

He frowned and said to Joanna, "I suppose you're here about this disgusting business with Mike."

His choice of adjective surprised her, but she only nodded.

"Why don't you wait, then? I'm sure they'll return soon; they knew what flight I was coming in on." To the housekeeper, he said, "Would you bring us some coffee, please? We'll be in the sunroom."

The woman nodded, took Douglas's suitcase from his hand, and went out. Joanna followed Douglas to the rear of the house, where a long room with windows on three sides—an addition of 1960s vintage—overlooked the sea. This was Phyllis's particular domain, a normally cheerful space decorated in cool blues and greens and filled with comfortable furniture and healthy plants. Today, however, the room was cold from the gusting winds that chilled the large expanses of glass. The lawn that sloped down to the cliff was puddled in places, and the sea beyond it was steel gray and turbulent.

Douglas took off his overcoat and tossed it on a chair, then noticed the chill temperature. He adjusted a thermostat that regulated the electric space heaters below the windows, and motioned for Joanna to sit. She took a platform rocker she had always favored, and he sat on a couch across from it. "Coffee will be here soon," he said. "That should warm us up."

"I imagine after New York, this doesn't seem so cold," Joanna said. "I heard they had snow this week."

Douglas nodded.

"You were there on business?"

"Yes, they called me there to discuss my opening a new office in San Rafael—I'm with Hodges and Harlin, the brokerage, you know. We're a new firm, very aggressive, and it's quite a coup...." He paused. "Of course, my news is now completely overshadowed by Mike's latest escapade." As he said his brother's name, his lips drew together in disapproval.

"How did you find out about that?"

"Well, first Mike called me at my hotel early yesterday morning—it would have been about four-thirty here. He didn't say anything was wrong, just asked me when I'd be back and mumbled something about needing to talk to me when I got in. But he sounded strange, and it's unusual for him to get in touch anyway, let alone at that hour. I didn't know what to make of it. Then—last night—my father called. He wanted me to drop everything and come home. As if I could help.... But fortunately my business was finished anyway, so I came. It's always been like that; Mike gets in trouble and everyone else's life stops dead."

Douglas rummaged in the pocket of his suitcoat and extracted an airline ticket folder, as well as several other papers and receipts—the detritus of travel. As Enid entered with the coffee, he crossed the room and tossed them into the wastebasket next to Phyllis's little Louis XIV desk, then returned, taking a cup from the housekeeper's outstretched hand.

Joanna set her saucer on the table next to her and held the cup between her palms. It was still cold in the room, and she felt more like plunging her fingers into the coffee than drinking it.

Douglas drank his coffee in noisy gulps, seeming disinclined to continue the conversation. Finally Joanna said, "I stopped by the gallery before I came here, looking for your father. Who on earth is that new assistant?"

"The punk rocker? Her name's Abby something-or-other. Quite a change from Jane, isn't she?"

"Yes. What happened to Jane?"

Douglas poured himself more coffee. "She got a better offer from another gallery."

"I'm surprised Marshall didn't try to top it."

"He couldn't—it was that much better."

Joanna thought of the sparsity and poor quality of the paintings on display. "Is business bad?"

"The economy's bad. And when the economy's bad, the sectors where people spend their discretionary income are the first to suffer."

"Does that include the brokerage business?"

"Yes and no. In the case of my firm, we're taking an aggressive stance, trying to move counter to the trend. But in a business like my father's, it's better to retrench."

She helped herself to a second cup of coffee, in order to keep her hands warm. "Is that what Marshall's doing—retrenching?"

"Yes. Next month the gallery moves to a new location near Fisherman's Wharf."

"What!" Marshall had been in his space on Sutter Street for decades; Joanna could not imagine him anywhere else. Besides, the galleries near the wharf were strictly tourist-oriented—and notoriously tacky.

Douglas frowned at the disapproval in her voice. "It's unfortunate, but true. Rents in that downtown area have become exorbitant. On Sutter Street they're up to a hundred, even a hundred and twenty-five dollars per square foot. The same around Union Square and Post Street. The only costlier places in the country are parts of Fifth and Madison Avenues in Manhattan, Rodeo Drive in Beverly Hills, and Michigan Avenue in Chicago. Father should have made this move years ago."

"But..." Joanna hesitated. Any objection she could pose would merely be based on sentiment. She didn't like to see a gallery that she considered an institution disappear—as Marshall's surely would after a few years in such a disadvantageous location.

As if he could hear what she was thinking, Douglas said, "It's not so bad, Joanna. Father's going to have to retire one of these days, anyway."

That was another shock. She had simply never thought of Marshall—or Phyllis, for that matter—as old and retreating from their active participation in the art world. They were both too dynamic, too vibrant.... And then she remembered how tired and thin Marshall had looked at the de Young the other night. Maybe Douglas was right; maybe it was time he retired.

But she had come here on business, not to pass the time in idle talk. She turned the subject back to Mike. "Have you seen much of Mike lately, Douglas?" she asked.

Again his face took on the pinched look. "No, I have not. He seldom favors us with his presence, unless he wants something. Father tells me he was passed out on the couch the morning after the painting was stolen, but before that it had been months since he'd set foot in the house."

It was interesting that Mike had come home shortly after the theft. "Did your father mention how Mike behaved that morning?"

"How do you think he behaved? Hungover and surly as ever, I'm sure."

Joanna was surprised at the vehemence in Douglas's words. His tone was not merely the disapproving one he had used before, but something very close to hatred. She said, "It sounds as if you don't care very much for your brother, Douglas."

"Why should I? He's been nothing but trouble for this family since the day he was born. Always in and out of trouble; thrown out of this school, gotten into another; picked up by the cops, bailed out; wrecking this car, being bought another; knocking up this girl, paying her to have an abortion. And every time he got into a scrape, it was a family crisis: Drop everything, no matter what it was; run to Mike's side, support him; pull together, for Mike's sake. Never mind what anyone else needed, never mind what *I* needed. Mike's the only one who counts, because he's their..." Douglas stopped abruptly, looking surprised at his own tirade.

"He's their what, Douglas?" Joanna asked.

He shook his head and reached for his coffee cup.

Joanna studied Douglas. That nondescript brown hair: It was not the Wheatley blond, a color that—she had once commented to David—was appropriate to their last name. Nor were his features like the rest of the family's; Marshall's and Mike's were full and ruddy, and even Phyllis's prominent bone structure had none of the sharp edges of Douglas's. And that gawkiness: While tall, the three other Wheatleys were well coordinated, graceful.

An art dealer with an adopted son in his twenties. She was certain now what Douglas had started to say. "He's their natural son, isn't he?" she asked. "You were adopted."

Douglas let out his breath in a long sigh. "Yes."

"And a few years later Mike was born."

"Yes, just the way you always hear about it happening. Childless couple adopts, and next thing you know they have a baby of their own."

"And you've always resented him." Joanna injected a note of sympathy into her voice—sympathy she wanted to feel for Douglas, but couldn't. If only he weren't so *unlikable*....

Douglas responded to it, however. "It's hard *not* to resent Mike. All my life I've tried to do everything just right. I felt I had to be the model son, had to try harder, because my parents were good enough to take me into their home, give me a name. And then Mike came along and never did anything right. But they still loved him more."

"Are you sure of that?"

"Why else would they run every time he needed them? When *I* did anything right, all I got was a pat on the head."

"Maybe they felt you were so self-sufficient you could take care of yourself."

"Oh, I've been through all this with myself, time and time again. I'd tell myself that the squeaky wheel gets the oil, or whatever that old saying is. But it didn't really help." He looked uncertainly at Joanna, as if he doubted he should go on, then continued anyway. "Sometimes I'd do horrible things to Mike."

"Like what?"

"Well, when he was a baby, I'd sneak into his room and pinch him when he was asleep, so he'd wake up and cry. I'd take toys of his—ones I knew were particular favorites—and throw them in the garbage. Once he was building a ship model and I smashed it and made it look like a heavy book had fallen off the shelf above the desk onto it. I even . . . you don't want to hear this."

"It's okay, Douglas, tell me."

"One time when we were at Aspen on a family trip, I fixed the binding on one of his skis so it would jam. He fell and broke his ankle. I didn't mean for it to be that serious, but secretly I was glad."

Joanna shook her head slightly. This was certainly a side to Douglas no one had suspected before.

He said, "Why am I even telling you all this?"

"It's probably something you've needed to talk out for a long time. And I understand. Really I do." But did she? She hadn't had siblings, hadn't had anyone she'd needed to vent such rage upon.

But then she remembered her father, her rage at him when her mother had killed herself. Maybe she *did* understand—a little.

"Did Mike ever know you were doing those things?" she asked.

"That's the funny part: He did, but he never told. He never even said anything to me, but he'd give me a look, and I could see in his eyes that he knew. And shortly afterward, he'd get into one of his scrapes, and all our attention would be focused on him."

It was an interesting family dynamic, Joanna thought—and a distressing one.

"The only time he ever said anything," Douglas added, "was after the skiing accident. He was in bed at the hospital where they'd taken him, and Mother had left us alone for a few minutes. He looked me straight in the eye and said, 'I'll get you for this some day.' And then he smiled at me."

Joanna was silent, picturing the scene. Douglas looked down at his coffee cup; the hand that held it was trembling. He set the cup carefully in its saucer and seemed about to speak when Phyllis's voice called out to him from the hallway. He stood up just as she hurried through the door.

Joanna was taken aback when she saw her, so great was the change in her appearance in only two days' time. Phyllis's face was sallow, the skin drawn tight with tension; her upswept coiffure was unkempt, strands of hair straggling down; the colors of her pants and sweater clashed badly, as if she'd dressed without really looking at what she was putting on. But it was her movements as she entered the room that spoke most eloquently of her disturbed state: They were erratic, graceless, and—worst of all—unsure. Until now, Joanna had never known Phyllis to display the slightest lack of confidence.

"Thank God you're back!" she said, moving toward Douglas. Then her eyes rested on Joanna, who was just rising from the rocker. "Oh, Enid didn't say who—"

"Joanna came to ask about Mike," Douglas said.

"No doubt she did." Phyllis's tone was decidedly unfriendly. "Unknown to us, she's been doing a good deal of that during the last few days."

Douglas frowned, looking from his mother to Joanna.

Before he could speak, Phyllis said, "Would you excuse us for a moment, dear? There's something I have to say to Joanna."

"Certainly." He picked up his overcoat and retreated, looking relieved at the dismissal.

Phyllis crossed her arms over her breasts and went to the largest window, which faced directly onto the sea. Her motions were choppy; she seemed to be holding herself tightly in check. Joanna waited as she stood staring out for a long moment.

Finally Phyllis said, "Why didn't you tell us about Mike?"

"You mean about his phone calls to Great American."

"Yes. You knew about them from the first, didn't you? You knew about them that night you talked with Marshall at the reception at the de Young. You had to have, because you told him you'd come to San Francisco to work on the theft of the Hals."

"Yes, I knew."

"And the next morning you had coffee with me and chatted like an old friend, when what you really wanted was to pry information out of me about Mike."

"That wasn't the reason—"

"It was."

"Phyllis." Joanna went to stand beside her. In spite of the electric heater at the baseboard, the air off the huge window was icy. "I didn't chat with you 'like an old friend.' I was being a friend. Even though Mike had made those phone calls, I didn't believe he really had anything to do with the theft, and I thought if I could see him, talk with him, maybe I could spare you the pain of even knowing what he'd tried."

Phyllis kept her eyes rigidly on the gray sea. "By 'what he'd tried,' do you mean extortion?"

"I guess that's the legal definition of it. I thought of it more as a prank."

"A prank." Phyllis's shoulders sagged, and she leaned forward, her forehead against the glass. "He's too old for pranks, has been for years."

Joanna put her arm around her shoulders. "Come on, Phyllis, sit down. Let me get you some hot coffee."

For a moment she thought her old friend would lean on her, allow her to lead her to a chair. But instead Phyllis straightened and moved away, again staring out at the Pacific.

She said, "Everything's falling apart."

"No, it will be all right."

"Not again, ever. Mike is out there, somewhere, hiding. And Marshall's been out since dawn looking for him. And if I know Douglas, he's upstairs in his room hating Mike for putting us through all this." She placed her right hand against the glass, fingers spread wide. "And the goddamned rain keeps coming down. If this keeps up, we'll slide right down onto China Beach."

"It's rained this hard before and nothing like that has happened," Joanna said. "This house is built on bedrock."

Phyllis laughed harshly. "The house, perhaps, but not the family. And not our friendships, either. You weren't a friend to us, Joanna, no matter what you claim. If you'd been a true friend, you'd have told us about Mike immediately."

"Phyllis—"

"No, no more talk." She took her hand from the window and crossed her arms once more. "Just go, Joanna. Please go."

Joanna started to speak, then thought better of it. Words were of no use to someone in Phyllis's distressed state. She contented herself with a quick squeeze of her old friend's arm, and quietly let herself out of the house.

FIFTEEN

IT WASN'T UNTIL SHE SLIPPED behind the wheel of her car that she thought of the Wheatleys' cottage near Devil's Slide.

The slide was a perilous area along Highway One, some twenty minutes south of the city, where the road snaked along a shelf on the cliffs above the sea. Periodically, during heavy rains such as had fallen this month, mud and rocks showered down onto the highway from the towering palisades on the inland side; often the momentum of the avalanche carried on over the precipice into the sea—and took part of the road with it. The residents of the small beach towns south of there would then find themselves cut off from the city, with no recourse but to cross the rugged hills much farther south, to the freeways in the center of the peninsula. For years they had proposed to the California Coastal Commission that a bypass be constructed as an alternative to Devil's Slide, but last year—for political reasons that Joanna hadn't taken the trouble to decipher—the measure had once again been turned down.

As she recalled now—prompted by Phyllis's words about her home sliding down onto China Beach—the cottage stood on a promontory near the south end of the slide. A white elephant that had been passed down through the Wheatley family for generations, it was now dilapidated and unused, protected from vandals and tourists by an electrified security fence. Occasionally Marshall had threatened to deed the land to the state—

it was one of the few parcels of privately held property along that stretch of the coast—and Joanna assumed he would eventually do so. But something, possibly sentiment, had up to now prevented him from relinquishing the cottage, and it remained a lonely, rustic outpost above the Pacific.

It was also, she thought, a perfect place for a fugitive to hide. And neither Phyllis nor Marshall would have revealed its existence to the police if they suspected Mike were there.

Tapping her fingers on the steering wheel, she debated driving down there. The cottage was situated high up on the bluff, and in order to reach it one had to scale several hundred stone steps cut into the steep incline. And if the security gate were shut and activated—as it surely would be if Mike were hiding within—there would be no way of getting close enough to investigate. Or would there? Joanna thought about the fence, a simple precautionary measure she herself had recommended when the cottage had twice been broken into by transients. She didn't really have the proper tools to bypass it, but perhaps...

She started the car and drove west, skirting Lincoln Park Golf Course, on her way to the Great Highway. The road wound past the area around the Cliff House, where it was crowded with people from tour buses even on this rainy day. They clustered under umbrellas, craning their necks out toward the Seal Rocks, hoping for a look at the sea lions that usually gathered there. The weather was so inclement that the rocks were barely visible, and any self-respecting sea lion would be huddled with his companions in a cave, or wherever such animals went on bad days. But tourists, Joanna reminded herself, would be tourists rain or shine; she'd been one often enough herself to know that.

The city beaches were deserted, with only an occasional slickered figure walking their sands. Soon Joanna turned the car onto Skyline Boulevard, heading toward the junction with Route One. Ahead lay the St. Francis Riding Academy—a ramshackle stables-on-the-sea where many of the city's young people learned to ride— and she felt a pang of regret mixed with guilt. E.J. had mounted his first horse there. E.J., who was now off God knew where, venting his anger at her and David and Eleanor in one manner or another. E.J., about whom she had scarcely thought since Rafferty had walked into the apartment the night before.

The guilt intensified. Let it be, Joanna, she told herself. Let it be.

The wide sweep of Route One branched off Skyline north of Pacifica. Monotonous tracts of boxy houses were diminished by the vast expanse of the sea. The freeway curved down to the coastside town, and filling stations, fastfood restaurants, and the flat roofs of storage sheds began to clutter the landscape. The freeway became a highway with traffic lights; it passed ugly condominiums, an uglier rock quarry, and another deserted beach before it rose into a eucalyptus grove and wound into the hills. The smell of the trees, heightened by the rain, was bitter, medicinal, yet vaguely pleasant.

The highway—down to two lanes now—leveled out above a deep valley. A hitchhiker in a yellow hooded slicker stood on the muddy shoulder, leaning on a backpack that was covered with an olive green tarp. In spite of her self-imposed prohibition against picking up riders, Joanna briefly considered stopping for him; he reminded her of E.J., who perhaps at this moment was shivering somewhere in the downpour. But then she acknowledged both the sentimentality and impracticality of the notion; she was almost to Devil's Slide and would have to drop the boy off before he'd even settled down in his seat. She passed the pathetic figure with mental apologies, crested another hill, and began the steep descent above the Pacific.

A sign at the roadside depicted a car with skidmarks behind it. Joanna tested her breaks, shifted into a lower gear. The road twisted toward the looming cliff wall, then out toward the guardrail that was all that stood between her and the sheer drop to the water and rocks below. Every so often there was a graveled overlook where, on better days, motorists stopped to savor the view. Today they were all deserted, as was a large parking area where picnickers normally left their cars before descending the slopes to a protected cove. Promontories rose on the sea side; one of them was crowned by an odd structure that she thought was the remains of a World War II gun emplacement.

Here and there were signs of recent landslides; scars on the mountainside, piles of rubble that had been bulldozed to the side of the road, Cal Trans equipment standing in readiness in a declivity where the inland cliff gave way to a small box canyon. The hazards of an especially rainy winter had already threatened Devil's Slide, and Joanna glanced anxiously up at the towering granite, wondering how much longer the mud and rocks would withstand this latest downpour, how long the road would remain open.

The promontory where the Wheatley cottage was situated should be just around the next curve, Joanna estimated. She checked her rearview mirror for traffic behind her, saw nothing, and slowed to a crawl. As the road bowed outward once again, she saw the rise of land, topped by wind-warped cypress trees that all but hid the slate roof of the little building. There was a wide parking area—mostly mud and ruts today—in front of the chain-link fence, and in it sat a black late-model Lincoln. The security gate stood wide open.

She pulled off the road into the parking area, got out of her car, and hurried over to the Lincoln. Its doors were locked and when she peered through the windows, she could see nothing that would identify its owner. Footprints—large ones, probably a man's—led through the mud from it to the bottom of the stone steps that scaled the promontory. Before following them, Joanna took down the car's license plate number, then went through the gate and began the steep climb.

The steps were slippery with rainwater and moss, the railing rickety where it had not completely collapsed. She climbed slowly, buffeted by a strong wind, glancing back occasionally to gauge her progress. Halfway up she paused, out of breath and thoroughly soaked, and looked around. The promontory blocked her view to the south, but to the north she could see the curve of the cliffs and the gray surf roiling around the rocks below. From up here the sound of the waves was a murmur, punctuated by a muffled boom whenever one broke on the jagged offshore outcroppings. Gulls soared overhead, shrieking as if in protest at the weather.

When she reached the top of the steps, she could see the cottage, nestled in a cypress grove some twenty yards away across ground that was overgrown with gorse and ice plants. Only a narrow break in the vegetation indicated that there had once been a path, and when she began to follow it, she was surprised to find it paved with round slabs of stone. As she approached, she studied the cabin.

It was of wood, weathered to an almost silvery gray and splintering in places. A fieldstone chimney rose on the right-hand side, and on the left, a tall cypress tree bent so low its branches rested on the slate shingles. The front door of the little house had once been painted red, but now it was faded to a dirty pinkish color; on either side of it were high leaded glass windows that reminded her of the one in the Alpine chalet room display at the de Young. The side of the cottage with the chimney was exposed and open to the winds off the sea, but the grove of trees seemed to embrace the rest of the structure. To the south, the slope was covered with more cypress, and from here Joanna could see the coastline in that direction too; the cliffs became less rugged and the curve of the land gentled as it flattened into farm country and small seaside towns.

She was only a few feet from the cabin's door when it began to open. Even though she had known someone must be here, her heart began to beat harder, and she stopped, putting a hand to her throat. Marshall Wheatley looked out, his face eager and expectant, but when he saw Joanna, the life went out of his expression. He stood, frozen as she was for about ten seconds, and then he laughed. The laugh was harsh and weary, as full of pain as the sag of his shoulders, the sudden downturn of his mouth.

"Never expected to see you here, girl," he said.

"Were you looking for Mike?"

"Seems we both are."

"Yes." Joanna paused, awaiting an invitation to enter. When none was forthcoming, she went up to the door. Marshall sighed and moved backward. She stepped past him, shaking off water and removing her sodden hat.

The room was a small one, wood-timbered and dominated by the fireplace on the right-hand wall. Although nearly devoid of furnishings, it contained an old sofa and a trestle table around which stood four straight-backed chairs. An oil lamp on the table and a pile of newspapers and wood next to the hearth attested to recent occupancy. Two doors—one at the rear, the other at the left side—opened off the room, but both were shut.

Joanna said, "Has Mike been living here?"

"It would seem that way. Someone's been using it. How recently, I can't say."

"Did you see any evidence of a break-in?"

"No. That security fence you told us to get still works, even after all these years."

"Then whoever has been here would have had to have a key."

"Right."

"Is there any way a person who wasn't a member of your family could have gotten hold of one?"

"Not easily." Marshall sat wearily on the edge of the sofa. His color was more pasty than it had been at the reception at the de Young; his eyes were more deeply sunken; and his hands, which he now let dangle between his knees, trembled. "You know us Wheatleys and our keys," he added. "They're kept on a pegboard in the pantry at home. It would be hard for a stranger to get his hands on any of them."

"So it must have been Mike who was here."

"Probably."

Joanna looked around the room. "May I inspect the rest of the cabin?" she asked.

Marshall looked up at her, eyes narrowed under his shaggy white brows. "You investigating the mess?"

"Yes."

"For who?"

"S.S.I. And the insurance company."

"And the police?"

"Not really. You know how these things work: The safety of the Hals is the real issue. I'm not out to apprehend a thief."

"What about a murderer?" Marshall asked. "You out to catch whoever killed Reed?"

She hesitated, the image of Wilson Reed's body flashing into her mind. "Of course I'd like to see whoever killed Mr. Reed caught. It was a horrible thing. But..."

Marshall waited.

"But I don't have any experience with murder; it's best left to the police. My job is to get the painting back." She looked at him and saw the bunched muscles in his jaw relax. Belatedly she realized he had been afraid that she thought Mike had committed the murder and was planning to turn him in.

"Marshall," she said softly, "I don't think Mike killed Mr. Reed. He doesn't have it in him."

He looked down at his dangling hands. "How would you know what a person has in him?"

"I can sense these things. Mike's not a killer."

"It's kind of you to say so, but I don't really believe you can tell. I don't believe any of us can actually know anything like that about another person—not until we've stood in his shoes."

She had heard something similar to that recently. Oh, yes, herself saying to E.J., "You can't possibly understand a situation until you've lived outside it." Quite probably, Marshall was right.

She said, "I'd still like to search the cottage."

He didn't look up. Finally he said, "Ah, the hell with it. Look around all you want. You won't find anything; *I* didn't find anything."

She started with the door at the rear of the room, beyond the trestle table. It opened into a small bedroom—no more than ten by ten feet—that contained a folding cot with a green plaid blanket and a chest of drawers made of rough pine. The single window was covered with plain brown rough-woven curtains; when she parted them to look out, she found herself staring into the dense lower branches of a cypress tree. The light that entered was enough, however, for her to make out an outline roughly the size of a suitcase in the dust on the dresser. She went through the drawers and found nothing, then took the blanket off the cot and shook out the sheets and pillowcase and examined the thin mattress. Again she came up empty-handed.

Leaving the room, she closed the door softly and crossed to the one opposite the fireplace. Marshall still sat on the couch, head bent forward over his hands; for all she knew, he could be asleep.

The cabin's third room was a kitchen: black iron woodburning stove, old icebox, sink with a bucket half full of water sitting on its drainboard. The cottage, Joanna knew, had no running water or electricity; there was an outhouse on the property and probably also a well from which the water had been drawn. An old-fashioned hutch was the only cabinet space; she went up to it and looked inside. Surprisingly, it was stocked with supplies: canned goods such as sardines and vegetables, an unopened box of corn flakes, some crackers. She went to the icebox and found in the bottom of it almost a bagful of cubes such as you could buy from an ice machine; some Jack cheese, a carton of milk, a stick of butter, and a surprisingly good bottle of white wine rested on the shelf.

Strange, she thought, that Mike would have taken his suitcase but left his food behind.

She continued to explore, finding a small supply of dishes, pots and pans, and utensils in the bottom of the hutch. There were paper napkins and towels, disposable salt and pepper shakers, a large supply of matches, and oil for the lamp she had seen in the other room. In the open space under the sink was a plastic garbage pail; it reeked of something fishy, and she saved it for last. When she had been through everything else, she went to the main room for a section of newspaper. Marshall was definitely asleep, leaning forward heavily and snoring. She wondered whether she should try to move him to a more comfortable position, then decided against it. Better not to risk interrupting this badly needed rest.

Back in the kitchen, she spread the newspaper on the floor and upended the nearly full trash can onto it. The fishy-smelling garbage was crab claws—a large number of them. There was also an empty wine bottle—of a similar vintage to that in the refrigerator—and a profusion of artichoke leaves. Mike *had* been living well while in hiding, she thought.

Unwilling to handle the garbage, she got a wooden spoon from the hutch and began to turn it over. There were steak bones, crumpled paper towels, a paper bag from Safeway, and a small spiral notebook. She reached eagerly for the book, which was smeared with grease, wiped it off on one of the pieces of paper towel, and opened it.

Obviously it had been discarded because it was used up; it contained only two pages. They were covered with notations in a large, spiky hand. Mike's? She'd have to ask Marshall. The notations were names and addresses, all in the city, and all in the area of the Sutter Street gallery enclave. She recognized a number of them as well-known dealers.

Art dealers. Why had Mike carried a listing of them?

She turned that page and with a shock saw an additional address; there was no name appended to it, but that didn't matter—she recognized it as Rex Malauulu's New Apia Bar.

Not Rex's address—*hers*. What was Mike doing with the address of her apartment?

Quickly she replaced the garbage in the pail and went to the living room. When she shut the door behind her, Marshall's head jerked up. "Huh?" he mumbled, looking around.

"It's just me, Marshall," she said. "You dozed off for a little while."

"Uh." He rubbed his eyes like a sleepy child. "You find anything?"

She held out the notebook. "Just this. Is that Mike's handwriting?"

Marshall stared at the book, turned it over, then opened it and read the list of names.

"You'd recognize Mike's handwriting," Joanna said, "wouldn't you?"

"Yes."

"Well, is that his? Does he make that sharp upward stroke on the f? Or cross his sevens that way?"

Marshall continued staring down at the little notebook, turning it again so the manufacturer's name—

Oficio—caught the light. Finally he said in a tired voice, "Yes. It's Mike's."

"But why would he have a list of local art dealers?" she asked. "Surely he knows who they are. And on the next page, he has the number of the building where my San Francisco apartment is. Why—"

Marshall handed the book back to her. "I don't know. I don't know anything anymore."

She sat on the arm of the couch, staring into the blackened fireplace as if answers lurked there. "Marshall, when I talked to Douglas a while ago—"

"Douglas?" He looked at her as if he couldn't place the name.

"Douglas just got back from New York. I saw him at your house. Anyway, he said you'd told him Mike was passed out on your couch the morning after the painting was taken."

"Right."

"How did he seem?"

"Seem? Cross as a wounded grizzly bear. There was a phone call for Douglas sometime after five A.M., and it woke him up because he was practically sleeping with his arms around one of the extensions. He woke me up, thinking the call was for me, and the way he slammed the receiver down practically broke my eardrum." Marshall stood slowly, one hand on the back of the couch. He seemed fragile, as if his bones were brittle and might snap. Joanna jumped up and took his elbow, but he shook off her hand.

"I'm not dead yet, girl," he said in his old testy way. "But we'd better get going; Phyl will worry if I don't check in, and it's doing us no good sitting around this dump." He looked around the room, then moved toward the door. "Come on," he added. "I can use your company on the climb down to the road."

She tucked the spiral notebook into her purse and followed him. The rain was blowing inland now; the wind buffeted them as they made the long descent. Joanna pretended to be afraid and kept her hand securely tucked in Marshall's, so she could save him in case he slipped on the wet, mossy steps. Or vice versa.

SIXTEEN

WHEN JOANNA GOT BACK to the S.S.I. offices at a little before two that afternoon, she found Nick in the reception area, rummaging through a file cabinet drawer. His gray-black hair was tousled, and his shirttail—slightly frayed—hung out over the belt of his jeans.

"Goddamned son-of-a-bitching thing, where *is* it anyway?" he said. Then, without looking at her, he added, "Oh, you're back, are you? Changed your mind."

"Yes," she said. "I—"

Nick swung around, his craggy features creased in irritation. "Not *you*. I *know* you're back. Rafferty told me. I thought you were the secretary."

"Well, this is a cordial reception."

"Sorry." He slammed the drawer shut. "I'm in one of my rages. The secretary quit, and I can't find the file on the revamping of the de Young security system."

"I never even got to meet her. Why'd she quit?"

Nick looked guilty and ran a hand through his hair, which only messed it up more. "I, uh, was in another one of my rages all morning."

"I see." Joanna skirted the desk and went to the bank of file cabinets, reaching for the drawer marked D.

"Don't bother," Nick said. "I've already looked there. And under Y. No go."

"Maybe it's somewhere on the desk." She looked dubiously at its cluttered surface. The other night she had thought that a pack rat might have taken up residence there; now it was clear that he'd also moved in his entire family.

"I've checked," Nick said.

"Oh." She stared glumly at the file cabinets for a moment, then pulled open the M drawer. The file was there, under "Museum, de Young."

"God," she said, "what kind of intellectual giant have you been employing?"

"One who will work for less than ten dollars an hour." Nick took the folder from her outstretched hand and started for his office.

Joanna followed. "What are you doing with that?"

"Refreshing my memory about the museum's security. I'm hoping to come up with some idea about how the painting got out of there. You want to go over it with me?"

"In a while. Right now I'd like to borrow some space where I can use a phone and do some quiet thinking."

Nick stopped and turned, wearing his shark's grin. Joanna immediately felt uncomfortable. He went to the door of her former office and flung it open with a flourish. "Here you are, madame."

Hesitantly she stepped into the room. She hadn't been in there since the day over three years ago when David's doctor had called to say he'd been taken to the hospital, and she'd known the end was near. And now, just as when she'd entered the apartment on Tuesday night, she felt as if the years had fallen away. Her pictures—color blowups of David, E.J., and herself on various vacations—were still on the walls. The glass-fronted display case of treasures from their travels—Indian pottery from Santa Fe, myrtlewood carvings from Oregon, shells from Florida, glassware from New England—still stood against the opposite wall. Unable to speak, she turned to Nick and raised her eyebrows in a question.

He nodded encouragingly. "It's all there. I've kept a close watch over the years."

"But—why?"

"Well, I've had to let other people use the desk and filing cabinets from time to time, but I told them right off not to move anything, and I made sure they didn't take—"

"No, I mean why didn't you just pack all this up and send it to me?"

"Oh." He looked embarrassed, shifting his weight awkwardly, like a boy caught passing notes at school. "Well, you know I've always hoped you'd be back. And when that happened, I wanted things to be nice for you."

Joanna turned from him, tears stinging her eyes.

"Jo?" Nick's voice was worried.

She couldn't answer.

"Jo, you're not mad at me, are you? It's just that I kept hoping. You were what made this company, and I hated to lose you."

"No, Nick," she said quietly, "I'm not mad. This is the best possible homecoming."

"Then you *are* back to stay."

"I didn't say that."

"But you'll consider it."

"I don't know." She looked at him and saw the shark's grin was back in place.

He said, "You'll consider it." And then he went out, beginning to whistle as he crossed the hall to his own office. The tune was "Happy Days Are Here Again."

Joanna sighed and shut the door. She went around to the wall behind the desk and straightened a picture that hung on a slight angle. It was of E.J., aged thirteen, astride a big chestnut horse at a dude ranch in Montana. The stirrups looked too long for him, and the expression on his face—this was after only three lessons at the St. Francis Riding Academy—was one of sheer terror. Was that the day he had fallen off and vowed never to ride again? She couldn't remember. All she recalled was that he had been back in the saddle before sunset. Had he been more resilient then, or did he still have the ability to bounce back after adversity?

Forcefully she banished the thought of E.J. and sat down at the desk. This was time for work, not worrying over circumstances she could not control. From her bag she got the spiral notebook she'd found at the Wheatley's cottage, and laid it on the blotter in front of her. There had to be some reason why Mike had made the list of these particular dealers—but what? Was there some common denominator that linked them?

She had always kept the phone book in the bottom righthand drawer of the desk. Now she reached in there and came up with it—this year's Yellow Pages, A through L. Nick really was trying to woo her back by providing every little necessity, she reflected. The phone book was only two months old, and from all appearances previously untouched by human hands; she was afraid to look in the center drawer, for fear she'd find it full of newly sharpened pencils.

She set the book in front of her, next to the spiral notebook, and turned to "Art Galleries, Dealers & Consultants." Moving down the list, she checked each dealer's name—most were familiar to her—against the ad for his gallery in the phone book.

Anglin, Herbert; the Anglin Gallery; specializing in original prints, sixteenth century to present. Chadsey, Kenneth; Braun and Breakstone Galleries; specializing in French Impressionist and Postimpressionists. Graf, William; The Graf Galleries; specializing in contemporary paintings from Latin America. Livingstone, Stephen; Stone Galleries; specializing in nineteenth-century American art. Payant, George; St. Francis Fine Arts; specializing in contemporary works by Western artists.

So it went, with very few commonalities appearing among the people on the list. In fact, as far as Joanna could tell, the only norms were that they were male and San Francisco art dealers. Few specialized in the same type of art; none even had their galleries in the same building. Finally she turned the page to the H's and checked Malcolm Halsey's phone number. The art dealer was on another line, but promised to call her back as soon as possible. She waited impatiently, drumming her fingers on the blotter and staring down at Mike Wheatley's odd, spiky handwriting.

When Halsey finally returned her call, she read him the list. "What can you tell me about these people?" she asked when she had finished.

There was a pause. She could picture Halsey pursing his lips contemplatively. "Well," he finally said, "they are all respected—and respectable—dealers."

"Meaning . . . ?"

"They would make no unusual transactions on the side."

"Is there anything you can think of that these men have in common—other than being respectable dealers?"

Another pause. It went on so long that Joanna said, "Mr. Halsey?"

"I am thinking." His voice was faintly annoyed. Then, "Let me hear the list again."

She read it slowly.

"Herb Anglin I know," he said. "A man of about sixty, very distinguished. Kenneth Chadsey is the same age, but not so elegant. Graf is downright sleazy, hangs around with—well, I won't go into that, it's not relevant. Livingstone is a fine fellow, maybe fifty-five or -six; we've played racquetball—"

"Mr. Halsey, start with the age of all these men. Are they within the fifty-five-to-sixty range?"

Silence. "I would say so. Yes, definitely."

Joanna wrote "SF art dealers/male/55-60" on the blotter. "What about sexual orientation?"

"I beg your pardon?"

"Are they heterosexual? Gay? Bisexual?"

Halsey, who was rumored to be a closet homosexual, sounded shocked. "Well, I'm sure I don't have access to *that* sort of information!"

"Think: Are these men married?"

"Oh, well...Livingstone is. Also Payant, Chadsey, and Anglin. Graf—God, he's got himself a dreadful wife. Dresses as tastelessly as he—"

"Mr. Halsey," she said, "as far as you know, are *all* of the men I've mentioned married?"

"Yes, I believe so."

"What about children? Do they have any off-spring?"

Again he paused to consider. "Herb Anglin has a boy and a girl, both grown. The same with Kenneth Chadsey. Payant has a son at U.C. Davis—wants to be a veterinarian or some such odd thing. Livingstone...I seem to recall a son also. Was there something about the Air Force—a flyer, perhaps?"

Joanna felt a rising excitement. "Do you think we can safely assume that the sons are all in their twenties?"

"I would say so, given the fathers' ages."

"Thank you, Mr. Halsey. I owe you a drink—several—for helping me with this."

"I'm glad to be of assistance, my dear. And I'll cheerfully accept any number of drinks, so long as they are not the house wine at that Chinese restaurant." He paused, then added slyly, "I'm sorry I can't tell you which of those sons is adopted."

"You've given me more than enough information." Joanna hung up, smiling. It hadn't taken Halsey long to realize what line of inquiry she was pursuing; unfortunately, it also wouldn't take him long to pass the information around on the street.

Well, she thought, it fit. It fit very well. Then she flipped the page and stared down at the address of the New Apia. *That* was what didn't fit. Or did it? It all depended on how much time had elapsed since the original list had been made and this address had been noted. And any number of other things depended on when this notebook had been discarded because it was no longer needed—

There was a knock on the door. She glanced up in exasperation and called out a grudging welcome. Rafferty looked in, somewhat hesitantly, as if he were worried he might have the wrong office.

Joanna had been afraid that when she next saw him she would feel awkward at best, and at worst realize that last night had been a terrible mistake. But now there was none of that, only the same comfortable feeling, spiced with warmth and excitement. She took her mind off the problem of the notebook for a moment and allowed herself to enjoy the pleasing contrast between his mane of silver gray hair and his deeply tanned face, the graceful way his muscular body moved beneath his brown business suit. He came around the desk and leaned over to kiss her, then ruffled her hair.

"You're a real curly-top in rainy weather," he said.

She smiled up at him. "I know. I used to hate it—would wrap my head in layers of rain hats trying to keep the curls down. Once I even contemplated a plastic bag."

He went back around the desk and sat opposite her. "And now?"

"Now I've learned to worry about the important things." Her eyes moved back to the notebook on the blotter.

"So," he said, "tell me what you've found out. I assume you've found something, or you wouldn't have those worry lines between your eyebrows."

"Yes, I've found something, but I'd rather hear what you've been doing first."

"Well, things were dead at the office, and I figured my assistant could handle any calls that came in. Nick is working on the theft from the standpoint of museum security, so I thought I'd pick up where you left off with the dealers."

"Any luck?"

"Not really. Nick gave me a list of people to talk to, ranging from the semicrooked ones you hadn't gotten to, on up to those who appear to be beyond reproach. I got the same results you and he did—no one had prior knowledge of the theft. But I also remembered what that fellow—Halsey—had said about the man who was asking about a dealer with an adopted son, and just for the hell of it I threw that into my questioning."

Joanna leaned forward, elbows on the blotter. "And?"

"He'd talked to several of the people I saw this morning. Same description—tall, balding, the scar on his neck, raspy voice, electric blue eyes."

"What?"

"I said, the same—"

"No, the eyes. Electric blue?"

"That's right."

"How many people told you that?"

He considered. "Now that you mention it, only one. A dealer named Kenneth Chadsey, has a gallery specializing in Impressionist works. You know him?"

"Slightly."

"Chadsey has a son in his twenties, living up in Sacramento. This fellow came into the gallery and asked him point blank if the boy was adopted. He isn't."

"But what about the eyes? Everyone else who talked to the man said he wore sunglasses, even inside."

"I guess he had to take them off because of the situation at the gallery. It's being remodeled, and the electricity in the office where I met with Chadsey—and where our mysterious man probably talked with him too—is off. Has been for quite some time, because the electrician who was doing the work quit and is taking the gallery to court over something. Chadsey's mad as hell about having to work in a room where you need a Seeing Eye dog."

"And this visit took place around the same time as the others we've heard of?"

"Yes, a little over three weeks ago." Rafferty got a small notebook similar to the one in front of Joanna from his coat pocket. "The twenty-first of October, to be exact. Chadsey remembered the date because it was the day after the contractor walked out."

"And the man didn't give a name?"

Rafferty smiled. "Oh, he did—John Jones."

"Or a reason for his inquiring about the son?"

"The most overused of all—something about an inheritance the boy might be able to claim."

Joanna thought for a moment, then said, "Electric blue eyes," and looked down at the notebook, where Kenneth Chadsey's name was second on the list. She turned the page, stared at the address of the New Apia, then turned the book over and studied the manufacturer's name. "Rafferty," she said, "I have to make a couple of phone calls."

While she thumbed through the Yellow Pages, he got up and began to prowl the office, stopping here and there in front of the pictures of her, E.J., and David. She had told him a great deal about her past—although by no means everything—the night before; now, she supposed, the photographs were fleshing it out for him. Normally she would have taken such interest as an invasion of her jealously guarded privacy, but with Rafferty it pleased her. And she sensed that the future would prove he had a right to know these things—and more.

She selected the largest office supply store in the directory—H.S. Crocker—and dialed their number. The clerk who answered referred her to a second clerk, who did not recognize the brand name of the spiral notebook. He went away and returned some minutes later.

"We don't carry that brand, but the name's familiar to the boss," he said. "If you want to hold, he can check on it."

"Thanks, I'll hold." More minutes went by. Rafferty was standing in front of the display case, staring at a pottery bowl from New Mexico. She covered the receiver and said, "You can open the case if you want to."

He did, taking out the delicate piece and running his fingers over its irregular surface. "Jemez?" he asked, naming the tribe to which the potter belonged.

"Yes. You're familiar with Indian crafts?"

"Just the pottery. I've traveled a fair amount in the Southwest, and have a small collection, mostly Hopi. We'll have to go down there someday, if you like that kind of country."

"I do." Apparently Rafferty held the same visions of the future that she was entertaining.

The clerk at the office supply store came back on the line. "We checked our catalogs, and Oficio isn't listed, but my boss remembered where he's heard it. It's a Spanish firm, headquartered in Bilbao."

Another confirmation. "So this kind of notebook is probably unavailable in the United States?"

"If we don't carry it, it's unlikely anybody else does."

"Do you think it would be commonly available throughout Europe?"

"It's probable; they're a pretty large manufacturer."

"Thank you very much." She hung up and dialed the familiar number of the New Apia. Rex's wife Loni answered and told her to call upstairs at their apartment; Rex was on a break. Joanna dialed the second number—also familiar—and waited until the receiver was lifted and Rex's voice said, "Come in." It was his standard way of answering the phone; she'd never been sure whether he was grammatically confused or merely did it because he thought it funny.

"Rex," she said, "it's Joanna Stark. I have a question for you."

"Shoot."

"Do you remember a few days ago when that man came looking for me? The one you told I was living in Sonoma?"

"Sure."

"Will you describe him again?"

"Tall, gray hair, sunglasses, trench coat. If I believed what I see on TV—but I don't—I'd say he was a private eye."

"His hair—did he have a lot of it, or was he balding?"

Rex hesitated, and Joanna knew why: Under the Forty-niners cap he habitually wore, Rex himself was going bald. He didn't like to mention such a subject. "It was pretty thin on top," he said reluctantly.

"Anything else that you remember?"

Silence.

"What was his voice like?" she asked.

"Rough, like he had a bad cold."

"Any scars?"

"Uh . . . yeah. On the side of his neck."

"And you didn't see his eyes."

"Nope, he wore sunglasses the whole time. Say, I thought you said that was your business partner."

"I thought so too, at the time. Thanks for the information, Rex." She hung up before her landlord—who had a bartender's penchant for gossip—could ask any questions.

Rafferty was back in his chair, watching her intently. He said, "What was that all about?"

She looked down at the spiral notebook. Her pulse rate was elevated, and for a moment the letters inscribed on the pages seemed to blur. It was incredible, she thought, that after all these years so many things were coming to a head in four insane days. But it was happening, and she'd have to see it through in as rational a manner as possible.

She took a couple of deep breaths, and in a moment felt calmer. She reached out, hit the intercom button on her phone, and when Nick picked his up, said, "It's me. Will you come in here, please?" To Rafferty, she added, "The three of us had better discuss this together."

In about thirty seconds Nick entered, the de Young security file tucked under his arm. He nodded to Rafferty, set the file on the desk, and drew up a chair. "What's happening?"

Joanna said, "I'm going to tell you something, and I want to ask you not to interrupt—"

"I never interrupt."

She rolled her eyes at Rafferty.

"Sorry," Nick said.

"I'm anticipating you interrupting," she went on, "because initially what I say will sound crazy. And there's a great deal of reasoning behind it that I can't explain. Also, you think I have a fixation in this particular area—"

"Parducci!" Nick said. "Not this again!"

Rafferty glanced at him in annoyance. "Why don't you shut up and listen to her?"

Nick shrugged, unoffended. "Why not, if she's determined to speak?"

"Thank you, Nick," Joanna said with wry emphasis. "And you're right—I'm going to talk about Parducci. Antony Parducci," she added for Rafferty's benefit, "is—as Nick mentioned Tuesday night—an Italian art thief. He specialized in Dutch paintings, and used an M.O. similar to that which appears to have been employed in stealing the *Cavalier*. Around 1976, he stopped doing jobs himself. It's my theory that he became a broker."

Rafferty said, "And you think he's the one who placed the order for the Hals."

"Yes."

"Why?"

"I've made quite a study of Mr. Parducci—mainly because I had the misfortune of knowing him at one time, and I dislike him a great deal."

"I thought you disliked all art thieves," Nick said, apparently seizing the opportunity to needle her in return for her earlier sarcasm.

"I do. Any art lover who isn't a crazed collector does. But Parducci is special."

"How so?" Rafferty asked.

"Most thieves are daring but somewhat stupid. Typically they're young men who are out for a quick buck and a few thrills. But Parducci made a true profession of stealing, and he had the sense to get out when he reached his prime. A man like that is a challenge to any investigator."

Rafferty nodded. "Yes, I remember a couple of others like that. Unfortunately, I never got to apprehend them."

"Then you understand about my"—she grinned evilly at Nick—"so-called obsession with him."

Nick grinned back, in a mock malicious manner. "Get on with it, Jo."

"Gladly. What I have to say is simply this: Parducci's here in San Francisco."

"Ah," Rafferty said, "the man who was asking about the dealer with the adopted son."

"Yes."

"But I thought his description wasn't familiar to you."

"It wasn't, until you mentioned the electric blue eyes."

"That doesn't seem enough to base your assumption on—"

"Wait a minute." Nick held up one hand. "What in hell are you two talking about?"

Quickly Joanna explained. When she had finished, Nick said, "That's all very interesting, but Steve's right—do you realize how many people in this world have bright blue eyes?"

"I have other reasons for believing the man is Parducci. First, this notebook." She held it up. "It contains a list of local dealers, all of whom have sons in their twenties who may or may not have been adopted."

Nick said, "Is that Parducci's handwriting?"

"It's been identified as Mike Wheatley's, and I found it in the place where he's apparently been hiding. I think Mike wrote this list out for Parducci. The notebook is a brand that can only be purchased in Europe, where Parducci most likely was before he came to San Francisco. And Mike also supplied the address of my apartment here in the city." She flipped the page and showed it to Nick.

"So?"

"Parducci went around there earlier this week, and my landlord told him I live in Sonoma now. So Parducci went up there and talked to...a friend of mine. What he said to him, coupled with the description Rafferty got, convinces me it's him."

"What did he say?" Nick asked.

"I can't go into that."

"Come on, Jo, you can't hold out on us."

She thought for a moment. "All right. He told my friend that he was there to give him a message from his father."

"Is this friend the adopted kid that Parducci—if it really *is* him—was looking for?"

"Yes."

"Why was he doing it?" Rafferty asked. "As a favor to the natural father?"

"That's what he implied to my friend. He said he and the father were friends, and they both thought he had a right to know who his parents were."

"Who is this friend of yours?" Nick asked.

"It doesn't matter. It's not relevant to this case. But the man was Parducci; you'll just have to trust my judgment on that."

Nick stared at her, started to say something, then apparently thought better of it. His craggy face flushed slightly with annoyance. As if to deflect some of his irritation, Rafferty said, "So what do you think happened? Parducci came here to arrange for the theft of the Hals, and . . . ?"

Joanna was silent. Parducci's main purpose in coming to San Francisco had been to lay hands on the *Cavalier*. Locating E.J. had been secondary, and on the surface seemed a little odd, but she thought she understood why he had done it. A man reaches a certain age—as E.J.'s father was now—and he feels youth and vigor slipping from him; one way of recapturing that is through his offspring. It was natural that he would now want to know his son.

But locating E.J. had turned into more of a chore than Parducci had counted on because he'd gotten the details of his adoption a little skewed, thinking the man to be a dealer rather than an attorney whose clientele were

mainly prominent figures in the art world. That much of
what had gone on was clear, but after that the details of
the affair became muddied.

Parducci had gone around asking dealers about a man
with an adopted son—they knew that. Eventually his
inquiries would have led him to Marshall Wheatley,
whose elder son *was* adopted. And the connection with
Marshall might have inadvertently led him to Mike.
Mike then might have supplied the list of other dealers
with sons his age, but why had he also given him Joanna's city address? *He* couldn't possibly have known E.J.
was adopted; until yesterday morning she herself had
been the only person here in California who did know.
And why would Mike have known the address of her
apartment, anyway? When she'd visited him at his studio in the old warehouse, he'd barely remembered her.
It might have been an act, but she didn't think so—no
one as hungover as Mike had been could act that con-
vincingly.

And then there were other questions that bothered
her: What had Mike been doing with Parducci's notebook in the cottage at Devil's Slide, where he'd thrown
it away? How—as evidenced by his phone calls to Great
American—had he uncovered so much information
about the theft? She was still convinced that Parducci
was too much of a professional to let such details slip; no
one with Parducci's exacting standards would have enlisted the aid of anyone as unreliable as Mike. And who
had killed Wilson Reed? From what she knew of Parducci, he was no more of a killer than Mike. And where
was Mike now? For that matter, where was Parducci?
That was the important thing—locate Parducci.

"Janna?" Rafferty said.

She looked up and saw Nick frown at the unfamiliar nickname. Perversely, she decided never to explain it to him.

Rafferty went on, "About Parducci—"

"I've got to find him," she said. "If I can get to him, chances are I can get to the Hals."

"But you didn't connect the original descriptions with him, so he must have changed radically since you knew him. Can you even recognize him?"

She's just been wondering the same thing. "I don't know. Part of the change has to be due to normal aging, in which case it shouldn't be too difficult. But he may have altered his appearance deliberately. His voice, for instance: No one could say what his accent was—and I admit he didn't have much of one back when I knew him; his English was nearly perfect."

Rafferty frowned and tapped a knuckle against his chin. "That voice—everyone described it as rough or raspy. And there's the scar on his neck. Was that there when you knew him?"

"No. Why?"

"It's the kind of scar that's typically left by a thyroid operation—an uncle of mine had one once. What often happens is that the person's voice is affected; sometimes it's reduced to a whisper, sometimes it's merely abrasive."

"Well, if that's the case, maybe he hasn't made a conscious effort to change his appearance. I must admit the voice was the detail in the descriptions that threw me off the most. Maybe it's just all the work of time."

Nick said, "He's making some effort to disguise himself—wearing sunglasses all the time. I don't understand why he didn't just change his eye color with contact lenses."

Joanna smiled smugly. "Because Parducci is one of those people who can't tolerate lenses."

Both men looked surprised. Nick said, "You must have known him pretty well."

"As well as I ever want to."

When she didn't go on, Nick looked disappointed and fingered the folder on museum security, which lay on the edge of the desk. "All right, go ahead and be vague. I'm willing to accept the fact that the mysterious Mr. Parducci is in San Francisco. But proceeding on the assumption that he ordered the theft, we're still faced with the question of how the hell he got the painting out of the museum."

"Wilson Reed—" Rafferty began.

"Reed couldn't just have walked out of there with the *Cavalier* tucked under his arm."

"But no one saw him leave," Joanna said.

"Wrong!" Nick's triumphant look rivaled her earlier smugness. "I went back over to the de Young this morning and questioned the personnel some more. What I found out was that Reed left the museum on his break, around four that morning. Due to confusion caused by the other guards taking their own breaks, no one realized he hadn't come back. But they are certain that he left empty-handed."

"Interesting."

"Yes. And remember—the painting didn't turn up at the rod and gun club, *or* in Reed's car, *or* at his home."

"The killer could have taken it from either the car or the club," Joanna countered.

"Dubious."

"Not really."

"Jo, there's no way that painting could have gotten out of the museum, given the security setup and the circumstances surrounding the theft."

"But it did, didn't it?"

Nick sank back in his chair, deflated. "Yes, it did."

Rafferty had been watching their exchange with amusement. He seemed about to speak, but Joanna forestalled any further conversation by getting to her feet and putting on her raincoat.

"Where are you going?" Nick asked.

"To ponder the problem in a more conducive setting—at the de Young. Maybe being there will give me an idea."

As she left the office, the two men looked at one another. Their expressions seemed to say, *"Women!"* Joanna smiled, picturing them heaving a joint exasperated sigh as soon as the door closed behind her.

SEVENTEEN

THE CORRIDORS of the de Young were hushed and deserted, partly due to the bad weather and partly to its being only an hour before the museum's five o'clock closing. Joanna went past the bookshop, where two clerks chatted behind the counter, warming their hands on mugs of coffee, then began retracing the route along the west hallway that she and Marshall had followed only three nights before. She moved slowly, glancing at the glassed-in cases of Greek amphorae; their colors—terra cotta and black—were repeated in the red orange tiles and black marble border of the floor.

Almost halfway down the corridor, she paused, then turned into a gallery and crossed it to a second room, nodding with satisfaction when she saw it was empty. This was where the sixteenth-century Spanish paintings hung, among them three El Grecos. The gallery's vaulted wood-paneled ceiling dated to the fifteenth century and had once graced the palace of the dukes of Maqueda, near Toledo. In spite of its high arch, its dark gilded surface gave the room a closed-in, brooding atmosphere that suited Joanna's mood perfectly. She sat down on a small window seat, her back to the rain that sluiced down the glass, and contemplated a marriage coffer and two convent chairs that stood against the opposite wall. The low chest made her think of a coffin, which in turn reminded her of Wilson Reed. She looked away and shivered, hunching her shoulders against the cold air that came off the panes of the window.

What she next focused on did not make her feel any better: It was El Greco's *Saint Peter*, his face filled with an infinite sadness. Sorrow—in no way so profound, but painful nevertheless—began to seep into her consciousness, eradicating all the warm feeling that seeing Rafferty had generated. What good was it to look to the future, she wondered, when she and others whom she had cared about had made so many irreversible mistakes in the past?

Sternly she forced her mind away from the question and turned her eyes to the next El Greco—*Saint Francis Venerating the Crucifix*. She'd never particularly cared for religious art, save for a fourteenth-century Madonna and Child in the Italian Renaissance gallery, which for some reason made her feel a link with antiquity that no other artwork had ever provided. This formalized scene, however, done with the artist's characteristic elongated figures and sharply contrasting colors, was something she could dismiss while thinking.

All right, she told herself, reason it through again. Parducci comes to San Francisco, a city he's never worked in before to your knowledge. Because he's unfamiliar with the territory, it takes him longer to establish a contact with a Fagin than usual. And while he's trying to accomplish that, he decides he may as well also ask about the man who adopted E.J.

All right: Through his inquiries, Parducci makes contact with the Wheatleys. Mike somehow finds out about his arranging for the theft of the Hals. Dammit—that is where the logic breaks down. Parducci is too much of a pro to let Mike know about this. And...what else is wrong here?

Of course—it's too much of a coincidence that Parducci used Wilson Reed, a man whose wife used to work for the Wheatleys, as his confederate inside the museum. Reed's involvement is what ties Mike in with the planning of the theft. Did Mike put Parducci in touch with Reed? Again, that doesn't make sense. Parducci wouldn't use Mike; a drinker and a talker is too much of a risk.

Start at the beginning, she told herself. You went to see Mike at his studio.... No, start further back than that. You went to see Tony Capello at Islais Creek Resort. Capello said Mike had claimed—while in his cups—that he was going to "get rich and get even because of the fellow in white." He had revenge in mind, and Capello thought it would be "damned sweet." Revenge....

And then she thought of Douglas Wheatley, clutching his empty coffee cup in his trembling hand as they sat in Phyllis's sunroom that morning. Douglas, quoting Mike after the skiing accident he himself had caused. Quoting Mike as saying, "I'll get you for this some day."

Revenge....

Joanna stood up and hurried from the gallery. She was about to turn right toward the front entrance when a movement at the far end of the empty corridor caught her eye. Glancing back there, she saw a tall figure in a too large trenchcoat cross the alcove between the Alpine chalet and French Regency rooms and disappear down the rear hallway. It was a man, slightly stoop-shouldered and walking in a peculiar shambling gait. Joanna had forgotten that characteristic walk—probably because it had not been so pronounced when the man was younger. But age has its way of accentuating distinctive traits, and now she could recognize him, even from this distance.

She stiffened and bit her lip to keep from crying out. Her scalp began to tingle, and a chill shot through her body. For a moment she couldn't move, and then she rushed down the corridor after Antony Parducci.

When she rounded the corner at the end of the hall, Parducci was entering the narrow passageway to the Dutch gallery. Briefly Joanna wondered what she would do when she caught up with him, but then she dismissed the thought and merely followed with a doggedness born of years of frustration and pent-up anger. When she entered the gallery her heart was pounding.

The gallery was deserted. She looked to the left, into the still roped-off room where the Hals had been, and found it empty. The only other way out of here was through a smaller gallery that led to the space where the Rubenses and van Dycks hung. She went that way, but saw no one.

For a moment she stood still, resisting an impulse to stamp her foot in aggravation. Parducci had always had a lot of nerve, but it took real brashness to come here so soon after the theft. Why *had* he come? He was no amateur with a compulsive desire to visit the scene of his crime. And there had been a purposeful swiftness in his walk, as if he knew exactly what he was after and only needed to get there. *Where*, then?

Joanna hurried through the archway and started down the east corridor, past two galleries that she knew to be dead-ends. A noise came from her right, where the eighteenth-century Italian paintings were displayed, and she stopped, then tiptoed over and peered around the edge of the archway. Inside was one of the security guards, just finishing a low-voiced conversation on his walkie-talkie. He saw Joanna and said, "Closing in half an hour, miss." Then he added, "Oh, it's you, Mrs. Stark."

The man looked familiar, and she thought back to her interviews with the security staff. He was one of the guards who had been on special duty for the reception Tuesday night. "It's Mr. Chen, isn't it?"

He looked pleased. "Yes, ma'am. Is there something I can help you with?"

She went all the way into the gallery. "I was following a ... business associate, and I seem to have lost him. He's a tall, balding man in a trenchcoat, walks with a stoop. Have you seen him?"

"I've seen plenty of men in trenchcoats today, but none in the last fifteen minutes. The place has cleared out early."

Where the hell had Parducci gone? she wondered. The logical destination of someone using the east corridor was the American wing; he'd probably bypassed these galleries and gone there. "Thank you anyway," she told the guard.

"Sorry I can't help. Do you plan to remain after closing?"

"Perhaps."

"Then it would be best to check in at the security desk next to the entrance, just so they'll know you're here."

"I'll do that."

Mr. Chen nodded and left to make the remainder of his rounds.

Joanna went to the archway and looked up and down the corridor. As she was about to turn toward the American wing, Parducci appeared in the doorway of the first gallery she had passed up. He went to the next room, looked in, and then started her way.

Panicked, she stepped back and whipped around to face the nearest painting. Its formalized figures blurred into a meaningless swirl of colors as she listened for

Parducci's footsteps. Would he recognize her after all these years? she wondered. Probably not from behind. But what if he came up next to her, looked at her face? Unlike him, she hadn't changed all that much....

The footsteps came along the hallway and stopped at the archway. Joanna continued staring at the painting, assuming the almost supplicating pose that most people—for some reason she'd never fathomed—seem to feel necessary for viewing works in a museum. For a moment she could hear Parducci's breath wheezing slightly as he stood in the entrance. Then there was a rustle of clothing, and his footsteps went back into the corridor.

Joanna sighed softly and waited until the sound of the steps was distant, then hurried to the archway and looked after him. He inspected the gallery across the hall but didn't go inside, then moved on a diagonal and did the same on this side. Finally, as she'd expected, he rounded the corner, bound for the American wing.

What the devil is he looking for? she thought. Well, there was one way to find out—keep following him. If she was lucky she'd figure out why he came here and also be able to trail him to where he was staying. He couldn't have taken delivery of the *Cavalier*, because once that happened he'd leave the city—and the country—immediately. So if she could just stay with him, she stood a damned good chance of intercepting that delivery and getting the painting back.

She left the gallery and moved quickly down the corridor, trying to minimize the tapping of her heels on the terra cotta tiles. The American galleries were carpeted, and she stepped onto the thick pile with relief—an emotion that was heightened when she saw the gallery was not deserted. A young man was sketching in front of a

de Peyster portrait; a couple stood next to a Hepple-
white highboy, admiring its satiny finish; three schoolchildren rushed past her, their mother vainly trying to
slow them.

Joanna adopted her typical museum-goer's pose once
more: hands thrust in coat pockets, chin slightly elevated, smiling faintly to show that she really *enjoyed*
this. All the time, her eyes darted about, searching for
Parducci. When she spotted him, he was moving toward the rear of the U-shaped gallery, pausing briefly to
read the information card next to an Empire secretary
filled with stemmed glassware.

She trailed after him, stooping at the secretary herself
to allow him time to enter the bottom of the U. When she
rounded the corner, he was striding purposefully toward the nineteenth-century works. She took up a vantage point in front of Whistler's lengthily titled *The Gold
Scab, an Eruption in Filthy Lucre*—a murky green por-
trayal of a demonic piano player with clawlike append-
ages, which would surely have made the artist's fabled
mother slap his hands and demand he return to more
sane and sentimental renderings.

Joanna maintained her supplicant's stance and moved
her eyes to the left. Parducci was examining the information card next to a Queen Anne lowboy. He straightened abruptly and moved out of her line of sight, into
the last side of the U. She followed, and when she spotted him again, he was making a jog into an alcove where
the Copley portraits—including the new acquisition that
had been honored three nights ago—could be seen. He
leaned forward in front of a tall case clock and read the
descriptive information, then turned back toward her.

In her eagerness to catch up with him, Joanna had
moved closer than she should; now she stood less than

four feet from him, gazing intently at a portrait of a pompous white-haired man with a large stomach. Parducci stopped, his eyes on her, and remained very still. In the periphery of her vision, she saw his face crease in a puzzled frown. Then he whirled and started out of the gallery at an accelerated pace.

If he hadn't already realized who she was, it wouldn't take him long to figure it out. Joanna went after him, abandoning all pretense of being just another browser. The three schoolchildren cut in front of her, laughing and shrieking. She stumbled over the smallest boy and had to stop and grab him by the shoulders to keep him from falling. Parducci hurried along the hallway toward the lobby.

Joanna gave the little boy a none too gentle push toward his mother and continued her pursuit, heels tapping loudly on the tiles. As Parducci reached the steps that led down into Hearst Court, he hesitated and looked back at her. Recognition flooded his features.

Joanna stopped, amazed at the change in his appearance and feeling the same icy chill as when she'd first seen him in the west corridor. He had aged, very much so, but his eyes were still the same: a shocking blue green, sunken deep in his skull, burning intensely. Joanna had seen various things ignite that fire, but now the fuel was shock and hatred. Their eyes locked and she stood still, afraid to go any closer. Then Parducci plunged down the steps into the great hall.

Mr. Chen, the guard she'd spoken with earlier, suddenly appeared in Joanna's path, a questioning look on his face. She said, "Excuse me, I must catch up with my friend," and ran down the steps after Parducci. He was moving even faster now, toward the rear of the court.

Joanna broke into a run as he went up the far steps at a trot and disappeared into the Dutch gallery.

A startled guard materialized in the archway to her left. When she saw that he recognized her, Joanna called out, "It's okay," and rushed toward the steps. As she entered the Dutch gallery, Parducci was just hurdling the velvet rope that barred entrance to the room where the Hals had hung. Joanna followed, ducking under the rope just as Parducci cleared its twin on the opposite doorway. As she bent, her foot slipped on the highly polished floor, and she stumbled and almost fell. Parducci sprinted across the next gallery and through the swinging doors that led to the conservation labs in the basement.

Joanna regained her balance, and as the doors flapped shut, she began to smile maliciously. "Got you, you bastard," she said. What Parducci didn't know was that there was no other exit from the basement.

She went toward the other doorway. The parquet squares of the floor creaked beneath her feet, and the sound echoed in the half-empty gallery; without the Hals and the grandfather clock and wardrobe—which must have been part of the Wheatleys' loaned collection—it seemed cavernous. The last gallery was deserted, its early religious paintings frozen and timeless; no guards were visible in the corridor.

Joanna paused in front of the swinging doors, considering how to deal with Parducci. She could wait for him to emerge once he'd realized his mistake, but the man had infinite patience. He was capable of remaining down there all night if he saw any advantage to it. She could summon the guards and have them drag him out, but Parducci might slip away while she went to find them, and apprehending him wouldn't insure the safe return of the Hals, anyway. The best resource, she decided, was to go downstairs, confront the man, and strike a bargain. When faced with probable defeat, Parducci had been known to rethink his options and take the least damaging alternative.

Joanna pushed the swinging door open and began her descent. The stairwell was concrete-walled and dimly lit; the low-wattage bulbs gave off an eerie amber glow. She heard no voices or other sounds; the staff went home at four-thirty, and it was now close to five. For a moment she felt a strong urge to turn and flee to the safety of the security station at the front of the building, but she restrained the impulse. That was undoubtedly what Parducci expected her to do; by following him down here, she had the element of surprise on her side.

A number of doors opened off the basement hallway; Tapestry Conservation, Painting Conservation—a laboratory for the care and preservation of every type of treasure the museum possessed. The doors were all closed, and the ventilation system, which maintained the temperature and humidity at a level most conducive to the safety of the artworks, hummed quietly. Joanna tried the door to the office of the Conservator of Paintings, and found it locked. The others were similarly secured, but directly ahead at the end of the hall the entrance to the large storeroom stood open.

When she reached it, she felt around inside the door jamb for a light switch. There wasn't one. The dark room was silent; she couldn't hear so much as a breath being drawn. The air was dry and chilly in there, filled with stale, dusty odors that she associated with old attics. As Joanna's eyes became more accustomed to the gloom, she could pick out glass-fronted cabinets, racks of paintings, and tapestries furled around rollers. Toward the back, where the shadows were thickest, she saw a group of bulky upright shapes, massed together in the center of the room like people at a cocktail party.

People? Joanna drew back, then realized the response was foolish. Moving forward again, she squinted through the gloom at the strange figures. To the left was what appeared to be a man in a frock coat.

What on earth . . . ?

And then she remembered the costume exhibit. It had gone on most of the fall, a special display of fashion down through the ages that had taken up all of Hearst Court. The show had closed only last week, and obviously not all of the mannequins had been undressed and dismantled. What a perfect place for Parducci to hide!

But surely he must know she was here. She cleared her throat and said, "Parducci?"

Silence.

"Why don't you come out? I know about your placing the order for the Hals—I want to make a deal."

No reply.

"You've probably heard that I own part of a security company; we're working with the insurance carrier and we're prepared to make a generous offer for the return of the painting. Let's talk about it."

There was a rustle toward the back of the room, behind the costumed figures. Then all was silent once more.

Anger began to replace Joanna's apprehensiveness. She moved forward slowly, toward the figure in the voluminous white material. When she reached it, her fingers encountered the cool slickness of satin. She stopped, hand on the mannequin's shoulder, and said, "There are other things we have to talk about, Parducci."

This time a rustle came from her left. She whirled and bumped into something that was clothed in a stiff brocaded fabric. The figure rocked back and forth, and she steadied it before stepping around it.

"Parducci," she said, "I want to know why you were looking for—"

Something rushed at her from straight ahead. It hit her in the chest, a heavy blow that knocked the breath from her. She reached out, grabbed what she thought was a hand, and felt cold metal. Then she fell backward into the billowing folds of satin. She hit the concrete floor, feeling a sharp wrenching in her back, and the oncoming figure collapsed with a hideous clanging in pieces around her.

Armor, she thought dazedly; he had knocked her down with a suit of armor.

Footsteps slapped down the hall as she thrashed about in the sea of slippery satin, waving the suit's gauntlet like a baton. Furiously she hurled the metal hand into the blackness and struggled to her feet. As she started to run, one foot slipped on the satin and went out from under her. She grabbed the voluminous white skirt and pulled herself up on it, then lurched toward the door, feeling as if she were trying to run on ice.

By the time she had careened down the hall and up the stairway, Parducci was out of sight. She raced through the gallery and down the west corridor toward the main entrance. Above her own labored breathing she heard the bell signaling the day's closing. Several visitors were filing out past the security desk under the watchful eyes of a guard. Joanna pushed past the line.

A navy blue arm shot out and grasped hers just above the elbow. She looked up into the stern face of an unfamiliar guard. "For God's sake, let me go!" she said, jerking back. The man hung on tight.

Over his shoulder she spotted Mr. Chen emerging from the security room. "Tell him to let me go!" she called.

Chen stepped forward. "It's okay, she's with the security firm."

The first guard looked puzzled and momentarily relaxed his grip. Joanna wrenched free and ran through the entrance.

The rain was driving down hard now, and it was almost full dark. The wind whipped up wavelets on the reflecting pool and tossed the leaves of the big palm trees about. Joanna ran down the walk to the side of the road and scanned the Music Concourse. There, in the shadows among the gnarled plane trees, she saw a tall figure move in Parducci's shambling gait.

Heedless of traffic, she started across the road. A yellow cab screeched on its brakes inches from her, and the driver's angry voice told her what she should go do to herself. Joanna kept running.

Parducci was two-thirds of the way across the Music Concourse, heading for one of the tunnels that went under the opposite roadway. In her low-heeled shoes, Joanna could not hope to gain on him, so she kicked them off and kept going, her bare feet slapping on the wet, icy ground. Parducci disappeared into the mouth of the tunnel.

Joanna put on speed, feeling a rock cut into the sole of her foot. She emerged from the grove of plane trees, raced along the paved walkway, and entered the tunnel. Parducci's figure was silhouetted at the far end, and then he was gone, scrambling up the slope beyond, and melting into the blackness next to the Academy of Sciences.

Joanna stopped, panting and drenched for the second time that day. There was no point in further pursuit. The alley next to the Academy opened onto Middle Drive, where Parducci probably had a car waiting. If not, he could simply disappear into the heavily wooded ravine on the opposite side of the road. There would be no way of finding him in this blinding rain and darkness.

She stood staring into the tunnel for a moment, then felt her foot, finding it was bruised but not cut. Finally she turned and went back to look for her shoes, a desolate feeling settling upon her. She knew she had mishandled the situation—mishandled it very badly. Parducci had been trapped there in the basement, and instead of summoning security to deal with him, she had tried to be a hero. And, as with many would-be heroes, she had gotten her comeuppance.

She finally located one shoe at the base of the Concourse's central foundation. The other turned up in a puddle under a nearby plane tree. Sitting on one of the stone benches to put them on, she wished she were inside someplace warm and dry, instead of perched on this icy, wet piece of furniture.

And then the desolation lifted. The time she had spent following Parducci was not a total loss after all. Though the man had escaped, before that he had provided her with the answer to an important question.

She knew how the *Cavalier* had gotten out of the museum. And she also knew where it was now. With any luck, if she hurried, she would still be able to recover it.

EIGHTEEN

ON ANY OTHER RAINY NIGHT, the sight of the welcoming lights of Sea Cliff's mansions would have warmed Joanna. Now they only heightened her sense of being exiled from warmth and comfort. The Fiat's heater had dried her somewhat, but she still felt damp and out of sorts. She drew up in front of the Wheatley home—from which she really *had* been exiled—and went up the walk to the door. While she waited under a dripping cypress tree for an answer to her ring, she wondered what she should do if barred entrance.

Finally the porch light flashed on and the door opened slightly. Phyllis peered around its edge with a quick thrusting motion of her head that reminded Joanna of a frightened animal emerging from its burrow. When the light touched Phyllis's features, Joanna drew in her breath, shocked at how much she had changed since that morning. Earlier she had been tense and distraught, but now her jaw hung slack and her eyes were dark-circled and vague. She stared at Joanna for several seconds, then started to cry.

Joanna stepped inside, shut the door behind her, and put her arms around the older woman. Phyllis felt fragile, an insubstantial shell that might easily be cracked by the sobs that shook her. As Joanna held her and murmured meaningless phrases of comfort, she wondered if this state of near collapse was merely the culmination of the toll the past few days had taken, or if something catastrophic had happened. Finally Phyllis's crying ebbed. She drew in a shuddering breath, like a small child who has spent all emotion, and moved away, fumbling in the pocket of her sweater for a handkerchief.

Joanna said, "Is anyone home but you?"

Phyllis shook her head, touching the handkerchief to her nose. "Douglas went into his office for the evening. And Marshall...I persuaded him to go to his regular poker game at his club. I thought it might take his mind off things. And Mike..." She covered her face with her hands.

Afraid she might start crying again, Joanna said briskly, "Why don't you go into the sunroom and sit down?" She took Phyllis's arm and began steering her toward the back of the house. "I'll find Enid and ask her to bring us some tea."

Phyllis allowed herself to be led to the sunroom and tucked under an afghan in her favorite chair. Joanna closed the curtains against the bleak night, checked the thermostat to make sure the heat was up, and started for the door. Halfway there, she said—as casually as possible—"Oh, by the way, where's the furniture that came back from the de Young?"

If the odd question surprised Phyllis, she didn't show it. She gestured vaguely toward the south wing of the house and said, "In what used to be the boys' playroom."

Joanna knew the way. She left the sunroom, her footsteps soft on the deep red oriental runners in the hall, and detoured by the kitchen. Enid, the white-haired housekeeper, was sitting at the table, talking in hushed tones with a young woman who must be the maid. When she saw Joanna, her lined face became hopeful.

Joanna said, "Enid, do you think you could fix Mrs. Wheatley some tea?"

The hopeful look became one of relief. "She's going to eat, then? She hasn't eaten all day."

"I don't know, but maybe if you put something she especially likes on the tray..." Joanna went all the way into the kitchen and let the door swing shut behind her. "Enid, has anything happened since I was here this morning?"

The woman paused, teakettle in hand. "What do you mean?"

"Anything...well, bad."

Enid turned and began filling the kettle with water. "I'm sure I wouldn't know, ma'am."

"Please—I'm an old family friend. I'm trying to help."

The younger woman, whose presence Joanna had almost forgotten, spoke. "You'd better tell her."

The housekeeper set the kettle on the stove burner and adjusted the gas flame beneath it. When she faced Joanna she studied her for a moment, as if trying to gauge her sincerity. Finally she said, "Mr. Wheatley returned here mid-afternoon. His car had broken down, and he'd walked from the service station on Geary Street. He was wet and cold, and Mrs. Wheatley fussed over him."

"He's been ill, hasn't he?" Joanna asked.

"Yes."

"What is it—cancer?" Until she said the word, she hadn't consciously considered it, but once it was out, she realized she had suspected it all along. Marshall's gaunt, wasted appearance was much as David's had been as the disease made inroads.

Enid hesitated, then nodded. "I wouldn't say anything, but you've already guessed. It was diagnosed three months ago. Mrs. Wheatley's taken it well; the boys haven't been told yet. He's not in much pain, and he's cheerful. Well, you know Mr. Wheatley—he's naturally a cheerful man."

Until this week, Joanna thought. "Thank you for confirming it, Enid. It helps to know. Go on about what happened this afternoon, if you will."

"Finally Mr. Wheatley convinced her he was all right. They spent an hour playing gin rummy in the sunroom. Mrs. Wheatley isn't a very good player." Enid sighed. "I guess that was what made her decide he should go to the poker game at the club. She said he needed a game that was a challenge. Then Mr. Douglas came down and said he was going to his office to clear up some work that had piled up during his trip east. He offered to give his father a ride, and Mr. Wheatley accepted."

"And that's all?"

The two employees exchanged glances. Enid said, "Not exactly. About fifteen minutes after they left, Mr. Michael paid a visit."

So that was the cause of Phyllis's upset. "What happened?"

"I don't know, exactly. I answered the door, and Mrs. Wheatley came running out from the sunroom and threw her arms around him. He...he pushed her away and went rushing back to the room where the furniture is put when it comes back from the museum. I guess he locked his mother out, because there was pounding on the door, and then an argument, and then he left."

"And you didn't hear what was said?"

"No, ma'am. I've found that in this house, it's better not to hear too much where Mr. Michael's activities are concerned. So I came back into the kitchen and tried not to listen."

"I see." Joanna could see the sensibility of Enid's approach to the problem, but she wished just this time the housekeeper had been less discreet. She looked hopefully at the maid, but she was now examining her fingernails with an air of remoteness. Probably the young woman had not heard anything more than Enid had.

"Thank you, Enid," she said. "I appreciate your confidence. If you'll take the tea to Mrs. Wheatley when it's ready, I'll join her in a few minutes." She went through the swinging door, across the dark dining room, and down a corridor toward the extreme south side of the house.

At some point since she'd last been in there, the playroom—or more aptly, the adolescent party room—had been emptied of its serviceable furniture. College pennants and posters of seventies rock stars were still tacked to the paneled walls, but they presented a strange contrast to the ponderous pieces of furniture that stood in the middle of the linoleum-tiled floor. Joanna switched on the overhead light and contemplated what was there.

Some of the pieces were crated, but most stood unconfined or merely covered with movers' padding. She recognized a sideboard from the French Regency room, the breakfront whose removal Phyllis had been supervising the other day, the bureau with the interior altar that Marshall had shown her, and the grandfather clock and wardrobe from the room where the Hals had hung. Interspersed with these were smaller tables and some chairs.

Her spine began to tingle as she moved through the jumble toward the grandfather clock. Its arched top cast a hump-backed shadow on the wall behind it, and its ornate gold face gleamed in the light from the overhead fixture.

Before she could reach it, however, she heard footsteps behind her and turned. Phyllis stood in the doorway, clutching her sweater around her. The light bounced off her glasses, and Joanna couldn't read the expression in her eyes, but her mouth trembled, as if she were afraid she might be scolded. Childlike was a description Joanna never would have applied to Phyllis, and the woman's timorous appearance unnerved her more than her previous tears.

Joanna said, "I thought you were going to wait in the sunroom so we could have tea together."

"I wanted to see what you were doing in here."

"Enid must be ready to take the tray in by now. Maybe you should be there, so she'll know where to put it."

Phyllis snorted, and for a moment she seemed almost herself. "She *knows* where to put it; she's been serving tea in there for years. Are you trying to get rid of me?"

Joanna was silent.

Phyllis came further into the room. "Mike wouldn't even let me inside when he was here. He locked the door, and afterward—" She stopped speaking, staring at the grandfather clock. "My God," she said, "what has happened to my clock?"

Joanna looked where Phyllis was pointing. The rear casing of the clock had been ripped off—and none too gently. It lay on the floor, edges jagged and splintered.

Phyllis rushed forward to inspect the rear of the clock. "Good God!" she said. "This is deliberate and vicious vandalism. The clock was in perfect condition when it arrived." Then she turned to Joanna, eyes widening. "Mike?" she said. "Why would he do this? He knows this clock dates back to 1725. He knows it's practically priceless!''

Joanna moved around the clock and examined it. As she feared, there was nothing inside except the works.

Phyllis began pacing, waving her arms furiously. ''I can't believe he would do this!'' she said. ''I can't believe it!'' Her anger seemed to have affected her like a tonic, breaking the sluggishness of shock, but Joanna was afraid she would work herself into an equally harmful state. She took her by the elbow and tried to steer her toward the door, but Phyllis broke away and went back to the clock, staring at it as if she hoped to find it miraculously reassembled.

Joanna said, ''Phyllis, did Mike have anything with him when he came out of this room?''

''With him? He rushed out so fast I hardly noticed.... Wait, yes he did. One of those heavy green plastic trash bags that we keep in the garage.'' She motioned at a second door that apparently opened into there, but kept staring at the clock.

''Was it empty or full?''

''It had something in it. What, I can't say.''

''This is important. Think: What was the thing shaped like? Did it looks as if it had sharp edges?''

''Yes. Corners. And it was a thin object. Rectangular. About so.'' Phyllis turned and spread her hands, measuring roughly two feet by three feet. ''It could have been ... Oh, Joanna, *no!*''

''I'm afraid so.''

Phyllis's face sagged in horror. ''Mike?'' Her voice dropped to a whisper.

''I don't think so. But he knew where it was.''

''In the clock?''

''Yes.''

"But who put it there?"

"Wilson Reed. He was commissioned to remove the painting from its frame and hide it in one of your pieces of furniture before the collection was scheduled to be removed from the museum. But I think it was supposed to go into something other than this clock."

Phyllis took an unsteady step and put a hand on the back of a chair for support. "Why?"

"Because the broker who ordered the theft doesn't even know where the painting is. He's not even sure it was placed in one of the pieces of furniture that were removed from the museum—I know that because I saw him there earlier, checking to see what pieces from your collection are still on display."

Phyllis ignored that and went back to the subject of Reed. "But why would Wilson do such a thing?"

"For the same reason he consented to the theft at all—greed. He probably decided to hold out for more money, and the best way to do that was to put the Hals in a place where no one else would find it."

"But why did he put it in the clock?"

"It's the least likely of all the pieces of furniture. But Reed was an amateur clocksmith, and not only did he know there was room inside there for the painting, but it was easy for him to open the casing and hide it."

Phyllis nodded. Her anger had abated, and she looked dull, defeated. "I remember him tinkering with our clocks when he lived here with his wife. Once he and Mike took an old mantel clock he had found at the dump completely apart, and they had it running in no time."

"That's why Mike realized what Reed had done with the painting—he remembered his hobby."

"You say that's how Mike 'realized' where the Hals was. But he wasn't the one who told Reed to hide it in the first place?"

"I doubt it." Joanna went to the bureau that contained the altar and tried to open it, but it was locked. She tugged at the door of the wardrobe, but it wouldn't yield. "Phyllis," she said, "who has the keys to these pieces?"

"They're on the pegboard in the kitchen pantry, where all the household keys are kept."

"So theoretically anyone could get his hands on them, if he knew where they were."

"Theoretically."

"Did Mike say anything to you when he left the house?"

Phyllis frowned, trying to remember.

"Maybe," Joanna added, "he said something about getting revenge on someone?"

"No..." She paused. "But...I tried to keep him from running off, grabbed his arm to try to stop him, and he pushed me away. And then he looked ashamed and said...he said something to the effect that there was still time to save the situation."

"Time to *save* the situation?"

"Yes. That's right."

It wasn't what Joanna had expected.

"And then," Phyllis added, "he said he was sorry, but he had to go or he might not be able to get through."

"Get through where?"

"He just said 'get through.'"

But suddenly it didn't matter that Mike hadn't clarified the remark. Joanna knew where he had gone—and suspected who he planned to meet. "Phyllis, may I use the phone?"

"Certainly. Take the extension in the sunroom." She turned back to the clock, strangely unconcerned with what Joanna planned to do.

Joanna watched her for a moment, then decided it was best to leave her alone. The events of the last few minutes had probably forced her back into her vague, childlike state—and perhaps for the present she was better off that way.

Joanna turned and hurried from the room, pulling Rafferty's card from her purse. In the sunroom—where a tray of sandwiches and cooling tea stood on a low table—she went to the phone on Phyllis's desk and tried his home number. He answered on the first ring.

"Where have you been?" he asked. "I was worried about you."

Quickly she explained what had happened, what she had found out, and the things she suspected. "Will you meet me there?" she asked when she had finished. "I'll need your help."

"I'll leave right now."

"Good. I'll probably get there first, but I'll wait for you." She replaced the receiver and fumbled with her purse, then dropped her car keys on the floor. As she bent to retrieve them, her eyes caught the airline ticket folder Douglas had thrown in the wastebasket that afternoon. She pulled it out, examined the remainder of the ticket. Then she stood staring blankly at it for a long moment.

Phyllis was nowhere in sight when Joanna let herself out of the house. Perhaps she was still mourning her grandfather clock; perhaps she had decided she'd had enough pain for one day and had gone to her room. Whatever the reason, Joanna felt relief at not having to offer any further explanations.

Douglas's discarded airline ticket had shed light on Mike's remark about "saving the situation." But Joanna knew the situation was already out of control, careening toward its tragic conclusion—much like the mud and rocks that might at this moment be crashing down Devil's Slide to the sea.

NINETEEN

JOANNA CRESTED THE RIDGE above Pacifica and began the sweeping descent toward the sea. The pavement was slick with rain, and the lights of the tiers of houses on the hills were diffused. Straight ahead the black waters of the Pacific were icy, storm-tossed, threatening violence and sudden death.

She shrugged off the grim thought and steered the Fiat into the slow lane, tightening her grip on the wheel. The downward curve of the road—with only the insubstantial looking guardrail between her and the sheer drop-off—made her edgy. On top of that she was experiencing a foggy disorientation; probably she was coming down with a cold due to the day's repeated soakings.

The rain began to ease up as the freeway leveled out in the coastal city. The fast-food, gas stations, and shopping malls beckoned through the heavy mist. Joanna put on speed, slipping through the last traffic signal on the amber, and switched her headlights onto high beam as the road climbed into the hills. The flow of adrenaline that had spurred her departure from the Wheatley home had ebbed; the tired, headachy feeling had taken over and her mind wandered, scenes from the last few days flashing vividly before her, as if in a slide show.

E.J., coming into her kitchen in Sonoma with a big smile and a bag of groceries...E.J., storming across the lawn and disappearing down the driveway...Marshall, his eyes shining as he greeted her at the de Young reception... Marshall, a defeated old man dozing on the couch in the cottage at Devil's Slide... Phyllis, an elegant lady sipping coffee in the courtyard cafe at the museum ... Phyllis, childishly creeping around the corridors of her own home... Wilson Reed, vital and smiling in the photograph taken at the Bayshore Rod and Gun Club... Reed, sprawled dead and bloody in the vandalized clubhouse... Rafferty, rising to greet her in Nick's office, his face coolly professional... Rafferty, reaching for her in the subdued morning light, all coolness gone.

Changes, she thought, that was what this week had been about. Changes. Their lives had all been touched by forces that none of them could control—forces that had been set in motion by an unknown stranger many thousands of miles away. A greedy art collector in Paris or Buenos Aires or Tokyo had decided he must possess the *Cavalier in White*, and eventually lives in San Francisco had been altered or destroyed.

The road emerged from the groves of eucalyptus. Although the rain had now stopped, mud ran down the sandstone wall to the right and flowed like lava across the pavement. Joanna's headlights illuminated a yellow Cal Trans sign warning of slide danger. She oversteered on the sharp curve and had to pump her brakes, the gritty road surface making the car's suspension system vibrate ominously.

Pay attention to your driving, she told herself, gripping the wheel until her fingers hurt and leaning forward to peer through the windshield. She switched on the radio, hoping to pick up a news bulletin that would tell how bad the slides were, but got only static. Well, soon enough she'd see for herself; the sea and the ascent to Devil's Slide were directly ahead.

In spite of the perilous driving conditions, her mind continued to turn over the events of the past few days. Mike Wheatley's boast that the disappearance of the Hals would make him rich and enable him to get revenge on someone...Wilson Reed's greed, which had precipitated his murder...the disappearance of the *Cavalier*, which in actuality had been inside the museum almost the whole time...Parducci's tour of the de Young, indicating he had no idea in which piece of furniture the Hals had been hidden...her own search of the Wheatleys' cottage, and the curious things she'd found...the removal of at least three keys—maybe more—from the pegboard in the Wheatley home....

It was only when her thoughts moved ahead to what she knew she would find at the cottage that she pulled her attention back to the present, forced herself to concentrate on the road.

The guardrail that flanked the first curve above the sea flashed white in her headlights. A shower of pebbles rained down into the left-hand lane, a couple of them bouncing up onto her hood. She braked to narrowly avoid a jagged rock in the middle of the pavement. The road bowed out toward the water, then in against the granite palisade. More debris had tumbled down there, and she had to weave to keep from damaging her tires.

Just around the next curve, amber lights flashed. Cal Trans trucks and equipment were moving out of the cut next to the small canyon, where she had seen them standing in readiness earlier in the day. A man in a bright orange slicker stepped forward and waved a flare, motioning for her to stop. She could see nothing blocking the road ahead, but this activity indicated the slides must be starting.

"Dammit," she said as she put on the brakes again and rolled down her window. "Dammit to hell!"

The highway worker leaned down and looked into the car. "How far are you going, ma'am?"

Then the road must still be open. "Only about a mile."

"I wouldn't recommend it. Bad slide danger ahead; it could go at any minute."

"Look, I've got to get through." She thought quickly and added, "You know the cottage that sits up on the last promontory south of here?"

He nodded.

"There's a man there who's...sick. I have to help him." It wasn't a lie, not at all.

"You'd be better off going back to Pacifica, crossing over, and approaching from the south."

"I don't have that kind of time."

The man hesitated and looked up at the cliff face. Joanna's gaze followed the path his eyes had taken. The wall looked substantial, permanent—but she knew how deceptive that appearance could be in slide season.

"Look," she said in desperation, "is this road open, or isn't it?"

The highway worker glanced back at her. His face was weary, as if he'd already put in a hard night battling nature's forces. "We've got orders to close it in another few minutes, but that slide's not going to wait until the highway commissioner says it's okay to let go. I'd hate to see you drive into the middle of it."

"I'll have to take my chances." She touched the accelerator, and the man stepped back, shaking his head.

As she drove off, she thought she heard him call, "Good luck!"

She moved slowly along the pavement, edging around a bulldozer that blocked the other lane, and then she was past the road equipment and rushing on into sudden blackness. Rocks skittered down to her left; one hit the trunk of the car with a clang that almost made her lose her grip on the steering wheel. The Fiat, she thought distractedly, would need body work and repainting after this ordeal, but that was the least of her worries.

After a quarter of a mile or so, a massive bluff jutted out above the sea, and she saw the eerie shape of the old gun emplacement that topped it silhouetted against the cloud-streaked sky. The road there was thick with mud and she felt the rear end of the car lose traction, steered into the skid as she rounded the curve. The car slid dangerously close to the guardrail before she could control it. The steering wheel, she realized, was slick with sweat from her palms.

A rumbling sound came from somewhere above and all at once debris showered down. Mud coated the windshield, momentarily obscuring her vision. She felt the rear end begin to slew again, twisted the wheel frantically. The mud slid down the windshield and onto the hood like icing sliding off a cake; through the streaked glass she had a glimpse of a boulder that marked the south end of the promontory. Then the force of the skid wrenched the wheel from her hands, spinning it crazily. She heard the screech and tear of metal as the car careened into the boulder; the impact jarred her against the steering wheel and knocked the breath from her.

The car stalled. She remained hunched over the wheel, fighting for air, numb to all sensation except the need to breathe. After what seemed like a long time, she sat up straighter, feeling a tightness in her chest with each inhalation.

And then she heard more rumbling high up on the cliff, felt the impact as more small rocks pelted down. She struggled with her seat belt, pushed her door open—at the last second remembered to take the flashlight and canister of Mace from the glove compartment. When she stood up beside the car her legs felt weak and there were shoots of pain through her chest. She ducked her head, put her free arm over it as feeble protection against the falling rocks.

The rumbling was louder now. There was a sudden crack, as if the cliff were being wrenched apart by giant hands. Joanna threw both arms above her head and began to run down the highway.

Follow the white line, don't get too close to the guardrail, for God's sake keep clear of the cliff....

The whole mountain is coming apart, get around this curve, don't look back....

Whose car is that crashed into the rail? Looks familiar....

Lights on the promontory, the cottage, thank God....

She reached the parking area in front of the cottage's open security gate and ran blindly past two vehicles standing there, to the steps that scaled the promontory. The stairway seemed more slippery than it had that afternoon; she scrambled upward on all fours until she was more than six feet above the highway. Then she stopped, panting, the pain in her chest sharper now. Only a short distance away she could hear the thunder of rocks crashing and bouncing down the cliff face.

Abruptly she remembered Rafferty and the car she'd seen back down the road, crashed into the guardrail. It had been a familiar-looking gray Buick—was it his? She couldn't remember what kind of car he had, just that it was nondescript. Had he gotten to Devil's Slide before her, realized the road would be closed at any minute, and gone on ahead? Was he somewhere out here, too? Or—God, no—back in that maelstrom of earth and rock?

She twisted around, the uneven surface of the step cutting into her knees, and peered into the blackness to the north. For an instant the night became deathly quiet, then the earth seemed to give a final cracking convulsion. Joanna watched in awe as part of the cliff face collapsed and slid over the road toward the sea.

TWENTY

THE SLIDE CONTINUED UNABATED for more than a minute, and then the unearthly silence settled once more. Joanna remained perfectly still until the sound of voices on the promontory above jogged her senses. Only then did she realize she had been holding her breath.

She let it out silently, hoping whoever was on the bluff wouldn't see or hear her. She tried to make out their words, but they were muffled and distorted by the wind. After a moment the voices went away and she thought she heard a door slam. Apparently they had gone back into the cottage.

But who was up there? Mike Wheatley, for sure; his old red van was one of the vehicles in the parking area. The other was a plain brown compact with all the earmarks of a rental car; most likely it belonged to Parducci. One other person should be with them but the slide might have prevented his arrival.

She waited for a moment, heard nothing but the surf and the wind, and finally continued her climb. The rain had ceased, but a gale had sprung up; it buffeted her as she scaled the steps, hunched over, her hands resting on the step above her. At the top of the stairway she saw the windows of the cottage glowing dimly across the expanse of gorse and ice plants. Still crouching, she paused for breath and glanced over her shoulder toward the north. The flashing amber lights of the Cal Trans equipment were moving slowly down the road toward the landslide.

Once again she thought of Rafferty, prayed that he'd been restrained from entering the slide area, or that he was safe somewhere nearby. Then she turned her attention back to the cottage and the job at hand—a job she might have to do alone.

The light in the small leaded-glass windows on either side of the door flickered; its source was probably the fireplace. On the left-hand side of the cottage, deep in the grove of overhanging cypress, a second light was faintly visible. Its beam was steady, and she guessed someone had moved the oil lamp she had seen on the trestle table into the kitchen. The darkness and small number of windows were clearly to her advantage. She'd easily be able to cross the iceplant-choked foreground and take shelter under the trees.

She moved quietly toward the low-hanging branches that draped over the left side of the structure. After listening and hearing no sound, she crept up to the nearest of the small windows and peered over the sill. All she saw was the flicker of firelight around the edges of the rough-woven curtains; the material—similar to that in the bedroom—was so thick it didn't even show shadows. No voices were audible, nothing at all except the wind in the dripping trees and the crash of the surf below.

She slipped further under the protection of the trees and moved along the side of the building toward the lighted kitchen window. The ground was uneven here and sloped sharply downward to the south side of the promontory. Low-growing cypress branches caught at her clothing and slapped wetly against her face. She felt her way along the cottage wall, splinters at her hands, and finally arrived at the window. It was larger than the others, covered in the same heavy cloth, and because of the ground's incline, the top of her head came only to the sill. The curtains were slightly parted in the center.

Joanna put her hands on the sill and chinned herself, standing on the tips of her toes so she could look inside. The oil lamp was sitting on the shelf of the hutch and the bottle of wine she had seen in the icebox stood half full on the drainboard of the sink. How like Parducci to serve drinks, she thought wryly, as if this were a gentlemanly, civilized meeting. He may have lost his hair, but not his style.

The door to the living room was open, but the angle of the window prevented her from seeing more than its frame. She came down off her toes and skirted the perimeter of the cabin—collecting more splinters on the way—in hopes that the bedroom window would afford some interior view. The room was dark, however. She contemplated taking out her flashlight and shining it through the small crack in the curtains, but decided against it. If the door to the bedroom was not closed, it would alert anyone in the living room to her presence.

Now what? she thought. She certainly couldn't march up to the front door and knock. Not unarmed except for a small canister of Mace.

She made her way back to the kitchen window and took another look inside. The bottle of wine was gone from the drainboard, and she cursed herself for not keeping a vigil here and seeing who had come for it. As she stared through the small opening, the oil lamp guttered and went out. The wind gusted around the cottage; she came back onto the flat of her feet, grasping the window casing for support. The wind was blowing hard enough to buffet her body.

She stepped back to steady herself and almost twisted her ankle on a protruding tree root. She could picture

herself losing her balance and falling down the rocky
slope behind her, rolling over and over and raising a
clatter that would surely alert the occupants of the cottage....

The image gave her an idea. Naturally they would be
concerned about slides on a night like this; they'd already come outside to witness the blockage of the coast
highway. But that wasn't the only place a slide could
occur, and if one seemed to be starting here on the
promontory, someone would come out to investigate.

Joanna let go of the window sill and moved carefully
down the slope, feeling the ground for cylindrical rock
that would fit her hand. Then she tucked it into her
pocket and made several laborious trips up and down,
collecting more rocks and piling them under the kitchen
window. It must have been half an hour before she felt
she had enough.

When she was ready, she took the canister of Mace
from her purse and placed it in her left-hand coat
pocket, within easy reach in case she should need it.
Then she checked the kitchen to see if anyone had re-
lighted the oil lamp. All was black. That bothered her,
because a person standing inside the dark room would
be able to see her, but there was nothing she could do
about that now. Keeping close to the cabin wall, she bent
down and began to push the rocks over the steep slope.
They made a terrific racket as they rolled and bounced
over its eroded surface, and the effect was remarkably
like the beginnings of a slide. She had nearly run out of
rocks when the front door of the cottage banged open
and the flickering light streamed over the ice plants.

Joanna shoved one last pile of rocks down the slope,
then shrank back as far as possible against the cottage
wall. As she took out the cylindrical rock she had found

and held it in her right hand, a thick, elongated shadow appeared at the corner of the building. Mike Wheatley rounded it, staring off into the cypress grove, and moved along cautiously, stopping at the top of the slope just in front of her. As the rocks reached the bottom of the incline and stopped clattering, he put his hands on his hips and said softly, "What the hell?"

Quickly Joanna moved up behind him, thrusting the rock's round, blunt tip against his spine. He jerked, made a small interrogatory grunt, and then stood still.

She said, "Don't move, Mike, and don't make any noise."

His back became rigid, and she knew the ruse had worked. He thought she had a gun. "Who are you?" he said.

"Joanna Stark. Remember?"

"Jesus, what are you doing here?"

"Just step back this way toward the wall." She wanted to talk to him out of sight of the window and in a more sheltered spot, so the wind would not interfere with their hearing one another.

He complied, moving stiffly.

She said, "I know what's going on, Mike. I know you found the Hals in the casing of the grandfather clock and brought it here to Parducci."

There was a pause before he said, "So what do you want?"

"The painting—and Parducci."

Again he was silent. "You can have the painting," he said, "but not Parducci."

"Why? What do you owe him?"

"Nothing. But he'll tell...they'll find out...oh, hell, all I want is for everything to turn out all right." His last words were like a plaintive cry from a small boy.

"You know it's too late for that, Mike."

He stood stiffly, arms pressed to his sides, saying nothing.

"How did you find out what was going on in the first place?" Joanna asked. "Parducci wouldn't have told you."

"I never even laid eyes on him until tonight. The way it was—look, can't you put that thing away and we'll talk face-to-face?"

"No, Mike. I can't. How was it?"

He sighed. "I crashed on the couch at my folks' house the night the burglary happened at the museum. Early the next morning, before five, the phone rang. The living room extension was on the end table right above my head, so I answered it and a familiar-sounding man asked for Mr. Wheatley. So I woke up my dad, and when I came back and went to hang up the receiver, I heard the man say, 'I took the Hals, but it's not where you told me to put it, and it's going to cost you plenty to get it.' It didn't make any sense to me—not then—and to tell you the truth, I was pretty hungover, so I went back to sleep. Later that morning, I asked Dad who it was that called, and he said it was just somebody looking for Douglas."

"When did it start to make sense?" Joanna asked.

"Later that morning. Mom called from the museum, said she'd forgotten the key to one of the china cabinets she had to empty out. She asked me to get it off the pegboard in the pantry and bring it over. I noticed a few other keys weren't on their hooks, but I didn't think much of it."

"And then?"

"Then I went to the museum, and while I was waiting for Mom to come up front and get the key, I got to bullshitting with a guy I know in security. He told me about the Hals being stolen and Wilson Reed disappearing, and he mentioned that the insurance company was Great American. He knew because his brother works for them and is friends with the guy who wrote the policy on the Hals. Anyway, then I remembered why the caller's voice had been familiar—it was Reed.''

"What did you do about it?''

"Went back to my folks' house and checked to see what those missing keys were. One was for that bureau that has the altar in it. The others were one of the sets to this cabin and the security gate. The next day I checked again, and the wardrobe key was back on the hook.''

That was what he'd been doing at the house that day she'd tailed him there from the Galerie des Beaux Arts. "But even before that you'd figured out that the painting was supposed to have been hidden in the bureau.''

Mike shifted his weight and Joanna eased the pressure of the rock against his back, so he wouldn't be able to tell that its shape differed from that of a gun barrel. "Well," he said, "I knew that it had to be inside one of the pieces of furniture that were coming back from the de Young. And since it was Reed who had switched the hiding place, I guessed it was the clock, because that was the last place you'd look unless you were a clocksmith like Reed. I was dead right about that, but wrong about the cottage. I thought it was Reed who was staying here, but now I know it was Parducci.''

Joanna knew she should have realized it was Parducci, rather than Mike, in residence. His taste for artichokes, steak, and good wine was too high-toned for the younger Wheatley son. "So," she said, "you decided you had a good thing going and could extort money from the insurance carrier.''

"Yeah. I made a couple of calls, and my girlfriend, Suzanne, made another. Just to whet their appetites."

"Were you hiding at Suzanne's place all along?"

"Yeah. When the cops came looking, I hid in the crawl space above her closet, and she let them go through the apartment so they'd be satisfied. They never even looked up, just pushed her dresses around some."

"What made you decide to stop trying to contact Great American?"

"I found out Reed had been murdered. Man, that scared me! And a couple of hours after that, I realized what the situation really was. And I knew I couldn't tell anyone. But I thought somehow I could save the situation. Maybe I still can, if you'll help—"

A voice called out from the front of the cabin, but the words were garbled by the wind. Joanna felt Mike start at the same time she did. The tall figure of a man wrapped in a raincoat appeared at the corner; in the backlighting, he was only a silhouette.

Mike shouted at him, "Run!"

The man hesitated, and whirled and loped clumsily through the iceplant.

Joanna pushed Mike away and went in pursuit, stumbling over tree roots and pushing branches out of her path. By the time she reached the top of the steps, the man was already halfway down to the parking area. She teetered and half fell, putting her right hand on the ground for support, then realized she still held the rock. She flung it after the fleeing figure, missing by a good three yards, and began scrambling down the slick, moss-coated stones. Their downward cant was even more treacherous when descending, and she slipped, her left leg doubling under her, and cried out in pain.

She had just regained her feet when a hand seized her shoulder in a painful grip. It yanked her around, and she stared straight into the face of Antony Parducci. His blue green eyes were narrowed to slits, his nostrils flared, his mouth pulled down in a contortion of hatred. Shocked at the controlled violence she saw there, she dropped her eyes and realized he was carrying a green plastic garbage bag under his other arm.

As she started to reach for it, Parducci shook her furiously and said, "You've always been a fool, *Mrs. Stark*, but don't be a bigger one than usual tonight. Get out of my way—and don't try to save him."

Save who from what? she thought, but she didn't have time to contemplate the question. Her fingers grasped the slippery plastic, and she felt the shape of the painting within.

Parducci realized what she was doing, but by then Joanna had the Hals in a death grip, pulling it from under his arm and wrapping both of hers around it. He tried to wrench it free, and for a moment they teetered precariously together. Then Joanna's foot slipped and she tumbled from the stairway, the *Cavalier* clutched against her body.

She felt a searing pain in her side as she sprawled onto the ice plant-covered slope of the promontory. The impact flipped her onto her back and she began to slide toward the edge of the cliff, her progress assisted by the slippery little plants. The plastic bag was still in her arms; she cradled it against her as if it were a child, desperately attempting to slow her fall with her feet. Only a couple of yards from the sheer dropoff, she slammed into the outcropping of rock and lay there bruised and winded—but with the Hals unharmed.

Parducci was watching from up on the stairway. He hesitated, started to step off into the ice plants, then stopped again.

Joanna heaved herself into a sitting position and fumbled in her left-hand pocket for the canister of Mace. It was gone, lost during her fall; if he came down after the Hals, he could easily overpower her.

Parducci still stood on the step, but now he glanced up at the promontory. Mike Wheatley had appeared at the top of the stairway. Parducci's head moved, obviously surveying the terrain between where he was and where Joanna sat. Then he began to run down the rest of the steps to the parking area.

Cutting his losses, Joanna thought with relief. She managed to stand, then set the garbage bag containing the painting high on the outcropping of rock. Her footing was precarious on the slippery ice plants, and she couldn't see well enough to climb back to the steps; she merely sat again and slid away from the cliff edge down the remainder of the distance to the parking area. When she got there, the brown compact that she'd assumed was Parducci's rental car was pulling away to the south. The other man, the one who had fled first, was running clumsily north on the highway.

Why run that way? Joanna thought. Why not run the way Parducci was going?

And then the meaning of "don't try to save him," became clear. She began running up the road too.

The man had reached the slide ahead. It was a dark hillock atop the roadway, amber light from the emergency vehicles flaring above it. He looked back, but Joanna couldn't see his face. Then he began to climb the debris.

She took a deep breath and summoned her last reserve of energy. As she raced toward the mound, the man fell and floundered around near the top. Her shoes pounded on the pavement, her breath came in ragged gasps; she felt her knees might give out at any second.

The man lost his balance and started to fall backward. He clawed frantically at a tree branch near the top of the mound, wavered for a moment, then sank to his knees, motionless.

Joanna reached the heap of debris and scrambled up, dislodging rocks and clods of earth. The man made one last move to right himself. Then he sank face down in the dirt.

She reached the top and collapsed beside him, putting a hand on his shoulder. For a moment the sound of their gasps mingled. Finally she tried to raise his face from the mud. He resisted her.

"Oh, Marshall," she said, her voice breaking. "*Why?*"

He remained inert, and it seemed a long time before he turned his head, cheek still pressed to the dirt. His face was mud-streaked, his hair hung down on his forehead, his faded blue eyes were dead.

"Just let me go, Joanna," he said.

"I can't. There isn't any place for you to go."

He didn't respond.

"Marshall, it would only make it worse."

"It couldn't possibly be worse."

"Of course it could. Think of your family."

He gave a harsh, cracked laugh. "That was what it was all about. My family." After a moment he sat up and looked over the piles of rubble to the north, where the lights flashed and the bulldozer moved back and forth, shoving debris over the cliff into the sea.

Joanna said, "You were going broke. And you knew you were fatally ill. Parducci came to you, looking for an art dealer with an adopted son, and he somehow sensed what poor shape you were in."

"The man's got a nose for a bad situation."

"He talked you into arranging the theft with Wilson Reed, so you'd have something to leave your family."

"Yes."

"But what about Reed—why did you kill him?"

He shook his head.

"It was because he turned on you, wasn't it?" Joanna said. "That early-morning phone call the day after the theft was for you, not for Douglas. Mike overheard some of the conversation; he believed he'd called the wrong person to the phone, just as I believed it when you told me the handwriting in the spiral notebook was Mike's, rather than your own."

"I meant neither of the boys any harm, Joanna. I only intended to confuse you. Both of them were innocent, so there was no way you could prove Reed had called Douglas or that Mike had written out that list for Parducci."

"But you did write it out. And you gave him my address."

"Yes, God help me, I did. He asked for it early this week, and I thought it might throw him off if I only gave him the location of your apartment. Don't know why he wanted it."

"That doesn't matter now." Joanna hesitated, listening to the sound of the road repair equipment. Somehow she had to get Marshall off this heap of debris and back to the cabin, but she sensed now was not the moment. Better to keep him talking.

"Because he believed what you said about the phone call being for Douglas," she said, "Mike saw it as a perfect chance to make some money and get revenge on the brother he's always hated. But after he heard about Reed's murder, he realized Douglas had been in New York that night—just as I did when I looked at Douglas's used airline ticket. Mike even called him at his hotel to confirm it."

Joanna paused, not wanting to put the next things into words, but all the same needing to know. "You went to the rod and gun club where Reed was hiding before the reception at the de Young Tuesday night. Reed thought you were bringing him the additional money he'd demanded, but you didn't have that kind of cash. You took the gun along, and shot him. Then you took the keys you'd given him. And later, you checked the bureau with the altar to see if maybe he had been bluffing. But why did you check it in front of me? Certainly you didn't want me to see where the Hals was."

"You wouldn't have—I distracted you by pointing out the altar while I just slightly opened the drawer where the painting was supposed to be. It's easy to misdirect someone's attention that way."

Marshall continued to stare at the moving amber lights as if hypnotized. After a moment, he said, "You make all my actions sound so cold-blooded. But none of it was intended. I took the gun along for protection; that old clubhouse is in a dangerous area. I tried to appeal to Reed's sense of friendship for the family, to his sense of loyalty. He said we weren't a family of human beings; we were just a bunch of rich bloodsuckers. And then he turned his back on me. Dismissed me as if I weren't there, as if we hadn't fed and housed him and treated him well all those years. You can imagine the rest."

Joanna was silent for a time. Finally she said, "Come back to the cottage with me, Marshall."

He glanced at her, then back at the amber lights.

"Please." She stood up and extended her hand. Finally he took it and allowed her to help him up. When he was erect, he squared his shoulders, took a deep breath, and looked down at her face. A faint light came into his washed-out eyes. "You've always been a good friend, girl," he said. "Always. But I can't go back there with you. Hate to do this, but I have to."

His hand slipped from hers, and he surprised her by bringing it up flat against her shoulder. With what might have been the last of his strength, he pushed hard. Joanna staggered and fell backward, sliding down the mound of rocky earth almost to the road. She cried out to him, then began to climb back up to where he stood, ignoring the agony of her bruised and cut body. Marshall raised his hand, as if in farewell, and vanished over the heap of rubble.

By the time Joanna had reached the top again, Marshall was far down the highway, running toward the work crew. The amber lights highlighted his clumsily fleeing form in steady flashes. He ran, stumbling and flailing, but in a strangely deliberate path. Ahead of him she saw the slow-moving bulldozer.

"Oh Marshall, don't!" She had meant to shout, but the words were a mere whisper.

Marshall ran, never deviating. The bulldozer moved closer. At the last second it seemed the driver had seen him, but it was too late. The huge blade, laden with debris, collided with Marshall's rushing form.

Joanna put her hand against her mouth and bit down hard, moaning.

The driver of the bulldozer made a frantic effort to stop, but in a freakish miscalculation, he lowered its blade. It scooped Marshall up and began carrying him along with the rubble. The gears ground, but the bulldozer kept moving toward the cliff's edge. Mud, rock, and the mortal remains of Marshall Wheatley cascaded over the precipice into the sea.

Joanna felt frozen with horror and shock. Then tremors of revulsion began to pass through her body. It was a long time before they quieted and she could climb wearily down the other side of the mound. After skirting more heaps of mud and rock, she reached the place where the work crew stood on the edge of the cliff, staring down into the roiling surf. They were silent as mourners at a funeral; one man had even taken off his hardhat and held it over his breast. When Joanna came up, they parted and let her through. There was no sign of Marshall's body in the waters below.

As she turned away and moved back, she spotted Rafferty approaching on foot from the north. His trenchcoat was stained and muddy, his silver gray hair stood up wildly, and his eyes flashed with fear. When he saw her, they glazed over with relief, and he opened his arms wide. Joanna stumbled to him and buried her face in his coat, feeling the tears begin to flow.

"They wouldn't let me through in the car," he said against her hair, "but I persuaded them to let me go ahead on foot. I had to find you. I had to know you were safe."

It was a long time before they broke apart and went to the cottage on the promontory, to tell Mike Wheatley about his father and to retrieve *The Cavalier in White*.

TWENTY-ONE

WHEN E.J. FINALLY returned home the next week, Joanna was sitting on the living room floor surrounded by papers from her files on Antony Parducci. She heard the front door open and glanced into the hall, thinking it might be Rafferty, who was driving up from the city for the big Thanksgiving feed she was putting on the next day. Instead she saw E.J. attempting to sneak down the hall—a difficult maneuver when laden with a bulging backpack. His eyes met hers and he said, "I don't want to talk about it yet." He kept going toward the little bedroom off the kitchen.

Joanna shook her head with a bewilderment that in no way canceled her pleasure and relief at seeing him. Then she looked back down at the clippings she was sorting and sighed. All afternoon she had been classifying them according to periods, much as art historians did with Picasso's paintings; but instead of designations such as Blue and Rose, Parducci's periods could be labeled with dollar amounts indicating the magnitude of his thefts. He had started with small jobs—a few thousand dollars or so—in the late fifties, and had worked his way into the million-plus range before his abrupt retirement several years ago. A final category, that of "broker," rounded out the picture; Joanna already had collected a stack of information on thefts she suspected had been ordered by him.

She crawled over to the fireplace and fed some clippings she'd culled to the flames. Then she returned to the center of the array of papers and sat cross-legged, chin on hand, staring at one of the few extant pictures of Parducci. He had been much younger then, with thick black hair and a jaunty lift to his smile. Even from her biased viewpoint, Joanna had to admit that he had been a hell of a good-looking man.

Parducci had vanished without a trace, of course, had probably been on a flight out of the country before the police had reached the cottage at Devil's Slide. The hours that followed—indeed the entire weekend—had been devoted to sorting through the various details of the case, writing reports, giving statements to the authorities, restoring the *Cavalier* to the museum. And to comforting the bereaved.

When Joanna and Mike had finally arrived at the Wheatley home, Douglas had been there with his mother. Phyllis took the news bravely, standing up straighter and shedding her earlier childlike guise, then drawing the young men to her for comfort. Douglas had actually put his arm around Mike's shoulders, the three of them forming a circle. Joanna hoped it was a sign that the Wheatley sons might someday bridge their lifelong differences.

Douglas had been able to explain how Marshall had gotten to Devil's Slide. The gray Buick that Joanna had seen nosed into the guardrail near the cabin had been familiar because it belonged to Douglas; his father had borrowed it, saying he would pick Douglas up at the office after his card game at his club. Mike supplied details about what had gone on inside the cottage: Marshall had come there for a scheduled meeting with Parducci, intending to tell him he couldn't locate the Hals and to urge him to leave town. Mike had arrived shortly afterward with the painting, willing to turn it over for nothing if Parducci would leave the family alone. Parducci had agreed, but had not allowed either Mike or Marshall to leave the cottage until he departed for the late-evening flight to Paris. The three men had sat in uneasy silence, drinking wine—which had been among the many supplies Parducci had insisted Marshall equip the cabin with—until Joanna had faked the landslide. Of course, Parducci had not caught his Air France flight; the police had not found out how—or *if*— he had left the country. Knowing that the thief was always more secure on European soil, Joanna suspected he had returned there, perhaps by way of Mexico.

He probably considers himself clever, she thought now as she gazed into the fire. He lost the Hals, but escaped unscathed. When he starts thinking about it, though, he'll be furious because I was the one who foiled his plans. He'll want revenge, and when he decides to come after me, I'll be ready for him. God, will I be ready for him!

E.J.'s footsteps came back down the hall. He entered the living room, munching on a celery stick, and sat down on a hassock near the fireplace.

Joanna looked up and said automatically, "Don't eat any more of that. There has to be some left for the stuffing."

"We're having turkey?"

"Yes." She had decided that lasagna was too bizarre—particularly on Rafferty's first Thanksgiving with her.

E.J. said, "Who's coming?"

"A nice couple who just moved here. He's in management at the winery; I think she's some sort of horticulturist. Nick Alexander. Mary Bennett." A good holiday meal was the least she could do for Mary; had it not been for her friend's sage counsel, she might not have returned to the city and recovered the Hals—plus recovered her confidence about moving ahead into the future.

After a pause she added casually, "Oh, and a fellow named Steve Rafferty." Good God, she thought, how am I going to explain his presence in my bedroom?

The laugh lines around E.J.'s eyes crinkled slightly. "Who's he?"

"Rafferty? He's . . ." Oh hell, get it over with. "He's a very close friend."

"It's about time."

"What?"

"I said it's about time. I was starting to worry about you. It's not good to be sexually frustrated." He bit emphatically into the celery.

At a loss for words, Joanna merely glared at him.

E.J. nudged the nearest pile of clippings with his tennis shoe. "What are you doing with all of this stuff about my father?"

Again he had dumbfounded her. She felt her jaw drop.

"Oh yeah," he said, nodding wisely. "I suspected it from the first—for a couple of reasons. For one thing, he was too intense to be just a friend of my natural father's. I guess he wanted to feel me out, see what kind of a reception I was likely to give the news." His mouth twisted ironically. "He probably decided it would be pretty unfavorable."

E.J.'s other reason, Joanna thought, couldn't have been the one she had for knowing almost at once that the man was Parducci: E.J.'s natural father *had* no friends— and certainly not one close enough to intercede for him with his long-lost son. Parducci had always claimed that forming personal associations would jeopardize his safety.

She said, "What else made you suspect?"

"I've got his eyes. He kept his sunglasses on, but when he was leaving, I caught a glimpse of his eye color. It didn't register until later, when I was on the plane."

She shook her head in protest. "You don't have his eyes! His are hard as agate; yours are...well, caring." Then she realized what else he had said. "What plane? To where?"

"Newark. And then a rental car to Tenafly." Suddenly his cheeks flushed with embarrassment. "Listen, Jo, about the money—I took it because I suspected you wouldn't tell me anything, and I thought I might have to finance my own investigation into my parentage. I can't pay it back right now, but on my way into town I stopped at one of the restaurants on the plaza. They think they'll need an extra bartender over the holidays—"

She waved the words away. "Never mind that now. You went to see my father?"

"Yes. I needed to know, but I couldn't think of anyone to ask. Then I remembered that David had always kept in touch with him, even though you didn't. He was the only person left who was remotely family, and I decided to give it a try."

Joanna laced her fingers together and looked away toward the fire. "How is he?"

"Pretty good. He's got a heart condition, but he keeps fit."

"Is he still married to that woman?"

"Millie? Yeah, they seem pretty happy. I think you'd like her."

She felt some of the old anger stir, then die. Let it go, she thought, let all of the past stay buried. "How long were you there?"

"Only a couple of days. They wanted me to stay longer, but I needed to think, so I hitched down to the Jersey shore. But in those couple of days I learned a lot."

"Such as?"

"Well, I began to understand why you and David kept the details of my birth from me all those years. Your father told me that what you'd done was really an unselfish thing. He said that it's the greatest thing a person can do, to put aside his or her selfish desires for the good of the child. He said that parents make mistakes, but it's the intent that counts. And he said that giving up your natural rights is one of the hardest and most caring things a person can do."

Tears stung Joanna's eyes. She couldn't look at him. She stared resolutely into the flames, remembering Paris, the cold winter, the shabby flat, the lack of money to put food on the table. And the fear—God, the fear!

She said, "I was twenty years old. I'd gotten involved with Parducci before I knew what he was. How *was* I to know—a scared kid from Tenafly? He left when I found out I was pregnant, but then he threatened to come back and take his son from me. That was the one thing I couldn't let happen."

"So you got in touch with David, as your father had always suggested you do if you were in trouble."

"Yes. He came to Paris and took you back home with him. I went the other way, to Italy, hoping Parducci would become confused and think I still had you with me. It worked."

"Did he follow you?"

"Yes. He caught up with me in Bologna, and when he realized you were gone, he beat me up. I was in the hospital for a week. When I got out, I started wandering around Europe and North Africa, finally ended up in Southeast Asia. For a while I had a job in an art gallery in Manila and considered settling there, but then I knew it was time to come to San Francisco."

"Why?"

"To be near you. I had no intention of contacting David or trying to see you. But I wanted to be there, in case you needed me. And all the time I kept track of Parducci, so he wouldn't show up and ruin your life."

"And then David walked into that gallery where you were installing an alarm."

"Yes."

E.J. was silent for a long time. He didn't speak until one of the logs on the hearth broke and sent out a shower of sparks that startled both of them.

He nudged the pile of clippings with his toe again and said, "So what are you doing with all this?"

"Parducci almost pulled off a job in San Francisco last week. I think he'll be back. And this time I'm going to get him." She looked up at E.J. and added, "I know he's your father, but he's also an evil man. I want to put him where he can't harm anyone again."

To her surprise, E.J. said, "Good for you." He got up, went to the fireplace, and threw the end of the celery stalk into the flames. Normally Joanna would have chided him for that, but now she didn't say a word.

When he turned, his smile was tentative, but a smile nonetheless. He said, "So what are we having for dinner tonight . . . Mom?"

A CHIEF INSPECTOR MORRISSEY MYSTERY

IN STO*h*Y PLACES

First Time in Paperback

KAY MITCHELL

LOVELY ENOUGH FOR A KILLER

Murder stalks the quiet English village of Malminster. There's no connection between the victims, except that they're all young and pretty.

The murders seem random, and the killer is very careful. All Chief Inspector Morrissey's got is a fattening file of paperwork and nothing to go on but the latest victim's diary. Worse, he can't get a feel for the mind of the killer he's hunting.

But the killer is watching him—aware that Morrissey is getting close. Perhaps it's time he introduced himself to Morrissey's eighteen-year-old daughter....

"Unpretentious, brisk, an engaging example of the village procedural." —*Kirkus Reviews*

A TONY AND PAT PRATT MYSTERY

Murder Takes Two

First Time in Paperback

BERNIE LEE

FINAL CUT

An unexpected trip to recording studios in London for advertising writer Tony Pratt and his wife, Pat, sounded fun and exciting—in spite of the rather off-the-wall bunch they'd be dealing with.

The tension was thick as London fog, but there were commercials to be made and sights to be seen. Until the eerie quiet of the studio was shattered by an unusual sound effect—that of a falling corpse—as a murderer began a very personal job of editing.

"One of the more engaging husband-and-wife sleuthing teams."
—*Flint Journal*

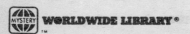 **WORLDWIDE LIBRARY** ®

MTTWO

A SUSAN WREN MYSTERY

THE WINTER WIDOW

First Time in Paperback

CHARLENE WEIR

SHE'D BEEN ONE OF SAN FRANCISCO'S FINEST—SEMI-HARD-BITTEN, CYNICAL AND HAPPILY UNATTACHED...

Until Daniel Wren blew in like a tornado, sweeping Susan off her feet
and back home to Hampstead, Kansas, new bride of the small town's
police chief. Ten days later Daniel was killed by a sniper.

Susan was an outsider—a city slicker, a woman, and worse, personally
involved in the case. She was also Hampstead's new police
chief...hunting for her husband's killer.

"Nonstop action and harrowing suspense." —*Publishers Weekly*